THE
WHOLE
TRUTH

THE WHOLE TRUTH

NANCY PICKARD

POCKET BOOKS
New York London Toronto Sydney Singapore

This book is a work of fiction. Names, characters, places and incidents are products of
the author's imagination or are used fictitiously. Any resemblance to actual events or
locales or persons, living or dead, is entirely coincidental.

POCKET BOOKS, a division of Simon & Schuster Inc.
1230 Avenue of the Americas, New York, NY 10020

ISBN: 0-671-88795-5

Designed by Liane Fuji

POCKET and colophon are registered trademarks of
Simon & Schuster Inc.

Printed in the U.S.A.

For my son, Nick

1

Raymond

The courthouse in downtown Bahia Beach, Florida, seems a pale, cool place to hold the evidence of so much passion. Divorces. Rape. Murders. Arson. Assault. Abuse of all kinds, by all sorts of people, upon all sorts of people. Daily, it parades past these bland, blond walls of the Howard County Courthouse, in Florida's Twenty-first Judicial Circuit. This is a place of stark contrasts and painful paradoxes, of quiet ironies and violent surprises. Outside the long narrow windows of the courthouse, the south Florida sun burns hot enough to scorch a tourist's skin, but inside, it's all shade and air-conditioning.

My fingertips feel dipped in ice water as I write these words.

They seem to promise a surprise or shock of some kind, although nobody in this courtroom is expecting one. We're expecting the jury to deliver a guilty verdict today, and we're all expecting to troop back in here in a couple of weeks to hear this same jury recommend the death penalty.

And yet, my own words seem to foreshadow something else.

Strange, but I don't have any idea of what that could be.

For the ten days of the trial of Raymond Raintree for the kidnapping and murder of Natalie Mae McCullen, I have scribbled notes with stiff, cold fingers. Now, as we await the verdict, I press

1

my fingers into my palms to warm them, before moving my pen again. I'm not using a laptop because the soft tapping of fingers on keyboards drives the judge crazy, and so she has forbidden computers.

Judge Edyth Flasschoen's courtroom—number three, second floor—is especially chilly, because she keeps the thermostat turned down exceptionally low. It's so cold in here I can smell the air-conditioning, a metallic aroma that gets up in my nose and stays there until I overpower it with garlic for lunch from one of the restaurants down on Bahia Boulevard. The judge takes good care of her jurors, though: no air-conditioning blows directly on them.

High on her bench, seated in her brown leather chair on rollers, the judge taps her microphone with a pink fingernail. She's a tough old broad, sixty-two years old, with a beauty-shop hairdo and the metabolism of a Florida mosquito. When I interviewed her for the true crime book I'm writing about this case, she said, "It's always too damned hot to suit me. I could go naked under my robes, and I'd still sweat like a pig in the brush."

"Get this show going," she commands her bailiff now.

Along with other spectators, I am seated on the back row behind the prosecutor's table. Picking which side to sit on each day has felt like choosing sides of the aisle at a wedding where nobody wants to sit behind the groom. The benches behind the defendant are full, but the people seated there look uncomfortable to me. Nobody wants to be mistaken for being sympathetic to Ray Raintree.

Judge Flasschoen is glaring at the defense team.

"I'm warning you in the audience and you attorneys up front, there will be no outcry over this verdict, whatever it is. You understand me?" Leanne English, the lead defense counsel, is getting the brunt of this lecture, which doesn't seem quite fair given that she hasn't done much to prevent the flow of justice toward conviction. If the only obligation of a defense team is to force the prosecution to prove the charges, then Leanne has succeeded admirably. Nevertheless, the judge is wagging a manicured finger at her. "Con-

2

tempt of court is no empty phrase in my court. You want your own trial? You want to experience what it's like to be a defendant? We can arrange that, for anybody who doesn't sit still and keep quiet."

Leanne, a trim little redhead in a crisp black suit, nods.

The jury hasn't liked her, but they've loved the state's attorney, Franklin DeWeese. He is a tall, handsome black man with an ingratiating manner and a name that oozes political promise. The prosecutor has performed superbly in this trial. He focused the jury's attention on the evidence that pins the defendant to the crime, and he distracted them from the two troubling questions that remain unanswered: No motive has ever been established, and nobody knows who the defendant really is.

Ray Raintree is a man without an identity.

In a country in which most people worry about how easily the facts of their lives can be accessed by strangers, Ray seems to have spontaneously generated out of thin air. Computerized criminal records haven't identified him, nor have fingerprint matching or DNA testing, either. He has no past that anybody, including me, has been able to find. This is not good news for a true crime writer with a book due on her editor's desk in two weeks.

In his closing arguments, Franklin emphasized, "It doesn't matter who Ray was or where he came from prior to the murder of Natalie Mae. It doesn't matter who Ray said he was after he killed her. The only thing that matters is where he was and what he was doing at the moment she died. At that moment, he could have been president of the United States in a former life, and it wouldn't matter. He could have turned into a Nobel Prize winner the next day, and it wouldn't matter. Ray can call himself anything he wants to, but if he is the one who murdered that child—and he is—we are all of us going to call him a killer. That's who he is. Ms. English will try to convince you that you need to know his motive for killing her, but I promise you the law does not require you to know *why* he did it. You only need to know *that* he did it. And you do know that, because we have proved it beyond any reasonable doubt. He kidnapped that child, he killed her, and he mutilated her body. That's all you need to know, in order to convict him."

He convinced me, and probably the jury, too.

But that's not going to fill the middle of my book with facts, and it makes me feel uneasy to think that my home state may execute a man with no identity. I don't know exactly why this should worry me—beyond my personal concern about my book—but it does.

The jury foreman is rising to his feet, with a paper in his hands.

On this day of the verdict, the foreman is wearing a light blue suit, white shirt, navy blue tie. He has red cheeks, slicked back hair, and he looks like he just drove into the big city from a farm. He looks somber, nervous, aware of the importance of his role and this moment. The other jurors are looking at him, as if they're afraid to look at anybody else for fear of giving their decision away, as if we don't all know what it's going to be.

I've attended a lot of trials, and I've seen a lot of jurors, and they almost all look scared and sincere at moments like this. Having served on a jury myself, I know just how they feel. Ray's on his feet now, along with Leanne and her team. Franklin and his assistants have stood up, too. There's a feeling in the room that we're all holding our breath, even though the verdict is predictable.

My own heart is beating faster than I would have expected it to.

"Members of the jury, have you reached your verdict?"

"Your Honor, we have," the foreman tells her in a strong, carrying voice. After a few phrases of official language, he finally says it: "We the jury find the defendant guilty as charged in indictment number six-seven-two. So say we all."

I'm surprised how deeply relieved I feel to hear it.

So much for my foreshadowing of a shock or surprise: This is exactly how this trial was supposed to turn out, and now it has, and I can write the final chapter.

Obediently, we maintain decorum in the courtroom.

4

And then we jump in our seats at a sudden, single loud noise.

Natty's father, Tony McCullen, has just slammed his beefy ex-boxer's hand down on the wooden railing which separates him from the state's attorneys in front of him. All by itself, that hand says it for all the rest of us: *Yes!*

My heart aches for Tony and for his wife, Susan. This verdict may be a necessary step in their healing, but it is also such small, small recompense for the loss of their sweet little girl.

Ray, himself, hasn't moved a hair since the verdict was read.

Leanne has put her left arm around him and is whispering something into his right ear. Franklin DeWeese has turned in an equally quiet manner to shake hands with his assistants, and now he's embracing Tony McCullen. The victim's mother, Susan, was a witness, testifying to Natty's whereabouts before the murder, so she has spent the other days of the trial seated on a bench outside this courtroom, surrounded by comforting friends and members of her family. Susan could have come in for this verdict, but when I saw her outside today, she told me she didn't want to be here for it.

"I want to watch him die," she told me, looking thin and haunted.

She doesn't want to have to see him at all before that final day.

After the verdict, the members of the jury—

The members of the jury are staring at Ray Raintree with odd expressions on their faces. What's going on up there? What's he done now? Jurors number six and seven glance at each other. Juror number one in the front row frowns. The juror to his left looks downright sick. Some of the other jurors are turning their faces away, as if they want to look anywhere except at Ray.

The judge doesn't seem to have noticed anything out of the ordinary. She's up there on her bench, gathering papers in preparation for setting a date for the sentencing hearing.

But something's up with the jury, even now.

I think I'll stand up as discreetly as possible, pretend I'm just stretching my legs, and see if I can detect what's happening up there. I have sympathized with the jury all through the trial, and not least because they had to face Raymond Raintree every day for ten days. From personal experience, I know he's hard to look at. Anybody who has ever stared into his creepy eyes hates the fact that his was the last face that child ever saw.

I see that Leanne English is about to say something to Franklin.

Oh, my god! Ray has just shoved her violently, propelling her across the aisle toward the prosecutor. Franklin yells, "Ow!" as she falls against him. Leanne screams, and she's clutching at Franklin's arms. He attempts to grab her, but she slips from his hands, and falls to the floor.

She's screaming again, and so are some other people.

The courtroom is erupting into pandemonium!

Ray has pushed his attorney out of the way, leapt across her legs, and he's charging toward Judge Flasschoen's bench.

"Kill me!" he's yelling at her. "Kill me now! Do it! Kill me now!"

Judge Flasschoen stands up. With her right hand, she reaches into the long black sleeve that drapes her left arm, and she pulls out a small pistol.

She takes aim, and shoots Ray.

Ray charges forward a few more steps before falling.

Oh, my god, a judge just shot a defendant!

I hear my own voice shouting, along with a dozen others, "Is he dead? Did she kill him?"

The Little Mermaid

By Marie Lightfoot

~

CHAPTER ONE

South Florida is laced with saltwater canals, all leading inevitably to the great Intracoastal Canal, which runs from Texas to Boston and which connects with the Atlantic Ocean. In Bahia Beach, alone, there is enough access to water to make the parents of children feel nervous all of the time. It's so frighteningly easy for a baby to wander only a few yards out of sight, and in the space of a telephone call, to tumble into the water. In Bahia Beach, there are 327 canals, most of them lined on both sides with residences. Many, many of those homes have children living in them, children who are warned from the time they can crawl, "Don't go near the water!"

Driving in the city is a matter of crossing many bridges, some of them drawbridges that open to allow larger vessels to pass, holding up long lines of traffic as they go.

But the majority of Bahia's bridges are small, pretty ones spanning narrow canals and made of concrete. An interesting way to see those bridges is to float under them in a small boat. Kids especially love that, unless it spooks them too much. Underneath a bridge it's a different world—a dank, shadowy cave where you can see barnacles on the bottom, and you can smell fish and salt water. But you have to wait for the tide to be low enough to do that, or you won't get under at all because the water that flows in and out daily from the Atlantic will be licking the underside of the bridge. As the tide retreats, the boaters who use the canals for fun and transportation can slide under by laying themselves flat in their little boats as the undersides of the bridges pass inches from their nose. But eventually the water level decreases enough to allow even a man as tall as six-foot-seven-inch Bradley Williams to pass under without ducking his head.

On the morning of June sixteenth Brad, fifty-seven years old and still sporting a thick crop of sandy hair, sat at the stern of his beloved seventeen-foot solid teak motorboat, *Carousel*. His wife, Jeannie, sixty-one and healthily attractive from all the tennis she plays, sat facing forward in front of him. She was knitting a vest for a grandchild as she and Brad leisurely puttered along on the reliable strength of *Carousel*'s eleven horsepower diesel engine. The little boat is a family heirloom that Brad himself meticulously maintains and which everybody on both sides of the family loves like a pet. Like an untiring pony, it carries them nearly everywhere, to Bahia Beach's boat-accessible parks and picnic areas, to the homes of friends who live on the water, even out into the ocean where it bobs like a cheerful, unsinkable brown seal.

This particular Tuesday morning, Jeannie and Bradley were motoring over to Brad's aged parents' residence on a nearby canal. The elder Williamses prefer to live in their native Maine in summertime, leaving their son and daughter-in-law to look out for their property. Checking on it every day gives Brad and Jean a nice excuse to hop into *Carousel* and enjoy an early morning cruise.

Above them, the busy streets of Bahia Beach, a city of

100,000 people, hummed with rush hour traffic. But down on the water, all was serene. Their little motor is a thoughtfully quiet one, so they can putter past backyards and barely disturb the peace of the upper-middle-class neighborhood where they and Brad's parents live.

To reach Brad's parents' place, they have to go under three bridges. At the first one, connecting Sunrise and Fourteenth Streets above them, Jeannie was so busy knitting and purling (to rush the wee vest into service for a Sunday christening) that Brad had to remind her to duck her head.

The tide wasn't out very far yet. The Williams bent way over to get under, but they were used to this. After more than thirty years of living near the water, they duck under bridges as casually as other people duck under tree limbs. Besides, Brad is so tall he jokes that he's spent most of his life ducking one thing or another.

So they took the first bridge easily. Jeannie never dropped a stitch. The vest she was making was all white, in honor of the occasion. The yarn was so delicate she worried that her fingers—roughened from years of sanding the teak on their boats—would catch the fibers and pull them out of line.

Even with her rush-job knitting, Jeannie didn't ignore the beauty all around them. Perfect green lawns tilting down to boat docks and to well-maintained stone and cement seawalls. Lovely homes. Royal palm trees. The chattering of wild parakeets. Yards boasting their own orange, avocado, or grapefruit trees, most of them sagging with their heavy harvest at this time of year. Several great-beaked pelicans perching on dock posts. Gulls swooping over tall masts. And a clear, sunny Florida sky overhead. It seemed a perfect morning, like almost every one to which lucky south Floridians awoke each day. Granted, the temperature was already ninety degrees at seven o'clock in the morning, but down on the water, it was pleasant.

Jeannie never tired of such days.

Bradley never took their good fortune for granted.

Mornings like this, they felt especially blessed, and they told each other so. Married twenty-five years. Three wonderful daughters. And now a first grandchild, a chubby blond darling named Melanie. Brad was already making her a "big-girl bed" shaped like a boat. When finished, it would rock with a gentle motion, just as if she were sailing on the sea.

The second bridge on their route was easy to navigate, too.

Duck. Under. Through to the other side.

Visitors to the Williams love these excursions in *Carousel*, even though it scares landlubbers to pass into the shadows below the street. It's a thrill, especially when they have to duck down really low, so low they're afraid they'll scrape their backs or knock themselves out on the concrete trusses. The Williams haven't lost any tourists yet.

Now, Jeannie and Brad saw the third and last bridge coming up. Beyond it, they glimpsed his parents' house.

"Hasn't burned down," Brad joked to Jeannie, in his laconic Maine accent, still pronounced even though he hasn't lived there since he was twenty.

"Somebody left their fishing pole," Jeannie remarked, traces of her Boston upbringing still as clear in her words as Maine is in his. "Looks like the cops caught him, too."

Sure enough, as they neared the third bridge, they saw a fishing pole lodged firmly between two of the concrete posts on the upper side of the little bridge. Fishing there was illegal, the Williams knew, but people did it anyway. There is amazing affluence in Bahia, as there is in Pompano to the north and Fort Lauderdale to the south, but the homeless flock there, too, and people have to eat. Personally, Jeannie wouldn't want to eat anything a person could catch from these canals. Maybe she's being persnickety, she says, but she never can help thinking of all those big boats on the Intracoastal and all of the pollution they surely must leave behind them, regulations or no. Not to mention industrial effluents. No, what is in these canals can stay there, in Jeannie's view. If she ever goes hungry, God forbid, she'd rather line up for soup at a shelter than to fish off these bridges.

As they slowly floated closer, they saw that the fiberglass pole was rigidly bowed and the line was very taut.

"Caught themselves an old inner tube," was Jeannie's guess.

"That dates you," Brad teased her. "Don't you know that tires don't even have inner tubes anymore?"

"I said it was an old one, didn't I?"

Bradley observed to himself that it looked like a substantial rig, like something his own fishing nut son-in-law might use to land a big, heavy swordfish, and not like a cheap old pole a tramp might use to snare a passing crab, or little sole. You wouldn't think anybody would want to go off and leave it there. Even if it was snagged on something under the bridge, they could have cut the line and saved the pole.

He throttled back to slow down the boat even more.

Now they could see that an officer in the brown and tan uniform of the Bahia Beach Police Department was peering over the side of the bridge. He had on a short-sleeved shirt, and they could see the sun glint off the badge above his heart. Sunglasses dangled from his left hand. He looked at where the taut line disappeared into the dark water beneath the bridge, and then he looked at them in their boat. He yelled out to them, "Can you see what's caught on the line down there?"

As Bradley eased *Carousel* as close as he could without running into the line, Jeannie slid over to starboard to try to get a look. At first, she couldn't detect anything, because the water was so shadowed beneath the overpass. But then she caught a glimpse of something darker . . .

A fish?

No! She recoiled instinctively, because her second glimpse showed her something that looked like hair, and she immediately thought: canal rat. Getting herself in hand, she looked again. No, the hair was too light, too long for—

Jeannie brought her hands to her mouth in dismay.

She cried out, and Brad knew instantly that something was really wrong. It shook him up terribly when his wife screamed, "It's a body! Oh, my God! It's a child!"

Jeannie doesn't remember saying that, or even screaming. What she remembers, what she can't forget, is that she saw a clump of sodden hair floating in the water, and at the end of it, barely still hanging on, there was a pink plastic barrette, the kind that a little girl might wear.

As the tide inexorably lowered that morning, it revealed to the horrified observers a small human body, a girlchild, hung from the bridge by the fishing line wrapped around her broken neck.

The uniformed officer ran down the bank of the canal and plunged into the water without even stopping to remove his shoes. If there was any chance of reviving her, he wanted to get her out of there immediately. But even as he felt salt water fill his leather shoes, his common sense and experience told him she'd been dead for a while: Her neck looked broken, her skin was shriveled, and her little body hung limp and heavy in the water.

He determined that she was, in fact, irretrievably dead. Since that was the case, it became important for him to leave her exactly as they'd found her, in order to begin in an orderly way the investigation into her death.

Now sloshing wet, he clambered back out of the canal.

A small crowd of pedestrians began to gather.

It was awful, watching her body gradually appear above the water, as the level dropped, first her head, tilted heart-breakingly and unnaturally to one side, then her small shoulders clothed in a white T-shirt so wet that her skin showed through. In a terrible irony, the T-shirt bore a picture of the Little Mermaid, a favorite movie character of little girls a few years back. The people watching also saw pink shorts, bare legs and feet, but only when the little girl's body was finally, gently, cautiously lowered into a police boat. Until then, it had to wait, hanging there for a much longer time than most of the spectators could bear, while police photographs were snapped, diagrams were drawn, notes were jotted down.

The child's hair hung in stringy clumps almost to her shoulders. Because the hair was soaked, you couldn't tell it was blond. Her hair looked the dark, nondescript color that blond hair looks when it gets very wet. The pink barrette still clung to its bit of hair at the end of one of the clumps.

Nobody wanted to leave her hanging there a second longer than necessary. But nobody wanted to make a mistake, either, which might prevent the person responsible for this crime from being apprehended and convicted. A certain deliberate speed was imperative, even if it did offend the civilians in the neighborhood. More than one person yelled at the officers down in the police boat on the water: "For God's sake, cut her down! Can't you at least cut her down?"

Down in the boat, there were two officers from the Bahia Beach Police Department marine unit, an invaluable branch of local law enforcement which was not "launched" until 1965. Back then, one sergeant and two patrol officers made do with a single thirteen-foot dinghy to patrol 135

13

miles of interior coastline and five miles of beaches. An impossible task, of course. Now, decades later, the department boasts a dozen specially trained marine officers assigned to several different types of boats. The one down on the water on this day was a twenty-five-foot Boston Whaler. The officers in the marine unit are basically water traffic cops—handing out speeding tickets, arresting drunk boaters—but the unit is also called out when divers or water access to the scene of a crime are needed, like this one.

The officers in the boat cut her down as soon as they could, but that had to wait until the crime scene unit gave permission for it. The alternative to lowering her into the boat was to haul her up by the fishing line. It wasn't that the officers on land were too squeamish or sensitive to do that, but if they did that, they ran the risk of mangling the neck wound, and causing posthumous injuries that might compromise the autopsy.

Everyone felt the relief of seeing the little body released from its noose, and the mercy of placing her into a black body bag. The marine unit removed her by water. In Bahia Beach, even the police department has boat docks—at Northeast Twelfth Street. It was faster and less public to take her that way.

Meanwhile, the bridge remained partially closed for a time, seriously annoying those motorists and boaters who didn't know why. But this was Bahia Beach, and they should have been used to waiting for bridges to open.

The Williamses, Brad and Jeannie, gave their names and address to the police, and then they followed orders to get *Carousel* out of the way. They continued on, terribly shaken, to Brad's parents' place. They didn't see the dead girl's body removed from the canal. Jeannie was thankful for that, because just seeing what she did see was more than she wanted to have to remember for the rest of her life.

14

That next Sunday morning at St. Pious Cathedral, Jeannie and Brad held hands tightly, and they both shed quiet tears at Melanie's christening. They thought of the ·other child and of the grandparents who grieved for her. By then they knew, as all of south Florida did, who she was, and who had loved her. "Life is very special," Jeannie told her daughters that day. "I'm grateful for every day of it that you girls are allowed to share with us on this earth." She thinks that for the rest of her life, she will mean that more than she ever did before, and she knows she will find it difficult to let her grandchildren out of her sight when she baby-sits.

The crime scene unit arrived at the bridge soon after 7:30 A.M.

The original uniformed officer at the scene, Sergeant Jimmy Clubman, accomplished a lot before they got there. Conscientiously, though uncomfortably, he labored away in his wet clothes and shoes. A young officer with only two years of experience on the force, Clubman has two small children himself. He felt shaken up by his macabre discovery.

"I was just driving my route." The sergeant explains how he slowly cruised the residential streets each morning. "I spotted this fishing rod stuck on that bridge, but I didn't see anybody with it. I figured they saw me coming, and ran away and hid, and they didn't have time to get their pole loose. I got out to look for them, because I figured they wouldn't go far, not with that nice pole stuck there."

He attempted to dislodge the rod from between the cement supports, but it was snagged so firmly on something in the water that he couldn't budge it.

"If those people in that little boat hadn't come by, I probably would have got back in my car and just left it there," he admits, "because when I saw how tight that line

15

was caught, I figured that was a better lesson to a fisherman than any warning I'd give him. It's real easy to get your line hung up on the crap that floats by those bridges."

Before the *Carousel* showed up, he pulled hard on the line a couple of times, but with no luck. Afterward, he shivered, not from being cold, but at the thought of what it would have been like if he had managed to yank the line up far enough to see what was caught at the end of it. He was glad that didn't happen. In his two years on the force, he'd seen awful things. He knew there were some things he didn't want to stumble across when he was alone. Having company, even if it was only two scared civilians, helped a little.

He knew he had to get down to business.

He told the Williamses to stay in their boat until the crime scene officers got there. "I felt sorry for them," he says. "I mean, what a thing to come across, when you just happen to be out for a morning boat ride." But he didn't have any time to waste on them. They'd have to comfort each other. He had to secure the scene as best he could by himself, using his own patrol car and orange cones he removed from his trunk, to block off the lane of traffic closest to the fishing pole.

He didn't think he should close both lanes, because these streets are man-made peninsulas, surrounded on three sides by water. If he shut down the whole bridge, the residents in their houses would be trapped for the duration of the crime scene investigation. They would be unhappy, and the fire department wouldn't like it either. When Clubman called in to his supervisor to report the body, and to request assistance, he asked her to call out the marine unit to help secure the area by using their boats to block access from the water.

Before anybody else arrived, Sergeant Clubman noted 7:12 A.M. as the time he found the body. He also recorded the temperature, ninety-two F., and reported the weather as being sunny, with a very slight breeze from the southeast, no clouds, ninety percent humidity.

He hoped that information—particularly the time, temperature, and humidity—could help the medical examiner determine time of death. The temperature of the water needed to be taken as well, but the officers in the crime scene unit could figure that out, as well as confirm the other data. He carefully wrote down a description of the body and the scene, including his observation that the victim's face appeared "peaceful." He expected the crime scene officers to make their own notes, but he hopes to make detective, himself, one day. He tries to train himself for the future, by thinking like a detective, noticing what they would consider important, and writing that down. He noted there was none of the eye-bulging, tongue-protruding awfulness of the face that would have been present if she had been strangled.

"Personally, I figured she didn't die from hanging from the fishing line," he says. "I figured she was dead before they hung her, and it seemed pretty obvious she was murdered. I mean, what else could it have been?"

Neither he nor anyone else investigating the death ever seriously considered the possibility that this was a suicide. For one thing, there was the extremely young age of the deceased. It wasn't that kindergartners never killed themselves; sadly, it was known to happen. But there was also the manner in which she was hung, which seemed impossible for her to accomplish by herself. They did toy briefly with the idea of this being some kind of macabre accident. Early on that first day, somebody with a warped sense of human capabilities suggested that maybe some kids played "fisherman," they used the child as "bait," and then they ran away, terrified, when they saw the consequences. But generally, the scene, the victim, and the method all screamed "homicide" at the police.

Clubman judged the victim to be around six years old.

That educated guess was right on the money. Her last birthday was May first. The child was white. Later, she was measured precisely and found to be exactly two feet eleven inches tall. Forty pounds. She was a little slip of a girl, with dark blond hair that was blunt cut at shoulder length, worn with long bangs. As everyone learned eventually, she had liked her mom to pull the sides of her hair back off her pretty face and fasten them at the top of her scalp with one of her legion of plastic barrettes, one for nearly every color she could name. She had dark blue eyes. None of the crime scene personnel knew that until later, because when they first saw Natalie her eyes were closed. For the men who cut her loose and then lowered her tenderly into the police launch, that was a mercy. Even the most inured among them find it hard to look a dead child in the eyes.

The Bahia Beach police identified her quickly.

Surprisingly, there wasn't a missing persons report out on her. But little Natalie carried in the right pocket of her pink shorts an identification card encased in protective plastic.

"My name is Natalie Mae McCullen. I live at 2533 Palm Sunrise, Bahia Beach, Florida. My phone number is 394-999-1232. My parents are Susan and Anthony McCullen. Please call them for me. Thank you."

It may seem odd that she carried that card, because she appeared to be old enough to be able to remember her own address and phone number. Neatly typed in black on white, the ID card almost made it seem as if somebody expected Natalie McCullen to be identified by strangers. But the real explanation for the card was printed on it in bold black letters: **I am deaf.**

It took all of about ten seconds for Sergeant Clubman's boss to realize that this was going to be a high-profile case conducted in the public eye. The killer almost seemed to have placed it there purposefully, in plain view. The victim, the method, and the neighborhood all added up to an important case as these things are measured. She expected the media to go crazy over it. Acting quickly, she shunted it down proper channels until two fine detectives, Paul Flanck and Robyn Anschutz, got assigned to the case.

Detective Paul Flanck looks Hispanic, but isn't.

"It helps," he says, "especially down here where it seems like every other person speaks Spanish." At the time he was assigned to the case of the little girl found hanging from the bridge, he was thirty-two years old, and a self-described "fanatical runner, weight lifter, and good ol' boy," originally from Fort Meyers, Florida. He was divorced, with no children. His perpetual hobby was taking Spanish lessons. "I can see the future," he says, wryly. It's a future, he means, in which English is the *second* language in south Florida.

That isn't an outlook that Detective Robyn Anschutz shares with him. At thirty-four and married to the son of a Cuban exile, she feels that Hispanics endure minority status, no matter what their population numbers. A pretty woman with short blond hair, a warm smile, and sober brown eyes, Robyn makes a striking physical match with her police partner. They are the same height, five foot ten, although Robyn's hair, back-combed a bit on top, gives her an illusory inch on him, which she likes to tease him about.

The topic of the Hispanic population is only one of many subjects that the two detectives were known to bicker about, almost like an old married couple. They are both frank enough to admit that theirs was not a pairing made in heaven. "Far from it," says Robyn, laughing, implying that it was a match made about as far from heaven as you can get—down on the first floor of police headquarters, in fact, where the top brass recognized each of them as top-rate detectives.

With her warm smile, Robyn gets felons to talk, and with his muscular, intense manner, Paul intimidates people without ever touching them. They were both known as dedicated cops. If any pair could produce quick, reliable results that wouldn't end up embarrassing the department, it was felt that Flanck and Anschutz could do it. They were expected to put aside their personal differences.

One of the few things they have in common—besides being good cops—was that neither has kids, not even stepkids. Paul asked later if that was one reason they were assigned to the case. "Was that supposed to make us more objective?" he asked their boss, the captain of detectives. "Did you think that we'd get less emotionally involved because of that? Because if that's what was supposed to happen, it didn't work."

He was told that hadn't anything to do with it.

Such misgivings came later, when in hindsight, every case can be conducted better and every Monday-morning quarterback will tell you how. On the morning of July seventeenth, the only thing that Detectives Flanck and Anschutz knew was that they were commanded to get to the scene as soon as possible. The detectives would rely on the forensic unit, which is part of the C.I.D., or Criminal Investigations Department. As Paul explains, "They're our crime scene unit, our specialists. They gather evidence at the scene, and they're responsible for preserving it and presenting it in court."

The organization of law enforcement bodies in the state of Florida is different from some other states. For one thing, there's no state police in Florida. There's a state highway patrol, of course, but their job is mostly what their name suggests: patrolling state highways. With no state police or state crime lab, a lot of authority devolves onto the sheriffs' departments of each county. Each county runs its own crime lab, for instance, and in addition, the sheriffs' deputies act as law enforcement for the smaller towns. But like Fort Lauderdale, Bahia Beach is large enough to support its own police department and to handle its own cases, from petty theft to mass murder.

The crime unit officers found important things at the scene.

But it was Paul who found the footprint on the Hatteras. And the ashes. And fingerprints on the fishing pole. And gouges in the ground where the perpetrator had dug in his toes to climb up and then dug in his heels coming back down. All of which would later be tied directly to the crime. And it was Robyn who sensed the truth, which would lead directly and with astonishing rapidity to the arrest of the suspect.

Knowledge of the murder of a child, and witnessing something like what the Williamses saw, tends to change people, sometimes dramatically. But as Paul says, "Hell of a way to learn it. I'd go back to being dumb ol' me, if that brought Natty back."

It's bad enough, a parent's worst nightmare, to be informed a child is dead when you know she's been missing and you've been desperate for news of her. If any fate could possibly be worse than that, perhaps it was what Natalie McCullen's parents faced that morning.

They didn't even know she was gone.

Apparently, Natalie slipped out of the house on some private little adventure of her own. It must have been after her mom kissed her and put her to bed, which was around nine o'clock, on Monday night, June fifteenth.

She was a bold little soul, by all accounts. Unlike most children, Natalie was never afraid of the dark. Whenever she played outside at night, Susan or Anthony always had to "call" her many times by flashing the porch light on and off when the sun went down. "Natty would have stayed out and played all night, if we let her," Susan says. "She always imagined she was born on a star." The child was a little star to her family, a sparkler who lighted their days and nights, a child who never met a stranger, who was outgoing and daring as a puppy.

When the McCullens' doorbell rang at 8:30 A.M. that dreadful Tuesday morning, Susan answered in her bathrobe, and found two detectives, a man and a woman, on her doorstep. They identified themselves, and then they asked her as gently as they knew how, "Are you the mother of Natalie Mae McCullen?"

"Yes, why, has she done something wrong? She's only six!"

"Ma'am—we're sorry to ask this, but do you know where your daughter is?"

"Of course, I do! She's asleep in her room!"

"Would you please check, just to make sure?"

"Why?" Susan didn't wait for their answer, however. Suddenly driven by the most overwhelming, sickening, soul-wrenching fear of her life, she fled from them, and ran down the hall to her daughter's room.

They heard her scream, "Natty! Natty, where are you?"

On the front step, Robyn Anschutz took a shaky breath, and felt her eyes fill, and her mouth tremble. Her partner tightened his lips, and simply thought, Oh shit oh shit oh shit.

"Where's my baby!"

Looking frantic and terrified, the mother ran back to face the police officers, who wished they could be any-where but there, delivering any news but what they had to say next.

They told her that the body of a little girl had been found—they didn't tell her how, not yet—and the child had a card in her pocket that identified her as Natalie Mae

McCullen. They described her, and her clothing. They told her that they believed that her daughter—who she had thought was safely sleeping—was dead. They said her daughter's body, if the child was Natty, was on its way to the morgue.

"It was," Paul Flanck said later, "enough to make you want to quit police work, and start mowing lawns for a living."

Making it even worse was the unavoidable fact that in the murder of a child the first suspects are always the parents. That meant interviewing Susan and Anthony McCullen during the first moments of the greatest shock and grief of their lives. It was very hard for either detective to believe that the beautiful, hysterical young woman standing in the doorway in front of them could so heinously have murdered her own child. "My baby, my baby," Susan McCullen screamed, before she collapsed to the floor, moaning, crying, screaming, "no, no, no." The muscular, good-looking young man who ran up behind her appeared so undone by the news of his child's death that Detective Robyn Anschutz's first impulse was not to interrogate him, but to hug him.

2
Raymond

"This is my courtroom!" Judge Flasschoen has put down her pistol and picked up her gavel, and she's pounding and pounding on the wooden surface of the bench. "Order! There will be order in my courtroom!"

Nobody pays any attention to her now.

We're all still angling to see what happened to the man she shot.

She sits down so hard that her chair rolls back to the far wall and slams against it, jerking her head so hard that her neck bones crack audibly into the microphone attached to her robes. She rubs the back of her neck, and withdraws into a display of silent judicial dignity while chaos explodes around her.

I get a quick glimpse of Ray, motionless below her bench.

Through the crowd, I see Leanne pick herself up and hurry to his side, where she kneels, and screams, "For god's sake, somebody do something! Call 911! We need a doctor!"

I flinch as the double doors at the back of the courtroom fly open and bang against the walls. Here come five Howard County deputy sheriffs surging in. Two of them, in the dark green short sleeve uniforms and gold badges of the department, take up posts at the back, not far from me, to keep people from leaving. Another one runs down the center aisle, and yells out, "Ladies and gentlemen, sit down and be quiet. Quiet! Take your seats. We'll get you out of here as soon as we can, but we need your cooperation right now."

Slowly, reluctantly, we spectators follow his orders, although within moments we're popping back up to our feet again, and the noise level rises to its previous roar.

Word filters back through the crowd that Ray is alive, but unconscious. When I hear that, I start inching my way forward, hoping no deputy will stop me. I want to see for myself, for my book.

"Excuse me. I need to get through. Thank you."

People are obliging, and move aside. A few do a double take, as if they've recognized me from my book jackets, or from magazine or television interviews. One of them even says, "Aren't you—?" and I nod, smile, and keep moving.

I get almost up to the front, and there he is—

I stop in my tracks, feeling weak-kneed at the sight of Ray Raintree lying facedown on the courtroom floor. For all the times I have written about murders, this is the first time I've seen an actual shooting. Cold bodies in morgues are one thing—I have viewed enough of them to get almost used to it—but a wounded, bleeding person I know . . . this is scary. I don't see any blood, so it must be soaking into his flesh and his clothes. His attorneys dressed him up in a white shirt, and dark trousers and a tie, trying to make him look normal. His black running shoes—they never talked him into dress shoes—lie still against the hardwood floor.

Maybe he's dead, and not just wounded?

I glance to my right, looking for Tony McMullen, and I see him sitting down among all the frantic people who are standing up around him. Natty's young father looks shell-shocked. As I watch, he leans over and puts his head between his legs, as if he's on the verge of passing out.

"Marie! Come on up here!"

I jump at the sound of my own name.

It's Leanne's paralegal, Manny Meade, calling to me.

Besides the judge and a few jurors, Manny is the oldest person on the other side of the railing that separates the players from the spectators. Jowly, overweight, always disheveled in flamboyant baggy suits, Manny looks more like a Damon Runyon character than a paralegal. I haven't yet figured out a tactful way to say that in my book, and I haven't decided if I really need to divulge that he is an ex-con who served time for fixing sporting events. As a former felon, Manny can't be admitted to the bar, but Florida law lets him get this close to it. He is sixty-three years old, a war veteran. "Oldest paralegal south of the panhandle," he likes to brag, although I doubt that's true.

I slide through the opening that he provides for me by shoving open the half-door through which witnesses come and go.

"Manny!" I hear adrenaline in my voice, and tamp it down. It feels unseemly to be so bloodthirsty for details. "How bad is Ray hurt? Is Leanne all right?"

"Don't know, Marie."

I turn to ask Leanne's cocounsel, Jaime Suarez, who shrugs, and says "You know as much as we do, Marie."

"Why aren't you guys up there helping her?"

"Leanne's got it under control," Manny claims.

"I don't want to touch him," Jaime says, with an expression of distaste. "Slimy bastard."

If his client could hear that, there'd be a malpractice suit. In an early draft of a chapter for my book I described Jaime as "tall, slim, well dressed, and fit-looking, a man with the deadpan expression of a prisoner of war, and the cynical mouth of a street thug." Then I erased it, because it's not my style to insult my subjects.

"Don't quote me, all right?" he adds, quickly.

"I won't, if"—I smile teasingly—"you'll tell me what Leanne said to Ray."

"When?"

"Right before he went off. She leaned over and whispered something into his ear. What'd she say to him?"

26

"Did she say something?" Jaime glances at his paralegal, who is at least thirty years older and an equal number of pounds heavier than he. Some people claim there's a similar difference in their IQs, with the advantage going to the older man. That's another observation I erased after I wrote it down. "Did you hear her say anything, Manny?"

The response is a jowly head shake: no.

"She put her arm around him," I remind them, although I realize they may not have seen it. "And she said something to him. And a couple of seconds later he went ballistic. You don't know what she said?"

Manny mutters comically out of the side of his mouth, "She said, 'Pay me before the first of the month, Ray.'"

I smile at his irreverent joke at their client's expense.

Jaime inclines his head toward the opposite side of the aisle. "So, Marie, you going to make them look like heroes, and us like jerks?"

"Marie never makes anybody look bad," Manny corrects him. "Except for the killers." He winks at me, before turning back to his young boss. "She isn't just a pretty face, she's fair to everybody she writes about. Don't you read her books?"

"Why, thank you, Manny."

I smile at the flattery.

"Who's got time to *read* about crime?" Jaime sounds aggrieved. "Besides, why would I want to pay money to see other lawyers get all the glory?"

Manny leans close to me, and says in a mock-confiding tone, "Jaime is only in the law to serve humanity."

"A man of principle, clearly," I reply.

"Yeah." The young man in question snorts. "Humanity. Like, Ray Raintree is human. Not."

This time his paralegal shoots a look up at him like a stern father warning a smart-mouthed son.

Jaime clamps his jaw, and shuts up.

"How can he be unconscious?"

I turn toward the skeptical voice which uttered those words, and see a gray-haired woman right behind the defense table. She's somebody I've noticed at the trial every day. When I asked a deputy who she was, he informed me that she's a "regular," a trial junkie who shows up at the courthouse for juicy cases.

"It was just a little-bitty twenty-two caliber gun," she says to me, with a dismissive wave of a hand. "I've got one of those for scaring squirrels away from my bird feeders. I don't think it could even kill a sparrow. You can't even bleed to death from a little-bitty ol' twenty-two caliber bullet wound. So how can he be unconscious?"

Manny says, "Maybe she shot him between the eyes?"

Jaime and the woman both laugh, but then the woman leans closer and says to me in a loud whisper, "I know what Ms. English said to him before the judge shot him. Do you want to know for your book? What she whispered to Ray? After the verdict? She said, 'Don't piss off the judge, Ray, she always packs a pistol!'"

"Thanks," I say, and write it down, feeling a bit shell-shocked myself.

I don't know whether to believe her, but I take down her name, making a show of spelling it right. She looks pleased and gratified. "I just love your books," she confides, and seems eager to engage me in a conversation about them.

But just then, the door to the little courtroom elevator slides open and two paramedics in navy blue uniforms step out, carrying a gurney and medical equipment. It gives me a tactful excuse to turn away, and start taking notes again. When the paramedics eventually lift Ray onto the gurney and carry him to the elevator, he looks completely out of it. His head lolls, turning our way, and it's obvious that she didn't shoot him between the eyes. There's a splash of blood in the middle of the white shirt. Small bullet or no, he certainly appears to be hurt and unconscious. Within moments, they've got him into the elevator, along with Leanne English and a deputy sheriff.

The elevator door slides shut.

The show is over.

"Good-bye, Ray," Manny Meade intones.

"Good fucking riddance," Jaime Suarez echoes.

A spectator begins to clap, and the woman behind us calls out, "Judge, Judge!" The applause swells, and soon it seems as if the whole courtroom is calling out for Her Honor. Judge Flasschoen rises to her feet. She lifts her arms. The sleeves of her black robe fall back, revealing a black strap attached to her left forearm, which must be where she secured the gun. She bows to the crowd, and they stomp, cheer, and whistle while sheriff's deputies vainly attempt to establish order.

During the celebration, I scribble a note about how unnaturally small and skinny Ray looked on the stretcher. He could pass for a child from a distance, or for a teenager up close. For an eerie moment, just as he was being lifted, I could have sworn that his eyelids opened a fraction, and that he looked directly at me.

When I look up, I find that the state's attorney, Franklin DeWeese, is staring at me with an unreadable expression on his handsome face. My heart does an embarrassing little skip, which makes me glad that hearts are not visible from the outside. I catch myself staring at his mouth, and I quickly shift my gaze to his eyes, which still doesn't make objectivity any easier.

I step closer to him, so he can hear me.

"Congratulations, Franklin."

"Thank you, Marie. You on their side now?"

"What? Just because I'm standing here?"

It amazes me, what people assume about my biases, when I try so hard not to show any at all.

"What are you going to do about the judge, Franklin?"

"If it were up to this crowd, I'd have to give her a medal."

"Well, Florida is a death penalty state, she just tried to beat you to it."

He smiles at that. "Even our electric chair is more efficient than this, Marie." The Florida electric chair is infamous for shorting out at the worst possible time. "We don't usually wound them first and kill them later."

"Where will they take him?"

"You want to see?"

"Yes!"

"Come with me, girl, we're outta here."

The prosecutor grabs me by an elbow, and instinctively, I move away a little. He drops his hand. More subtly this time, he steers me toward the same courtroom elevator where Ray, the paramedics, a deputy, and Leanne English have just gone down.

Side by side, we wait in front of the door, where we see reflected in its metal surface a black man in a charcoal suit and a blond woman in a pale summer dress. Our glances meet in the metal, but quickly slide away from each other.

The elevator thumps to a stop on our floor.

When the door finally slides open again, and we see what's inside, I start to scream. The same sheriff's deputy who rode down is now slumped inside of the elevator. He's a young man, can't be more than thirty, but now he's wild-eyed and there's blood pouring from a terrible wound in his face, and he's crying.

The Little Mermaid

By Marie Lightfoot

~

CHAPTER TWO

Once upon a time, Susan and Tony McCullen felt blessed.

They were young, still in love, the parents of a beautiful daughter and sweet twin boys. They got along well with their families. Tony had a decent job with a good future. To top it off, they lived in one of the nicest houses in Bahia Beach. Tony thought it was the deal of a lifetime, because they hadn't had to pay a cent for it.

"My boss owns it," Tony explained to anybody who was blunt enough to inquire how an auto parts salesman and a grocery store cashier could afford a home in one of the ritziest neighborhoods in Bahia Beach. "He comes down here a lot, but his wife can't. It's hard for her to get away. They have a lot of kids in schools all over the world, so she likes to stay in one place, so their kids know where to call home."

So here was this beautiful, four-bedroom, Florida-style ranch, complete with a three-car garage and a swimming pool, on one of the high-dollar canals in Bahia, just off the Intracoastal. It was an elegant neighborhood, where royal palm trees marched in even, towering rows down both

sides of the street and where homes sold in the high six figures, and more. Tony's boss didn't want to sell it, but he
didn't want to rent it to strangers, either. So he
approached his salesman Anthony McCullen and said to
him one amazing day, "Tony, would you like to move your
family into my house?"

For free.

Or, almost free. The McCullens paid for the utilities,
and by doing completely without air-conditioning and
using the ceiling fans, they cut those bills back to practically nothing. Their boss picked up every other expense:
lawn service, pool service, even house cleaning once a
month. He didn't even mind that they had three young
children and a couple of cats.

"What if we break something?" Tony asked him.

"Accidents happen," his boss agreed. "But I know you
and Susan, and I can't think of any people I'd trust more.
Something breaks, that's what insurance is for. Don't
worry about it."

"Don't you want to sell it?"

"Hell, no, we designed the damn thing to retire in, and
that's not so far away. I like that house. My wife loves it.
We'll live in it someday, but it seems a shame to waste it,
when a family like yours could be using it."

And so the McCullens moved in.

At the time, Tony and Susan were both twenty-seven
years old. Natty Mae was four, and the boys, Todd and
Troy, were eighteen months. Susan cried for joy when she
heard about the boss's offer, she cried the first time she
walked into the house, and she cried the day they moved
in. It meant a lot more than a free place to live. Now they
wouldn't have to pay rent on their apartment, or day care
for their kids. She could stay home without feeling guilty
because she wasn't bringing home any money. A lot of
pressure lifted from Tony's broad shoulders, too.

32

But Susan is a natural-born worrier, and their new and astonishing living arrangement didn't ease her mind entirely.

"This is way above our heads," she fretted to Tony. "How are we ever going to afford the electricity on a place like this? Our kids don't know how to swim yet. What if one of them falls in the pool, or into the canal out back?"

He said they could live without air conditioning, if they had to, and he'd teach the kids to swim, and all about water safety.

That helped, but it wasn't all that worried Susan.

"We knew someday we'd have to move out," she says, "and how would our kids feel then, having to go back to where we really belonged? It's hard to step down, after you've been living in the lap of luxury. My grandma used to say, 'How are you gonna keep 'em down on the farm, after they've seen Paree?'"

Her fears about money seemed groundless, at least for their first comfortable, fun year in the house. They were the envy of everybody they knew. They gave tours to their friends and family, and pool parties where everybody brought their own booze and nobody was allowed to get out of hand, for fear of breaking things, or offending the neighbors. They began saving for their own house, the much more modest one they hoped to be able to afford one day.

They were happy, their boss was happy, even if the other employees were jealous, and said so.

But as the McCullen family's savings grew, so did their desire for a boat, just a little one, to ply the canals that tempted them from the backyard. The house had a lovely wooden dock, and what was a dock without a boat?

And so, at the beginning of their second year of living there, they purchased a used runabout for $8,000, on credit, with a down payment, and named her the *Lucky Ducky*.

33

"I had no idea boats were so expensive to keep up," Susan says. They were midwesterners who'd lived in Bahia only for a few years, and they'd been too busy having babies and trying to support them to pay much attention to the multi-million-dollar business of boating in south Florida. "Man! We might as well have decoupaged that boat in hundred-dollar bills!"

Tony says it wasn't that bad, that Susan exaggerates about it, but there was a complete engine overhaul they didn't expect, and a zillion less costly repairs and items to buy.

"Do you know you even have to buy a special key chain for a boat?" Susan told her mother back in Dayton, Ohio. "You've got to have one that floats, in case your key falls in the water."

Somehow, expenses mounted, too, just from living in such an affluent neighborhood where it was nothing for moms to take a van-load of kids to McDonald's several times a week, sometimes more than once a day. And where Susan felt Natalie couldn't go to the nearby elementary school dressed a whole lot poorer than the other girls.

It was expensive, and they weren't even trying to keep up with the Joneses! They just didn't want their children to feel different or deprived, in comparison with their playmates.

"I didn't want them to feel ashamed," Susan says.

By the night Natalie died, Susan was regularly having trouble sleeping, worrying about making ends meet. "And I wasn't the only one on that block doing that," she claims. "One thing I found out from living there, was that rich people worry about how they're going to pay their bills, too." She was learning that people everywhere have a tendency to live beyond their means, no matter the size of those means.

The gift house was turning out to be a burden, in ways

they never expected it to be. She hated to feel ungrateful, but she began to wish that Tony's boss had never offered it to them, and that they were still living in their tiny apartment on a landlocked block in a blue-collar part of town.

And then the worst happened, and the house of their dreams turned into the scene of a parent's worst nightmare.

Tony McCullen has a sensible way of speaking that goes with his appearance. A former amateur boxer, he's six foot tall, solid and muscular, with an unusually long reach from shoulder to knuckles. When he was in the ring, his nickname was The Gorilla, because of that reach, and because he's hairy—lots of curly black hair, including on his arms, legs, chest, and back.

"He was good," Susan says loyally, of his days in the boxing ring, "but I told him that if he got his nose broken, I wouldn't marry him." She's only half-joking. The truth is that Susan did hate his fighting, and she insisted he quit, because she was scared to death he'd suffer brain damage.

"I loved her enough to do it," he says. Susan, a former beauty pageant contestant, was the prettiest and most sincere girl he'd ever known, and he didn't want to lose her.

"I thought he was really cute," Susan says. "And I didn't want to be married to a punch-drunk guy with a bent nose and cauliflower ears." It made her mad to hear people call him Gorilla. When he stopped fighting, she put her foot down one more time: no more nickname. His name was Anthony, a beautiful name. He was to be known henceforth by that name, or by Tony. No more Gorilla, at least not within hearing range of his new wife.

It tickled Tony, her concern for everything about him.

"I wasn't that talented, anyway," he confides. "She gave me an excuse to get out."

He's a straightforward kind of man, blunt, good with

words, intense and focused, which are probably traits that helped to make him a rising salesman for the Motor Land Company. When he was interviewed by the Bahia Beach detectives, he looked them right in the eye, "even when he was crying," observed Detective Anschutz in her notes on their initial interview.

The ancient Chinese believed there are secret forces at work in the world drawing together those people who belong together. Those "secret forces" were believed to be entirely beneficent. It was only when human beings willfully, obstinately, abused their freedom that the gods abandoned them to fate.

Eventually, it would be possible to trace the sequence of "willful, obstinate" human error that drew Ray Raintree toward the McCullen boat dock that night, at that time, out of all the nights, times, and boat docks in south Florida. It was also possible to track the "human error" that left a door invitingly open for a little girl to be drawn down to rendezvous with her killer that night.

"I almost always watch a little Leno in the family room before I go to bed," Tony miserably explained to the detectives. The late-night talk show starring Jay Leno, he meant. "It just relaxes me, I guess." In south Florida, *The Tonight Show* doesn't come on until 11:30 P.M.

"So about how long do you usually watch it?" Detective Robyn Anschutz asked him.

"I don't know. Through the opening monologue, not much after that unless he's got a really good guest I want to see. Dennis Rodman. Tanya Harding. Controversial people, especially sports stars, like that."

But Jay Leno's first guest that night had been a hog-calling state fair winner, which hadn't been compelling enough to keep Tony up any later. He turned off the television and the lights in the family room, and went off to bed.

"Did you check on the kids, Tony?"

He didn't that night, because he didn't always. All three of them were light sleepers, and it was a mistake to make any sudden noise that might waken them. Though Natalie was deaf, she was ultrasensitive to movement in the house. Wake any of the kids, both parents said, and you could count on a long night of trying to get them back to sleep again.

So he tiptoed past their bedroom doors, then on down the hallway to the room he shared with his wife. Telling the detectives all this, Tony broke down into tears and said that he wished he had taken a last look at Natalie. One final glimpse of her sweet, sleeping face. He wished he had, maybe she would have awakened, and then the worst thing that could have happened would have been a little delayed rest for him.

But he didn't open her door.

He didn't peek in one last time.

Among all the blessings that Susan and Tony counted before they moved their family into the free house, the three most important ones were their children. There were the twins, the Holy Terrors as Tony called them: Troy and Todd, a couple of identically adorable blond babies who shared a crib and every minute of their lives from the moment they were conceived. They were always inseparable, always on the move ("Even inside my tummy!" Susan recalls with an eye-rolling grimace), and always loud. "They do everything at top volume," their mother maintains. It's an irony, of sorts, since their older sister was never able to hear a single cry they made when they were babies, or a single word they uttered as they got older. By the time they were born, when she was two years old, she was already stone deaf.

Natalie was not born that way.

"It was an unusual series of inner ear infections that did it," her osteopathic pediatrician, Dr. Norma Battle, explains. "I've never seen one child get so many serious ones, in such rapid succession. They started before she was three months old, and it seemed as if we never got one cleared up before the next one struck. We could never get her sufficiently free of infection for surgery. By the time she was eighteen months old, she was almost completely deaf." The doctor, fifty-seven and a grandmother four times over, looks upset just remembering it. "I can't help but think that in another century, she would have died from the infections, long before the age at which she was killed."

The pediatrician admits, "I have seldom felt so helpless in the face of chronic infection."

She gives a weary smile when talking about those days.

"On the other hand, when Natalie went deaf, the infections stopped as if by magic. Almost for the first time in her life, she was free of pain. Deaf, but out of pain. In that sense, the deafness came as a relief, if you see what I mean. I think even her parents would agree that dealing with a deaf—but otherwise happy—child was easier than dealing with a child who was either screaming with pain, or stuffed with medicine."

The doctor sighs in telling it.

"After that, Natalie was about the healthiest little girl you'd ever meet. She went from sick, crying, miserable, to laughing and joyous—and deaf—practically overnight."

Why was the child so susceptible to ear infections?

The pediatrician shakes her head. *"Why* is the remaining big question in medicine, isn't it? The underlying philosophical conundrum. Why, really, does anybody get any disease? And why don't other people, all other things being equal, get it? We pretend to answer that, with camouflaging, hundred-dollar words like 'immunological defi-

38

ciency.' But there's always another 'why' underneath the last answer, and another one and another one under that.

"I don't know why." Dr. Battle, seated in her office, turns to stare out at a sunny day. She looks stricken. "I don't know why that one little girl appears to have been cursed by fate."

Natalie's parents do agree that dealing with a deaf child was easier—in the relative way these things have of being compared—than dealing with a screaming one.

"There were courses we could take to help us," Susan says. "There were books we could read, there was even a language we could learn to communicate with her. It sounds hard and sad, I know, but you've got to remember that we finally had a well child. She smiled, she was happy. She could play, instead of lying on the couch, all medicated. She just blossomed overnight, and I think it was because she was so glad to be out of pain."

Susan goes on to say, "The deafness was just something we learned to live with, and it was okay, because we finally had a laughing little girl, the boys had a sister they could play with. Does that sound strange to say, that it was okay with me that my child was deaf?"

She pauses, and then expresses a thought very similar to the doctor's. "Why did one little girl have to have so much suffering? She came on this earth and she suffered for almost two solid years and then she had just four years of a normal life, and then she died in a horrible way. What's the purpose in that kind of existence, I want to know, I really do want to know."

And why did everyone who loved her have to suffer, too?

Those were the agonizing "whys" that no police detective would ever be able to solve. They did think, however, that they correctly pieced together a probable scenario for Natalie's own actions on the night she was killed.

It is believed that she woke up for some reason.

A dream. A vibration in the walls of the house. A growing pain. We'll never know for sure. Natalie, herself, may not have known exactly what woke her up.

Her room was dark, but Natalie was never scared of the dark. She was too young to gauge the hour of the night, and smart as she was, she still couldn't tell time. For all Natty knew, morning and breakfast might have been only moments away.

At some point, she decided to get up. She must have turned on the overhead light in her room, because Susan found it on when she went racing down the hall to check on her daughter after the police came the next morning.

Natalie then dressed herself.

She put on clean underpants from her underwear drawer, leaving it open as her mom always asked her not to do. She put on the same pink shorts she'd worn on Sunday. She chose a clean T-shirt from a stack of neatly folded ones in a clothes hamper. The tee was one of her favorites, even though it was a hand-me-down from her cousin Ginny. It was a souvenir from the movie *The Little Mermaid*. Natalie had a video of the film. She and her playmates loved it. They watched it almost as often as they watched the newer Disney movies. Natty had first seen the movie while she still could hear, so she knew a few words and the music by heart.

Natalie fastened a pink barrette in her hair. She never went anywhere without wearing a barrette. And she grabbed her favorite bracelet—a row of tiny, linked, plastic hearts—although she couldn't fasten it around her wrist without somebody to help her do it.

Evidently, she did not put on shoes. None were missing later. Not her summer thongs for the beach, nor her pink plastic cutout sandals for the swimming pool, nor her tennies or her white leather dress-up shoes. Natalie wasn't supposed to go barefoot outside, but this time it appears that she did.

"I took it for granted," Susan says, "that Tony locked the back door. He always did. I never even thought about it."

Tony, who was sleeping, didn't think about it either.

She was very quiet as she slipped out of the house. If she had banged the door or the screen door shut, the boys might have awakened, and probably their parents, too. A noise in the night—unexpected, startling—is enough to make almost anybody bolt straight up in bed, exclaiming, "What was that?"

But she was very quiet, like a little mouse.

Susan found the inside door open in the morning. By that time the boys were up and playing outside, so she assumed they did it.

Natalie loved the feel of grass under her bare feet.

She may have walked directly to their dock, or she may have wandered a bit first. She probably wasn't in the least afraid. Not of the dark. Not of her own yard, or her own safe neighborhood where everybody kindly watched out for the little deaf girl when they backed out of their driveways. Unlike hearing people, she wouldn't have been spooked by strange noises in the night.

At some point, she ended up down at the dock.

Natalie wasn't afraid of the water, and she adored boats. "When there wasn't an adult around to watch her, it was a fight to keep her off of our boat," her mother told the investigators. "When we visited other people's docks, I kept my eye on her every minute, or else she'd be scrambling around in their boat."

She wasn't afraid of strangers, either.

"She never met a stranger," her father says. "We tried to tell her, not everybody was her friend, but it seemed like everybody really was her friend, because they were nice to her. Wherever we went, she smiled at people and they smiled back at her. She couldn't hear what they were saying, so they could be total jerks and she wouldn't even know it."

It is surmised that when Natalie reached the dock that night, she was attracted there by a cute little black and white boat slowly puttering down the canal.

The second of three calls connected to the murder of Natalie McCullen came into Bahia Beach 911 at 11:55 P.M. on Monday, June fifteenth, the night before her body was found hanging from the bridge. The call was from a woman who lived catty-corner across the canal from the McCullens and who reported a boat moving along the water. She thought it seemed suspiciously slow, suspiciously quiet. In south Florida, burglars have access from land and water, so residents keep an eye on both.

"Send someone to check on it," she requested.

"Yes, ma'am," responded 911.

The caller was Mrs. Marjorie Noble, an eighty-six-year-old widow who lived alone, and who was alert to untoward activity on her canal. At the time of the incident, she was reclining in the dark in the Florida room at the back of her home. If you've never seen one, a Florida room is a king-size screened-in porch, more like an actual room in the house, and frequently holding a swimming pool, as did Mrs. Noble's. She thought she heard something approaching from the east, where the canal opened directly into the much larger Intracoastal Canal.

Knowing that she couldn't possibly be seen, Mrs. Noble got up and peered through the screen as best she could. It wasn't unusual to see boat traffic at any hour on the canals, but Mrs. Noble suspected there were very few innocent reasons for people to be roaming about in a boat in her neighborhood near midnight. She felt that her

42

neighbors appreciated her watchfulness, which derived, she explained, from insomnia. Many nights, Mrs. Noble stretched out on her La-Z-Boy on the porch, watching for hours the slow, peaceful night go by.

Normally, an eighty-six-year-old person claiming to witness criminal activity at night was a defense attorney's dream. On cross-examination, the value of the senior citizen's eyewitness testimony could be respectfully demolished on the grounds of aging eyesight, hearing, and memory. Whether that was fair, or not, it could be done. But not in the case of Mrs. Noble. She was, in fact, a *prosecutor's* dream.

"I had the last of my cataract operations, only six weeks before," she told the jury.

"What effect did those operations have on your eyesight, Mrs. Noble?" Franklin DeWeese inquired courteously. The defense objected, claiming that called for an expert opinion she was not qualified to give, but Franklin calmly pointed out that she was the best expert on the view from her own eyes, and that he could provide the testimony of an opthomologist, anyway, if they liked. Leanne English, the lead defense attorney, did not like any of it, but the judge allowed Franklin DeWeese to carry on. A journalist covering the trial observed this was one of the times when Franklin looked like he was struggling to keep from looking smug, because this case was so easy to prosecute.

When Mrs. Noble was finally permitted to answer his questions, she said, "It restored my sight to twenty-twenty."

Actually, as her own surgeon would testify, the operation had left Mrs. Noble with slightly better than twenty-twenty vision.

Even that might have been demolished by the defense, except that this dream witness had two other gifts for the prosecution: binoculars and cassette tapes that came complete with date, time, and recorded descriptions!

"I wanted to kiss her," Franklin DeWeese says, "after reading her deposition. When I met her, I did kiss her. Nice little buss on her cheek. I hope she didn't mind; she didn't seem offended. I told her I loved her, and wanted to marry her." The prosecutor smiles, remembering her reaction. "Mrs. Noble said that would be all right, as long as I didn't have any objection to her continuing to go to her bridge games on Wednesdays. I said, heck, no, I'll even drive you."

It was no wonder the prosecutor was enamored of his witness. Not only was she sharp and clear-spoken in person, but she had that more-than-perfect vision, those binoculars, and those recordings.

"I am a bird-watcher," she testified. "You've got to have really excellent binoculars to be a serious bird-watcher. With mine, I can see the crest on a tufted titmouse from fifty yards away." A tit is a very small bird, as Franklin made sure to point out to the jury. Much tinier, by far, than a boat on a canal, or the man steering it.

As for her notes, Mrs. Noble kept a tape recorder and a journal by her side on the porch, where she spent most of her time. She started keeping the journal for medical reasons ("You wouldn't believe what those doctors want you to keep track of!"), but it turned into a sort of hobby in which she jotted down practically everything she did, said, or thought. When writing all that down became too burdensome, she switched to a little tape recorder that her son gave her.

From then on, Mrs. Noble talked into it just as if she were talking to another person, or to herself. Everything was there, on stacks of tiny tapes. Until the prosecutor subpoenaed them, none of the tapes had ever been transcribed, but each was dated, in Mrs. Noble's tiny script. (She did continue to keep the written journal, but only for notations related to her medical affairs.)

The tape player became a place for recording both the past and the present. There were thoughtful passages on the tapes, philosophical pieces derived from her many decades of life; some clever, rhyming poetry; memories to leave for her descendants, and, of course, a constant log of her activities, from brushing her teeth in the morning to watching the moon rise at night.

"I think I hear a boat. At this hour? My watch says it's eleven-fifty-four P.M. I'll use my binocs to look. It's a motorboat. Small. It's got some kind of ugly black-and-white design on it, like a checkerboard square. And there's writing on the side, but I can't . . . the number six, it's got the number six on it. I've seen it before, or one like it. I only see one person in it, looks like a boy, but surely not at this hour. If it is, what can his parents be thinking? He's got on a yellow shirt, pink pants, green baseball cap. Crazy outfit. He looks like a parrot.

"Eleven-fifty-five P.M. Called 911. I reported young man in boat. Got no business going up and down our canal at this hour. They said they'd send someone to check. They'd better just do that!

"Twelve-oh-five A.M. When I looked through my binocs again, I saw that same boat moving back down the canal. I mean, I heard it again, I didn't see it, because my view is blocked by that roof on my neighbor's boat dock, which they ought to knock down. I've told them and told them.

"Twelve-thirty-five A.M. Good grief, there are lights being flashed through our yards. Police? Well, they're just too late, if it's them. That boat is long gone."

It was, in fact, a patrol car checking the neighborhood from the street. A few minutes later, Mrs. Noble wrote down that she heard a helicopter overhead and then saw the canal cast into high relief in its searchlight. It was so bright that she saw a fish jump out in the water, as if it were rising to a bait of false sunrise. The Bahia Beach police had not sent the 'copter over especially to check out the 911 call; it just happened to be over the neighborhood and took a look.

Two and a half hours later, Sergeant Broyle Crouse, the forty-one-year-old pilot, reported seeing a small black and white boat five canals to the west. He recognized it as a Checker Crab water taxi, not a waterway prowler. Sensing no problem with that, he banked steeply toward the ocean, and whirred away. He reported seeing only one person in the boat, which was pulled up to a much larger boat docked next to the bridge.

Crouse had spotted the number six Checker Crab at the bridge where Natalie's body would be found the next morning. Most likely, she was already dead by then.

Unfortunately, due to a shift change in the police dispatcher's office, there occurred one of those communications bollixes that curse even the best of police departments. There had been an earlier call to 911 relating to the case. It came in at 11:45 P.M. from an angry boatyard owner who called to report that one of his boats was missing and probably stolen.

"Your name, sir?"

"Donor Miller."

He spelled it for her, at her request.

"You own the missing boat?"

"Goddamn right I own it, that one and five others just like it. Tell 'em to look for a black-and-white checkered boat with a number six on it. That's my boat, goddammit."

The dispatcher who directed Sergeant Crouse to look for a possible intruder on the water didn't know about that call, and so Crouse didn't know that at 2:30 A.M. he had spotted a boat that had been reported stolen. Neither were they informed that Mr. Miller called back at 2 A.M. to cancel his earlier complaint.

"False alarm," he told the 911 operator. "Boat was here all the time, goddammit. One of my idiot employees put it in the wrong slip."

"You want me to cancel your request for an officer, sir?"

"Oh, hell, yes."

It is department policy to send an officer to check out 911 calls, even if they are later canceled. It's a well-intentioned policy, intended to prevent the sort of situation that occurs when a gun is being held to the head of the person who is calling 911. The Bahia Beach police like to make sure everything is copacetic, by sending an officer to the door to inquire, "Are you sure everything is all right, ma'am?" Or, sir. But it is only rarely carried out, because there simply aren't enough officers to handle all the false alarms, plus the legitimate requests, too. A small-boat theft was a low-priority crime, anyway, especially for the night shift. Despite departmental policy, no police officer drove out to make sure that the boatyard property and the people on it were as secure as the owner claimed they were.

It appears then, that Natalie died sometime between 11:55 P.M., when Mrs. Noble put down her binocs to pick up the phone, and 2:30 A.M., when Broyle Crouse spotted the boat near the bridge.

3
Raymond

Ray Raintree has escaped from the county courthouse.

By the time I finally get home tonight, I know enough about how he pulled it off to be able to write about it, although I can't get further than two paragraphs into it without having to stop and take a few calming breaths.

I write, on my laptop this time:

He rolled off the gurney and grabbed the deputy's gun out of its holster just as the elevator door was opening on the basement level. It was cramped in the courtroom elevator, with barely enough room for all four people who were standing, plus the gurney with Ray. He took advantage of the tight space to create maximum panic and pain. As he came up from his roll, he flailed his arms around wildly, hitting people in their faces hard, causing them to cry out and to raise their arms to protect themselves rather than acting to prevent him from escaping.

Once he had the gun, he flailed it around, too, striking everyone in his path with the hard hurtful metal weapon. Blood was flying as he grabbed Leanne by the front of her suit and jerked her off the elevator with him, leaving carnage behind them. Like a wild animal with a victim in its claws, he came out of the elevator pushing his lawyer before him.

Both paramedics fell bleeding and screaming out onto the floor.

48

The doors closed, sending the stunned and wounded deputy back up.

I stop writing, needing to get up and walk around a bit. The man has sent four people to the hospital in conditions ranging from fair to critical. The poor deputy will need reconstructive facial surgery and they still aren't sure if bone fragments entered his brain. The paramedics have broken facial bones and gruesome bruises going clear to their bones, while Leanne English has a broken jaw and a dislocated shoulder from the way he manhandled her before releasing her several hundred yards from the courthouse.

I go back to my computer, and try again:

When the paramedics can talk coherently, they report their conclusion that Ray suffered an abrasion when the bullet hit him from the judge's gun. Sometimes bullets ricochet off the very bodies they're intended to hit. This was what both paramedics believe happened, because they didn't observe an actual hole in his chest where the bullet struck him.

If that's true, Ray is not only gone, he's healthy, and certainly in much better shape than his victims. The police have already pieced together what happened next. He ditched his bloody shirt in a trash bin. He ran down to the New River, which flows through downtown, not far from the courthouse. There, he stole a life jacket from one of the boats that's permanently moored on the river. He may have washed his face and arms in the river. Then he made his way back up to Bahia Boulevard and boarded a free trolley for tourists.

The small skinny guy in the running shoes, dark trousers, and orange life vest looked a little odd to the out-of-towners on the trolley. But he didn't look all that odd compared to other weirdos they'd seen on their vacations in south Florida. Probably wore swimming trunks under those trousers, and just would rather wear the bulky life preserver than carry it. He smiled at them. Uneasily, they smiled back. How old was he, anyway? Old enough to be out of school for the day? Strange-looking little person, they hoped he wouldn't ask for money. After a moment, as the trolley continued to fill up, they stopped staring, and ignored him in order to continue their sight-seeing.

With all of the tourists, Ray stepped off the trolley at the beach. He joined the mob of pedestrians strolling on the boardwalk. The last anybody saw of him, he was slipping into a public men's room.

And that is "the last known whereabouts" of Ray Raintree.

I get up from my desk again, and walk to my windows.

A guilty verdict, a shooting, an escape.

I decide to forgive myself for feeling a bit overwrought.

My sliding glass doors are open, and my air-conditioning is turned off so I can defrost after all the hours in Judge Flasschoen's frigid courtroom. I put my hands up to the screen, and feel the mesh on my palms. I can only imagine how the jurors are feeling. One of them told me that after the verdict Ray stuck his tongue out at them, obscenely miming a French kiss in their direction. That's why they looked so upset and repulsed before the shooting. As undone as I feel on this night, I picture them prostrate in their beds, staring at their ceilings.

Poor things, are they nervous with Ray loose out there?

I slide open the screen door, and step outside into my back-yard.

I live on the west bank of the Intracoastal Canal, on the southern edge of a private, gated cul-de-sac just north of the Bahia Boulevard Bridge. From any spot on the water side of this five-room house, I can pull the drapes to get a floor-to-ceiling view of the canal and bridge traffic. At night, with the lights from the bridge, the boats, and the houses across the canal, it looks like Christmas all year-round, and I feel very grateful.

Fifteen feet below my backyard, the turbulent waters of the canal slap violently and constantly against the seawall, precluding any safe harbor for my own or anybody else's boats.

I chose this site with an eye to security, front and rear.

At the entrance to the cul-de-sac, a round-the-clock series of armed guards courteously requests identification from visitors. Nobody drives in unless the guard has their name on a list, or verifies their welcome with a phone call. There is no access at all from the water, not unless intruders are willing to risk getting their boats battered to pieces against the seawall. The cul-de-sac property owners with boats moor them elsewhere, in private marinas with their own armed guards.

The developers named this enclave Isle d'Bahia, even though it isn't an island at all, and hardly even qualifies as a peninsula, being more in the nature of a gentle outcurving of land around a point of the canal. My neighbors jokingly call it Paranoia Park, but we all have our reasons for valuing the security. For me, it's a matter of taking precautions against the types of people I write about in my books, and also against a tiny but peculiar minority of my readers.

I step back into my house, close and latch the screen.

With Ray loose out there, I feel safe in here.

Not that I'd be a target of his. The killers I interview think I'm their best friend until my book comes out. Then they hate my guts, because I've told the whole world the truth about them, which isn't anything like what they tell themselves. The book I am writing about Ray and his terrible crime isn't out yet—isn't even finished yet, and may never be—so he shouldn't be hating me yet.

It's a little early in the publishing schedule for that.

I smile to myself, and walk to another window, another soothing view.

With the windows open, I can hear the water splashing.

This house is the smallest on the cul-de-sac, a two-story apricot stucco flat-roofed cube, Italianate, with green shutters. From the street, the house is nearly invisible behind six towering cypress trees, three on either side of the double front door, which is painted a lacquered green almost identical in shade to the cypresses. The trees, themselves, are visible for miles in either direction from the canal, and are a landmark to the water traffic. From the air or the water, I can pick out the location of my home even before the big bridge comes into view.

Other people can't easily see me, however.

Their visibility is limited from the water by the fifteen-foot cliff and the fact that the house sits on just enough of a slope to block the view from the decks of boats. I can see them, if they aren't directly under my windows, but they can't see me. From my three back doors—one each from the kitchen, living room, and office—it is, oddly, a bit of an uphill walk to stand over the water.

I turn and look around my home.

Some people wouldn't agree, but I think: How fortunate I am!

There's nothing like a shooting to make you value your life.

From my foyer, the house opens into one large sunny living and dining room, all glass along the south wall. The west wing is kitchen, with wraparound windows, and a half bath. To the east is my office, on the canal side, and a bathroom and a guest bedroom behind it. My bedroom suite consumes the entire second floor, but since the house isn't large, the area seems perfectly proportioned to my sense of space, rather than seeming a room for giants. Taking my cue from the apricot stucco walls of the exterior, I have decorated the interior in the colors of the Italian countryside, or of a bowl of ripe fruit—lemons, peaches, oranges, frosted grapes, and strawberries.

"Okay, that's enough self-congratulations," I say.

I return to my desk and computer, after placing an atlas to my left where I can see it as I type. I should be hungry, but I'm not. I haven't stopped to eat dinner or change clothes in the hours since Ray escaped, but have used the time to interview every official who would talk to me. Then I hurried home to get it all down. I know that when I stop, I will feel dirty, exhausted, and starved, but while I am writing, everything else disappears.

It's one of the reasons I write.

Now, I want to make the larger escape scene clear, especially to my readers who've never been to Florida.

"On maps, Florida looks like a state where it ought to be easy to catch somebody," I type, with frequent glances at the map beside me. This is the state where I live, but it's the things a writer takes for granted that are the places where she's most likely to err. "The farther down south they are when they first escape, the easier it appears to catch them. It's a peninsula, after all, with water on three sides, where a person ought to feel just about as trapped as on an island. Anyone who has ever tried to negotiate I-95 at any time, much less rush hour, knows just how trapped you can feel on the roads in Florida.

"From where Ray escaped, he couldn't run any farther south than Homestead, not unless he dived into Florida Bay, or let himself become all too visible on the causeway to the Keys.

"To the east from where he fled, there was only the Atlantic.

"The only through road directly west to the Gulf, from where he ran, was Interstate 75, also known as Alligator Alley, a toll road where it was easy to set up roadblocks.

"North to Georgia was a long, long way on foot, and the roads were heavily traveled whether he took A1A, Interstate 95, or crossed the state to continue on up 75, or even if he crossed into the middle to get to Highway 27."

But that's only on the one hand, I'm thinking.

On the other hand, in many ways Florida is uniquely suited to escapees.

The traffic and the crowds make it easy to hide, to pick up rides, to blend in. There may be water all around, but where there's water there are boats to steal, hijack, or stowaway. Jump the right ship, and a runaway can be stepping off in Colombia in less than a week. For every highway that's easy to blockade, there are dozens of little back roads connecting to other little back roads, many of them through Everglades, or swamp, or thick forest where a man can lose himself for a lifetime, provided he has the survival skills to forage for himself—or he forces other people to give him what he needs. Not only that, but many of the thousands of boats that tie up to Florida docks are empty most of the time, waiting for their owners to fly down from Indiana, or just to get a weekend free. Scores of houses sit empty a good portion of the year, too, waiting for tourist renters, or in new developments that are slow to sell.

In many ways, Florida is an escapee's paradise, and a law enforcer's hell.

This is assuming an escapee who knows what he's doing.

I write, "For any other escapee, Florida is a nightmare state of alligators, crocodiles, snakes, quicksand, mosquitoes, poisonous

53

frogs and insects, impenetrable mangrove, black bears, panthers, other violent criminals, and a thousand different ways to drown."

I like that last phrase, and pause to admire it.

Next, comes the search, itself:

"Not even twelve hours after his escape, Ray Raintree is a man being hunted down by approximately 250 law enforcement personnel. Sheriff's officers from Howard, Palm Beach, Broward, and Dade Counties join in the search, along with officers from the Florida Highway Patrol, local police, and the Coast Guard. Many of those wear body armor, carry 9mm assault weapons, and are equipped with nightscopes. Add to that: dogs and human trackers and helicopters, and you have as close as Florida law enforcement can get to 'no stone unturned.'"

I've heard that the governor will call out the Florida National Guard, if Ray doesn't get recaptured right away.

"That'll probably be close to a hundred military police and support personnel from the closest Military Police Company," a state highway patrol officer has told me. "They'll help with roadblocks and search teams. Most of them are civilian law enforcement personnel anyway."

The search teams are already fanning out over Bahia Beach and beyond, attempting to stymie Ray's access to escape routes. I wish I could write it from Ray's viewpoint, but I am probably never going to know about that. He is likely to die, or be killed in this attempt. Hardly anybody survives manhunts of this scope, and then lives to die in the electric chair, although Ted Bundy did it, and in this very state. Even if they bring him in alive, Ray Raintree will never tell anybody the truth about what it has been like for him to be out there alone with 250 guns pointed at him.

My desk phone rings, and I answer it.

"Ms. Lightfoot, this is Detective Anschutz."

"Hi, Robyn."

There is soft laughter. "Hi, Marie. It's hard to get out of official mode."

"Tell me you've got him back in custody."

"No, that's why I'm calling, we need your help."

"Mine? Sure, what can I do?"

"Captain Giancola—Cynthia—asked Paul and me to go over all our notes on Ray, because we're trying to give the searchers some idea of where he might go. You know what I mean? Like, what he might be expected to do."

"Good luck," I say, wryly.

"Ain't that the truth," the cop agrees, with matching sarcasm. "But here's the way the captain figures it: Paul and I interviewed Ray, you interviewed him, and you interviewed us about our interviews with him. Did you follow that?"

"I did, indeed."

"So the captain says we should all go through our notes one more time, to see if there's any clue there. It's a lot to ask. Would you do that?"

"Of course, Robyn, although I'm not optimistic."

"Me, neither. You got my number."

"I do, and at home."

"So you'll call me right away if you find anything."

"Will you call *me* if you find anything?"

The detective laughs. "God, there's a price to everything."

"Ain't it the truth."

"All right, it's a deal."

Well, this is interesting. And this is good, allowing me to return some of the many favors the cops have done for me in the researching of my book. They've sat patiently through interviews, put up with a million of my questions, even posed for photographs. I am happy to do this for them, and a little excited at the idea that I might find a tidbit of information that could lead them right to Ray.

I make myself a fresh pot of coffee, and then turn to my files.

After curling up on my living room couch, I start with my own chapters three and four, because they lead up to the spooky moment when Ray first showed up in his own story, a moment that doesn't even hint at the horror to come in chapter five.

The Little Mermaid

By Marie Lightfoot

~

CHAPTER THREE

*D*etective *Paul Flanck appeared to be just ambling around, not* doing anything in particular at the crime scene, but that impression was far from correct.

It is a widely held opinion in the police department that Paul takes a wider view of things than most people— like learning Spanish for the future. His boss, Captain Cynthia Giancola, likes to have Paul walk around crime scenes taking in the big picture. While others pick up—literally— the smallest details, Paul's job is to take it all in. The captain says it's like having close-up photos as well as panoramic shots. Both kinds are indispensable to the investigators.

That is why on the morning that the child's body was found, Detective Flanck slowly paced a wide perimeter, beyond the police barricades. At that very early point in the investigation, none of the officers at the scene knew about Mrs. Noble's call to 911 a little over seven hours earlier. Nor did they know about Sergeant Crouse spotting a Checker Crab at this bridge, from his helicopter.

Paul was thinking about the possible avenues of access

and exit for the killer. By car, it would be easy to drive up, drop the body on the fishing line over the bridge, drive away. By water it would be difficult, but still possible. He wondered if there was more than one person involved, perhaps one to hold a boat steady and at least one other to affix the fishing pole to the bridge. It was conceivable that there was someone in a car and somebody else in a boat. Paul didn't want to limit his imagination when considering the way it might have happened; he let his mind play with as many possibilities as he could think of, staying open to the persuasions of logic, experience, intuition, and good old common horse sense.

"I saw," he explains in his tough guy growl, "that there was really only one place down on the water to tie up a boat, and that was on the east side of the bridge." To Paul, that meant if the killer or killers came by boat alone, it had to have been from the east because until only a couple of hours earlier the water would have been too high for anyone to get from the west side of the bridge to the east, and the child was dangling from the east side.

On the east side only, there was a boat tied up to a dock. It was a big, beautiful Hatteras, Paul observed, estimating it (correctly) to be forty-seven feet long. The boat's name was scrawled across the back in flashy silver letters: *Overboard.* Paul smiled to himself when he read that. Did that mean the owners felt they'd been a bit extravagant— gone overboard—to buy it? It had a flying bridge all decked out for deep sea fishing. The gleaming, immaculate fishing yacht was tied up to a well-maintained cement dock at the rear of a private backyard from which you could climb a short but rather steep little grassy hill to the street and the bridge.

Paul saw that a boater could have stopped beside the Hatteras, tied up to one of the big metal cleats on her deck, and then used her swim platform and ladder to climb onto the aft deck. He could have walked right across her gleaming white fiberglass deck, climbed out of the Hatteras onto the cement dock, and then made his way up to the bridge, streetside.

In his imagination, Paul pictured a shadowy, anonymous figure doing just that . . . carrying a fishing pole, propping it between the railing of the bridge so the line hung down . . .

"No," Paul corrected himself. "The killer would have cast the line out, snagging his own boat with the hook, because how else was he going to get hold of the line again to wrap it around her neck?"

In the imagined scene, the killer then retraced his steps back onto the deck of the Hatteras, down into his own boat, where he grabbed the dangling fishing line, wrapped it several times around his victim's throat, and then lowered her into the water, letting the inflowing tide carry the body on the line toward the west, a bit under the bridge, until the line grew taut.

"Of course," says Paul, "my ideas were all bull if he arrived by car, or had an accomplice in a car."

But if the killer (he or she, at this point) had arrived by water, Paul worked it out that meant the killer had to have entered the canal from the east, or Intracoastal Canal side, because of the tide. (Later, that idea would connect with the fact that the Checker Crab Company was located only two and a half miles west of the Intracoastal Canal.)

No one else at the crime scene had looked at the private yacht behind the house yet. Paul saw two people standing in a Florida room, peering out at all of the commotion around the bridge.

He walked close enough to call out to them, "That your boat?"

In Florida, just because there is a boat docked at a house doesn't automatically mean it belongs to the homeowners. Many of them rent out dock space to other people. But a man in shorts and no shirt, appearing to be in his sixties, opened the screen door, and yelled back, "Yeah!"

Within minutes, Paul had from them a signed consent-to-search form. They were a retired couple from Oklahoma City, in their sixties, and visibly upset by the nature of the crime at their back door. They hadn't heard a thing, they told the detective. "What a terrible thing," the wife said, with tears in her eyes. She told Paul they had moved to Bahia Beach to be near their own grandchildren. Whatever they could do to help, they were glad to do. And so, he was soon on his way down their backyard to their dock to look at their yacht. He stood on the dock to which it was snugged, and gave it the once-over.

Nice, he thought, as who wouldn't?

A saltwater fisherman, himself, he couldn't help but think how great it would be to steer a beauty like this down around Government Cut on a Sunday morning, throw out a live crab on the end of a line, drop it into 150 feet of water, and hope for about a seventy-pound tarpon, maybe some kingfish and barracuda. It was hard not to be envious in a place with more than thirty thousand boats, some of them big enough to accommodate their own helicopters. But Paul figured he could have a decent retirement, or a big boat, but not both. Anyway, a man could catch a damn big fish off an eighteen-foot ketch, and it was the size of the fish that mattered to him, not the size of the boat.

Almost at once, he noticed a dark smudge on the otherwise pristine white fiberglass deck of the *Overboard*. Paul removed his own shoes and stepped onto the boat for a closer look.

The smudge looked to him like a large cigarette ash, flattened by someone walking on it.

If the killer had been smoking, maybe had a cigarette

dangling from his mouth, he could have dropped an ash onto the deck without realizing it. If the crime happened at night, as Paul assumed, the killer might not have seen the fallen ash, even if the white deck was illuminated by the moon or by lights. The smallest shadow would hide an ash, or this smudge. Standing there in his stocking feet, Paul noticed something else that gave his heart an excited jolt.

At the edge of the deck, right where someone boarding from another boat might have first set down a foot, there was the print of the toe of a shoe. Plain as day. With a distinctive V pattern sliced irregularly with the sort of individualistic "wear marks" that delight an investigator's soul, because they're so simple to match with the shoe that made them. If you can find the shoe, that is. If there was even a little water and dirt in the bottom of the killer's boat (this was still assuming the killer came by boat), and if the killer stepped into it before boarding the *Overboard,* then he would leave this imprint.

Paul backed carefully away.

He got off the yacht and pulled his shoes back on, before heading over to his colleagues to report his possibly important discoveries. They might be nothing, have no relationship to the crime. Or . . .

Sometimes, it pays to take the long view.

Paul Flanck's imaginings about a lone killer in a boat turned out to be almost exactly what had happened in the earliest hour of Tuesday morning.

Detective Robyn Anschutz says she did only one useful thing that morning at the crime scene, and that was to cater to a couple of her own idiosyncratic convictions. Having been trained with a generation of young cops who were fed FBI statistics and psychological profiles along with more traditional training, Robyn firmly believes two weird but verifiable ideas:

60

One: Murderers not only return to the scene of their crime, but they like to watch the investigation of it.

And, two: Many killers are infatuated with police work. They like to hang around cops, in other words.

And they really like to watch those cops work at the scene of the crime they committed. They like to be "helpful," and may volunteer in a search, for instance, and they enjoy the feelings of secret superiority they may experience while watching the "dumb" cops go down blind alleys or commit investigative errors.

Because she believes in the likelihood of both of those implausible events, Robyn took a good long look at every face in the growing crowd that morning. Cops. Media. Citizens. Everybody.

"I don't get to go to all that many murder scenes," she says, "which may surprise you. But I'm always bugging our still photographers and our video guys to include the spectators in their shots. I always want to see who was there."

She admits that she had never yet been able to match a spectator's face with the eventual suspect's—or convicted killer's— face, but she kept thinking that one day she would. Robyn likes to look over "spectator pictures" early in a case, so that she may recognize a suspect if she comes across him (or her) later.

"It was just this nutty hobby, you might say," she says, "until the Natalie Mae McCullen murder."

At that scene, that morning, indulging her heretofore unproductive hobby, Robyn noticed a wealth of typical south Florida faces. There were tanned, elderly women turned out in Lilly Pulitzer pinks and greens, and there were guayabera-shirted men in summer shorts or slacks. She noticed women in swimming suits, sundresses, shorts, halter tops, or tees. She saw bare-chested men. It was the usual mix of tourists, retirees, and hard-working residents, plus a sprinkling of the homeless men who sometimes haunted even the most posh boulevards. And her eye was definitely caught that morning by a figure she originally mistook for a boy. Dressed in an outrageously garish mix of yellow and pink, topped by a green baseball cap, he looked as if he had been wildly overdressed for the beach by his mother.

But on second glance, Robyn decided that the skinny, boylike body was more mature than that. It was a youngish man, Robyn decided then. She couldn't see his face under the bill of the cap, but she sensed how intently he stared at the busy activities of the police, and how very alone he appeared even while standing in the middle of a band of gawkers beyond the police barricades.

Robyn not only filed him away in her memory, she also sauntered over to the crime scene unit photographer and directed him to get a picture of "the fashion plate in the dirty pink."

"Maybe it was intuition," Robyn says. "Or, maybe it was experience. But if somebody told me that I had to pick the murderer out of the crowd, or die, I'd have pointed to him."

And she was right.

Locating and arresting the suspect turned out to be almost as fast and easy as identifying the victim had been.

"We should have known it was all too easy," Paul Flanck says, bitterly. "I should have known it was all bound to get more complicated down the line." But then, he's an admitted cynic and pessimist. "Protective coloration" Robyn calls it. She claims that some cops need that kind of attitude to protect themselves from overwhelming disillusionment. When Paul hears that, he laughs and retorts, "Oh, come on, Robyn, I'm a realist, that's all."

He adds, "The world can always prove to me that it's a better place than I think it is. In the meantime, I'll just go ahead and continue to expect the worst of it."

Robyn Anschutz remembers the exact pieces of the puzzle that came together with such amazing speed to point an arrow sharply at the Checker Crab Water Transit Company.

"We have a veteran chopper pilot, Broyle Crouse," she explains. "And when Broyle heard which bridge we found the body at, he remembered the water taxi he'd seen there the previous night. He didn't really think it was connected to the murder, but he called my partner anyway. They're old buddies from way back. They like to fish and fly together.

"So, Crouse tells Paul about how he saw the number six Checker Crab right up next to the big Hatteras parked—docked—on the northeast side of the bridge and how he saw one person in it. He thought it was a guy, he said. So Paul puts that together with the footprint he found on the deck of the yacht and the cigarette ash. And then we had the unbelievable break of that 911 call from the old lady who saw a black-and-white checked boat right at the McCullens' dock. And the other 911 call from the boatyard owner. Bing, bing, bam, everything came together all at once. It was the 911 operator who took it on herself to tell us.

"It was like everybody was upset about this little girl getting killed and how her little body was left like that to hang in public, and so everybody went on hyperalert and remembered the things they needed to."

Detectives Anschutz and Flanck obtained a search warrant.

Water taxis are a lot of fun. Tourists love them, and they're cheaper than cabs. Locals use them sparingly for special treats, like children's birthday parties, and for out-of-town guests. In Bahia Beach, there are three licensed companies that putter along the water routes, competing for hotel and restaurant business, and carrying tourists to attractions such as Ocean World down in Lauderdale, or even to shopping malls.

It's a wonderful ride, day or night.

During the day, tourists get a water's eye view of the fascinating boat traffic that rides the Intracoastal, and they can ogle the backyards of the mansions that line the canals. At night, they get a glamorous tour with all the glittering lights reflected in the black water. As the mayor of Bahia Beach says, "If I had a dollar for every time a tourist took a ride in a water taxi and said, 'Gee, I wish I lived here,' I could afford to run for governor."

At the time of Natty's abduction and murder, Checker Crab was the smallest and least successful of the water taxi businesses in Bahia. The other two operated out of tidy, attractive docks right on the Intracoastal. But the detectives traced Checker up a swampy little backwater bay off the New River. They drove into its gravel parking lot no more than three hours after Natalie's body was found at the bridge.

The developments in the case were moving very fast.

"What a dump," was Paul's verdict on the boatyard.

"Atmospheric," said Robyn, with wry diplomacy.

They were going in alone, but there was backup close by. "We didn't know if we'd turn up a suspect," Paul explains. "But we were definitely after the boat."

Surprisingly, considering how disreputable the boatyard looked, it seemed to have stayed out of trouble with the law. Its boats passed their mechanical inspections, the drivers didn't accumulate water traffic citations, and it even paid its taxes on time. It didn't get embroiled in local controversies, and it kept within the letter of the local zoning and occupational laws. To all appearances, it wasn't a bad corporate citizen of the county, merely a messy one. Even as an eyesore, it was pretty well hidden from general view, behind thick stands of mangrove, sea grape, and Spanish moss.

Detectives Flanck and Anschutz thought they understood the comparative tackiness of the company the minute they saw the owner. In Paul's judgment, "He looked like a loser."

"You the owner?"

"Do I have to admit it?"

The man's frank humor surprised them.

"You're not under oath," Paul joked, in response.

In Paul's and Robyn's view, the owner must at this point in the investigation be considered a possible suspect. He looked about sixty-five, and he was chubby, short, with a pot belly covered by a dirty white T-shirt over filthy blue jeans. He was balding, and his few strands of hair looked dark and greasy. Robyn found him unpleasant to look at. She flinched when she got a load of what he wore around his neck: a grimy silver chain with a small but real scorpion flattened between two glass circles that were held together by a silver rim. The man appeared not to have shaved in a couple of days, and his fingernails were long, broken, dirty. Still, he laughed good-humoredly at Paul's response, and waved an arm to invite the detective into his office. Before sitting down in there, Paul reluctantly accepted the handshake the man offered, over his gray metal desk. The desk looked, Robyn thought, like it was adrift in an ocean of unfiled paperwork.

The owner didn't offer his hand to the female cop, or look at her, or direct any of his comments toward Robyn. She was glad not to have to shake his grimy hand. It wasn't the first time she was ever ignored; over time, she has learned to use it, instead of resent it. She says it gives her the opportunity to watch everything, every nuance.

"My name's Donor Miller," the man said, fiddling with the flattened scorpion in the medallion on his chest. "I confess, I own this place."

Paul joked, "I don't have to beat it out of you?"

"Hell, I'm not *that* ashamed of it."

"Did you say Donor? Like blood—"

"Right."

"I gotta ask."

Mr. Miller sighed, and let go of his scorpion necklace. "I ought to wear a button. It'd say, 'Both my folks were drunks. They lived off money they made donating blood.' My name was a joke to them. I was, too, I guess. Joke's on them, though, isn't it? They're dead. I'm not. What can I tell you, Detective? My license expired, or something?"

"You reported one of your boats stolen last night."

The company owner looked surprised, but then he waved a hand dismissively. "Oh, hell, that's why you're here? That was nothing. I thought it was gone, but it was just in the wrong slip. When I went back later, I found it. I'm gonna ream out the dockhand who screwed up."

"Are you sure it was there the whole time?"

"Why wouldn't it be?"

"Could someone have taken it out?"

"For a joyride, like?"

Carefully, Paul nodded.

The owner shook his head. There was an old silver harmonica lying on his desk, and he picked it up and tapped one end of it into the palm of his other hand. "Nah. Wouldn't have had a key, and I've fixed them so they ain't easy to hot-wire. One of my stupid guys put it in the wrong slip, like I said."

"Which boat was it, Mr. Miller?"

"Which—you mean, like what number do I call it by? Well, I only have six of them, and it was number six."

"Would you show it to me?"

Robyn watched the owner blink. For the first time, he showed impatience. He put the harmonica down. "I told you, it was a mistake. Why you want to look at a boat that was never gone?"

"Got to put something in my report."

Donor Miller laughed at that. "Red tape! It's every-where! Okay, come on, I'll show you the damned boat. Hell, a report on a boat that wasn't stolen, ain't that a bitch?"

"Sure is." Paul, who has a soft spot for the "mouth organ," asked, "You play that thing?"

"This?" Miller picked up the harmonica, then tossed it carelessly down again. "This is for amateurs. Blues players who only know four chords and a slide. I used to be a musi-cian, but I don't play anymore. Make a hell of a lot more money in boats."

"I can believe that."

The detectives followed the chubby marina owner out to the docks.

On the way to the slips, they learned more about Checker Crab, without knowing if any of it was useful.

"How many men you got working for you, Mr. Miller?"

"What's today? Tuesday? Nobody's quit today yet, so I guess I still got eleven, although working might not be the word I'd use to describe what they do."

"Eleven full-time?"

"Oh, hell, no, only me and my main boat mechanic are full-time."

"So you've got, what, part-time drivers and part-time mechanics?"

"Yeah, I like it best if they can do their own repairs."

"All men?"

"Couple women, they all come and go, a lot of kids, you know, college kids working their way. It's a good job for them, it's easy, they make tips, and they meet the girls." He smirked. "Or the boys."

"What hours do you run?"

"Six A.M. to midnight."

"So it was around midnight you thought you had a boat missing?"

"Yeah."

"Do you recall the exact time you saw it wasn't in the right slip?"

That got him a sharp glance from the owner. "You gotta have that for your report, too?"

"You called into 911 at eleven-forty-five P.M."

"Okay, so it was however long it took me to walk up from the dock to the phone, after getting real pissed off and standing around and cussing for a while."

"How long, five minutes, ten minutes . . . between seeing the empty slip and calling 911?"

"Give or take."

"Not like an hour, though."

"No, nothing like that. What the hell difference does it make? Okay, say it was five minutes, maybe."

"Don't agree with me just to agree with me. Was it five minutes, or wasn't it?"

"Hell, I don't know! It's not like I was timing it. Five minutes sounds right."

"And what time did you see the boat was back?"

"It wasn't back, I'm trying to tell you. It was here all the time."

Robyn stepped forward for the first time. "Mr. Miller, your boat was seen at least twice last night, after midnight, on the water. Boat six. Checker Crab."

"What?" The owner stared at Paul, as if he were the one who had spoken. "Goddammit! Who took my boat? Why are you running me around like this, all the time you knew the truth that it was really gone?"

Robyn held up the search warrant they'd brought with them.

"We're investigating it in relation to a homicide."

"A what?"

"A homicide."

The detectives watched the man stare off toward the

68

dock they were approaching. They saw three black-and-white checked boats, three empty slips, and ten other boats of sundry sizes in larger slips.

"Shit." He reached for his medallion and held on to it. "One of my boats?"

"Who do those other boats belong to, Mr. Miller?"

"What? I rent out dock space to people."

They walked up to the head of slip six.

"When you made those calls to 911, Mr. Miller," Robyn asked him, "was there anybody else here at the time?"

"Have I got a witness, do you mean? Jesus. Do I need one? Hell, I had drivers coming and going. There might have been somebody here then. Jesus! Do I need a lawyer, or something?"

"Calm down," Paul said, bluntly. "These are just questions we've got to ask. If you didn't do anything, you've got nothing to worry about. We're interested in the boat. This it?"

"Yeah."

Robyn walked onto the wooden dock, while behind her, Paul asked the owner, "Has this boat been out since then?"

Miller shook his head, his volubility suddenly drying up. ("He looked scared to death," Robyn would tell their supervisor. She didn't enjoy frightening people, but it was almost unavoidable, since murder investigations scare both the guilty and the innocent.)

The open motorboat in the slip looked a mess, as if whoever had taken it out last had failed to clean up after himself, or herself. Looking down into it, Robyn saw a black tarp, a half-empty bag of grocery store popcorn, and several clear shoe prints.

And a child's bracelet.

"Paul!"

The bracelet floated in about an inch of water on the

69

bottom of the boat. It was a chain of little plastic hearts, each heart a different pastel shade of red, from deepest rose to palest pink. It was whole, not broken, as if its little owner had not been able to put it on her wrist by herself, and so had carried it with her, clutching it in her small hand.

Her partner and the marina owner walked over to look.

Robyn Anschutz felt a strange surge of conflicting emotions: exhilaration and a wave of sadness so strong she was afraid she might break down and cry, right there in broad daylight, standing between her partner and the tough old Checker Crab owner.

"What are you looking at?" Donor Miller asked them. "Listen, whatever happened, I didn't have anything to do with it!"

Paul Flanck's feelings weren't in the least conflicted when he saw the child's bracelet. He stared at Donor Miller and thought, Ask who got killed, you self-absorbed son-of-a-bitch. Ask about the victim you asshole. As he would say later, "I cuss, but not out loud. It's not professional. It may sound funny, but the fact that I restrain myself, I think it's one of the things that separates me from them."

The pair of detectives homed in fast and hard on the essentials of what they wanted to know.

"Who put this boat back in the slip last night, Donor?"

"I don't know."

"Why did you try to cancel your 911 call?"

"Hell, I got my boat back. Listen, what's this got to do with that homicide you said—"

"Who was the last person you knew of to take this boat out? Who's got access to your keys? Does anybody have their own key to it?"

"Wait a minute, wait a minute! I'm thinking I need to

70

call my lawyer. I ain't responsible if somebody's done something stupid with one of my boats. It's a goddamned bitch being a business owner these days. You can't mind your own business without getting sued. What the hell's my boat got to do with anything?"

"This boat was seen in the vicinity of where a child was killed."

"Killed. What do you mean, like murdered? Like a child molester, some pervert? Or, like in a boat accident? Was it a boat accident? Somebody stole my boat and hit somebody with it, and somebody got killed? That ain't my fault."

He pointed at boat six.

"There ain't a scratch on it."

"How do you know that?"

"Cause I'm looking at it! You can see for yourselves!"

"Let's go back to your office and check on who took the boat out yesterday."

"Paul!"

While he was distracting the taxi owner with disturbing questions, Robyn was quietly nosing around. The men looked over, and saw her standing with her hands on her hips, staring down into a battered metal trash bin on the dock just inches from the bow of boat number six.

"Come here," she said.

When the men were there to witness her actions, she slipped a ballpoint pen from her shirt pocket and used it to lift an object from the top of the trash in the bin. With a gesture that looked persnickety, she pulled out her own shirttail and used it to cover her free hand so that she could spread out the object without contaminating it with her own fingerprints. She displayed it to the men's view, as if it were hung on a clothesline.

It was a T-shirt, sodden, white, with the words CHECKER CRAB CO. in black letters. Opposite was a smear of reddish pink that looked like diluted blood. Above a pocket on the front were printed the letters RAY.

Detective Anschutz stared over the trash bin at the marina owner.

Quietly, she asked him, "Who's Ray?"

The Little Mermaid

By Marie Lightfoot

~

CHAPTER FOUR

Ray is just this weird guy I give odd jobs to."

That's what Donor Miller told the detectives when they asked him about the owner of the T-shirt in the trash bin. "I don't know anything about him, except he does what I tell him, as long as I keep it simple."

Detectives Flanck and Anschutz smelled an unpleasant aroma down by the docks, but as native Floridians they weren't alarmed. People from out of state might have recoiled, and exclaimed, "Who died here?" But as native Floridians, Paul and Robyn recognized the "fragrance" of a backwater bay. It was the smell of dead fish and of sulfur from the decaying layers of leaves that fell into the water from the branches of mangrove trees around the marina. This was, after all, part of the New River, a fascinating waterway that winds through scenery that is dramatic both by virtue of its content and its contrasts: From the parkways, bridges, and boat docks of downtown Fort Lauderdale, up the big branch into Bahia Beach, and back up the north channel to Lake Okeechobee, it's a biologist's dream, a boater's fantasy.

"What's his full name?"

"Raymond Raintree."

"Where can we find him?"

"Hell, he's always here."

Robyn Anschutz and Paul Flanck exchanged glances.

"You mind if we look for him?"

The boat owner sank down on a dock rail, and put his face in his hands. "No," he mumbled. "As if it makes any difference what I want. Shit. That little bastard. I'm probably the only person on this green earth who's ever been decent to him, and this is how he repays me. Shit."

Paul gazed at the man with loathing, and thought again, Ask about the victim. Just once. Pretend you care.

"Does this Ray have a criminal record?" Robyn asked. "Does he have a firearm?"

"Oh, shit. You may as well know. Hell, no, he doesn't have a record. He doesn't even have a Social Security card."

Robyn frowned. "How old's he? Are we talking about a kid?"

"An immigrant, or something?" Paul chimed in.

"No, no, he's just weird. He showed up one day a long time ago and I gave him some work, and he's been around ever since. Okay, I'll admit I don't even have him on my payroll. I just slip him some money now and then."

"Mr. Miller, does Ray own or possess any weapons we ought to know about? Pistols, shotguns, homemade bombs?"

"Thermonuclear devices?" The joke was said bitterly, angrily. "Hell, I don't know. I doubt it, he's not the type. He's not a fighter, he's a hider."

"A what?"

"A hider. Shy, I guess. Hell, if I looked like him, I'd be shy, too. He hasn't even got what you'd call a personality. He's a whatchucallit, hermit. The other men, they call him the hermit crab."

When Robyn heard that, she cast a sardonic eye at the

74

company owner. If ugly equaled shy, this guy ought to be living in a cave at the bottom of the ocean.

"So where's his . . . shell?"

"Huh?"

"Where does he live?"

"Here. Like I said, I'm probably the only one's ever been nice to him. I let him bed down on the boats. Wherever there's an empty bunk."

"I'll bet the boat owners love that."

"Like I tell them?"

"Can you take us to him?"

"I don't know exactly where he is. I could call him into the office, I guess."

Robyn looked at Paul, who said, "Okay."

They followed Donor Miller back up to his office, where he picked up a microphone and pressed his thumb onto a black plastic switch. "Ray, come to the office! Ray Raintree, come to the office."

Both of the detectives experienced a moment of dismay, thinking, What have we done? Far from luring their suspect to them, the loudspeaker page—which they heard booming out over the boatyard—might alert Raintree and drive him away. They were just about to panic, when they heard the outer door open.

"I nearly dropped my teeth," Robyn Anschutz said, of the moment Ray Raintree walked into her line of vision. "It was him. My guy in the gaudy shirt, the one I'd singled out at the scene of the crime. I mean, we didn't even have time to put our hands on the butts of our guns, and there he was, the very same guy! I'd told our photographers to take a picture of this guy. I couldn't believe it."

"You call me, Donor?"

The guy looked nervous. That was Paul Flanck's *second* thought. His first was less a thought than an impulse: to step back, to look away from the face of the strange-looking

75

person who stood in the doorway staring in at them from under the bill of a bright green baseball cap. Paul didn't know about the astonishment his partner was feeling at that moment, the chill of recognition oozing down her spine. What he, himself, felt was the same sensation he'd got one time when he'd stepped on a palmetto bug in his bare feet in the dark. Palmetto bug is the euphemistic name that Floridians give to the large, flying cockroaches that infest their paradise.

Paul's ex-wife had a saying about the criminals he arrested, whenever he showed her their mug shots. "Repellent creature," she'd say, with an expression of superiority and distaste that annoyed him. More often than not, she'd add something like, "Slimy under those rocks, isn't it?" It was true, but Paul had suspected that she also thought he was "slimy" for spending his life crawling under those same rocks to get those criminals.

Now, standing face-to-face with their probable murder suspect, Paul found himself thinking what his ex-wife would have said: Repellent creature, isn't he?

Is it a man, or a boy? Paul wondered.

"How old are you?" he blurted out.

The guy shrugged, as if he didn't know, but then he said in a voice that sounded high-pitched, strangled, and nervous, "Twenty-eight?"

"You tell me," Paul retorted.

The fellow nodded, as if confirming his own age.

Both detectives thought he could have passed for much younger than that, even a middle school student. Was he lying about his age? But why would he? The laws on juvenile offenders started flashing through Paul's brain, mixed in with images from the best books he'd ever read, *The Lord of the Rings,* by J. R. R. Tolkien. In those novels, there was a sickening and evil creature named Gollum, who had lived so long deep in the bowels of the earth that he had developed the appearance of a pale worm. It was an odd analogy for Paul to make, because this boy/man was actually tanned brown as dead leaves.

Later, Paul would try to make the analogy work, by saying, "There was a furtive quality about him, and nasty, like something that's been hiding in the swamp. I was standing there hoping I wouldn't have to pat him down, because I didn't want to touch him. I thought I'd give him a thrill, let Robyn do the honors."

"As if," snorted his partner, when she heard that.

Subsequently, people as diverse as reporters, attorneys, and other prisoners would attempt to define what it was about Ray that gave most people the willies. None would ever be satisfied with their own explanation of the phenomenon. Mostly, they'd end up saying, "I can't really explain it. You'd have to see him for yourself."

"These are cops, Ray," his boss informed him.

Robyn said sharply, "Would you excuse us while we talk to Ray, Mr. Miller?"

"You want me to leave?"

"That's the idea."

"I don't think I ought to. What if he says something that incriminates my boatyard? I could get in a lot of trouble I don't deserve."

The man, or boy, in the orange and yellow Hawaiian shirt and the pink Bermuda shorts just stood in the doorway, looking in. He didn't ask why they were there, or what they wanted from him. He didn't say anything at all in that first interview unless they asked him a direct question.

"These cops want to talk to you, Ray."

"Mr. Miller," said Robyn. "Please."

"You want me to stay with you, Ray?"

The man-boy shrugged, shifted his feet.

"You need a lawyer, Ray, you tell me, I'll call somebody."

Paul glanced at Robyn and his wry look said clearly, if silently, We're losing control here.

Robyn took back control by Mirandizing their suspect.

"Raymond Raintree, you have the right . . ."

It startled her partner, but she made the unilateral decision and acted on it, because it seemed to Robyn that the other man, Donor Miller, was turning out to be a loose cannon. With him as a witness to everything that she and Paul did in the next few critical minutes, she decided they'd better not take any chances with this suspect's civil rights. If he clammed up on them, she'd take the heat for it from all the Monday morning quarterbacks who would throw a fit at the early Miranda warning. But better that, she decided, than a jury who might be distracted by false claims of civil rights violations.

"Okay," the suspect said, to the terms.

"You don't want a lawyer?"

"No."

"You understand that anything you say can be used against you?"

"Yeah."

Donor Miller started to interrupt, and Robyn turned on him angrily and snapped, "Shut up. Now. You heard us read him his rights, you heard him say he understands. You heard him say he doesn't want a lawyer and he's willing to answer our questions. So either get out of here, or sit down and shut up. One more word, and we'll slap you with obstruction of justice. Got that?"

The boat owner looked shocked, but he sat down abruptly in his office chair. Dramatically, he clapped his hands over his mouth, thus managing to further infuriate the detective.

"And all the while," Robyn recalled later, "our suspect was standing in the doorway, with his mouth hanging open and his eyes bugging out. He looked like a goddamned dead fish."

Unlike her partner, she doesn't mind cussing out loud.

"I know the difference between them and me," she says, mocking Paul's reasoning. "And if other people don't, that's their problem."

When they escorted their suspect away, Donor Miller shouted conflicting orders at him: "You need anything, you make them let you call me, Ray! You got a right to a phone call! You keep your mouth shut about my business, you hear me? My business is none of their goddamned business!" And his last salvo was, "I don't want to find out some little kid got hurt 'cause of you, Ray!"

"Well, glory be," Paul Flanck said, sarcastically to Robyn, over their suspect's head. "I guess the man does care, after all."

Their preliminary questioning—and all of their subsequent interrogations—were like nothing the detectives had ever seen before. Since the same basic questions were thrown at Ray many times over the next weeks, a transcript of one of the early sessions recaptures the flavor of all of them. They were remarkable for the manner in which the suspect admitted to almost all of the facts, while completely denying the obvious truths that those same facts implied.

"Ray, did you take out one of Mr. Miller's boats last night?"

"Uh-huh." (Yes.)

"Which one?"

"Six."

"Boat number six?"

"Uh-huh."

"Where is it now?"

"In slip ten."

"When did you take it out last night? What time?"

"I don't know."

"What time did you bring it back, Ray?"

"I don't know."

The suspect didn't wear a watch, so this was possible.

"Where did you go with it?"

"I drove around the canals."

"Specifically, which canals, Ray? Show us on this map."

"I went up here . . . and here . . . and over here . . . and down there."

"You went down the canal between Royal Palm and Palm Sunrise?"

That was the canal where Natalie McCullen lived with her parents, in the house owned by her father's employer.

"Uh-huh."

"What time were you there?"

"About midnight."

It was five minutes to midnight when Mrs. Marjorie Noble called 911 to report seeing the black-and-white checked cab on her canal, the same canal where the McCullens were living.

"You admit you were there at midnight?"

"Uh-huh."

"How much time did you spend on that canal, Ray?"

"I just went up and came back down."

"Did you stop at any of the docks on that canal?"

"Yeah."

"Which one, Ray? Show us on the map."

"This one." A grimy, stubby finger pointed at the McMullens' dock.

"What did you do while you were stopped at that dock, Ray?"

"I saw a little girl."

80

When Robyn heard him admit that, she could only think, *Oh, my God.*

"What happened then, Ray?"

"She got in my boat."

"How'd you get her in the boat?"

"Popcorn."

There'd been a popcorn bag on the floor of the boat.

"She got in with you to get some popcorn?"

"Uh-huh."

"Did you kill her?"

"No, I didn't do that."

This was said with complete impassivity. The questions seemed neither to surprise him, or upset him.

"Do you know she's dead, Ray?"

"Yeah?"

"Did you kill her?"

"Huh-uh." (No, said as a little boy might say it, defensively, turning the "uh" into two syllables: "Huh uh-uh.")

"Who killed her, Ray?"

"I don't know." (Again, said as a child might say it.)

"Did anybody else get into the boat with you and the girl?"

"Huh-uh." (No.)

"It was always just the two of you, you and her?"

"Yeah."

"Did she get out of the boat and go off with somebody else, Ray?"

"Nope."

"So she was only with you?"

"Uh-huh." (Yes.)

"But you didn't kill her?"

"Huh-uh." (No.)

"You admit she got into the boat with you and there was nobody else with you, so tell us the rest of it, Ray."

The answer to that was silence.

"Where did you take her?"

"I don't know."

"You don't know? Show us on the map."

"I can't. I don't know."

Mrs. Noble had seen him on her canal at midnight. The helicopter pilot spotted him at the bridge at 2:30 A.M.

"Where were you for those two and a half hours, Ray?"

"I don't know."

"The last time you saw her, Ray, was she alive?"

"Uh-huh."

"She was alive? You mean . . . she was still breathing?"

Ray shook his head: No.

"What? But she wasn't dead? What are you saying?"

Again, a head shake for an answer.

"What the hell does that mean, Ray?"

Suddenly, Ray began to shout passionately, "She wasn't dead, she wasn't dead!"

That first time, they calmed him down by putting him in handcuffs and shackles. Both detectives felt relief when that was done, the kind of relief that comes from safely bagging a poisonous snake, or tranquilizing a rabid animal.

At that point, Robyn's worst fear was that this creepy guy who had done everything but admit outright that he'd killed the child, was smarter than he looked. She had an awful feeling that he, already knowing he was trapped by evidence, was from the start building up his own insanity defense, based on the idea that he was so nutty he didn't know right from wrong. In short, Robyn was afraid that she and Paul were dealing with a homicide suspect who only *looked* dull-witted, but who might be a hell of a lot smarter than they were, and several steps ahead of them already. It was one of the fears and ambiguities that many people after them would also struggle over, and few would resolve to their own satisfaction.

Holding Raymond Raintree in handcuffs, the detectives—Robyn specifically—summed up his own words for him.

"So, you admit you saw her, she rode in the boat with you, she wasn't breathing at the end, but yet you also claim she wasn't dead, and you didn't kill her?"

Their suspect was panting, his head was down, he was staring at the floor, and he didn't say a thing.

"That defies sense, Ray."

Silence from him.

"That's like saying you see the sky, but it isn't there." This was the first of a long line of metaphors and analogies that frustrated cops, lawyers, writers, and counselors would offer up to him. Others said, "That's like saying your own hand doesn't belong to you, Ray." "You might as well try to say you're not sitting here right now, Ray." "How can you keep denying the obvious? It's like describing yourself, but then saying that's not you!"

Over and over, he would give the facts that admitted Natalie was dead, and then he'd deny they meant that. Again and again, he'd admit every detail that irrefutably implicated him and nobody else, and then every time he'd deny culpability. With his own words, he proved he kidnapped and killed her. With his own words, he denied everything to which he seemed to be confessing.

It should have been a confession, but it wasn't.

It should have been a guilty plea, but it was not that, either.

"You know that book?" Robyn Anschutz says. "About how women are from Venus, and men are from Mars? I think Ray Raintree's from Pluto."

When the suspect's personal belongings were cataloged, it was a short list, but an incriminating one. There was a cheap guitar and three backpacks. One of them was full of

83

comic books. One had a razor, razor blades, toothpaste, toothbrush, a package of guitar picks, and a package of strings. It also held a child's red plastic shovel, and a small white envelope containing three baby teeth. Of course, the discovery of the teeth riveted and horrified the detectives, because of what it might mean: another murder, or two, or three? Were these three tiny ivory pieces the trophies of a serial killer?

The rest of the space in the second pack was crammed with a bizarre mix of prescription medicine with other people's names on it. The third pack held his clothes. That trio of backpacks would have seemed strange enough, but what also piqued the interest of the investigators was what they didn't find: no driver's license, no Social Security card, no bank book or checks, no bills either paid or due, no telephone numbers, no insurance cards, no photos or mementos. In fact, there was no paper at all on him or among his meager possessions, except for the paper in the comic books.

"It's just like the way he talks about the night of the murder," Robyn would say to Paul. "It's like he's denying his existence, while he's standing right in front of us."

The Little Mermaid

By Marie Lightfoot

⁓

CHAPTER FIVE

The chief medical examiner of Howard County began the autopsy on Natalie Mae McCullen at about the same time that Detective Robyn Anschutz discovered Ray's bloody T-shirt in the trash bin.

Dr. Adam Strough spoke the time into a microphone dangling above a silver table where her small body lay naked and apparently undamaged except for the mark of the fishing line pressed into her throat. Her body was ready for incisions.

Ordinarily, Dr. Strough might not have started an autopsy so promptly after receiving a corpse. Bahia Beach is a good-size city, and the medical examiner's office often has several bodies lined up to autopsy at any given time of the day or night, especially in the months of the most sweltering weather when citizens are most likely to annoy one another. But on this day, Dr. Strough put everything else aside, for the sake of the little girl.

"Three-oh-five P.M."

By four-fifteen, he finished the job of cutting through her skull in order to remove her brain.

"I don't know why I was so extra careful," he says, about how fastidiously he bared the raw hemispheres. "I didn't have any reason to think there was anything wrong inside. There was blood on her T-shirt, but not on her face, possibly because she hung in the water long enough to wash it away. She looked perfectly normal, except for the wound and bruising at her throat. But something told me to go slow."

Before the last piece of skull was removed, he exclaimed into the microphone, for the tape and posterity to hear, "My god! This child is missing part of her brain!"

But how could this be, when her entire skull was intact until he opened it himself?

Hours later, after X rays and scans, and excruciatingly careful dissection, he committed to the record his opinion: "It appears that the brain has been subjected, postmortem, to a procedure which has resulted in the mutilation of the brain and the removal of the deceased's pineal gland . . ."

His voice on the tape sounds astonished.

Detectives Anschutz and Flanck were still at the marina interviewing their suspect. By the next day, their supervisor, Captain Cynthia Giancola, would requisition a computer search to determine if any similar bizarre and awful amputation had ever been reported in any other known homicide.

Nothing would ever come up in the search.

It appeared to be a unique theft.

"The pineal gland is the most mysterious organ in the human body."

Chief Medical Examiner Strough found himself explaining to people as diverse as the police, the prosecutors, defense attorneys, the victim's family, psychologists, jailers, and journalists, and eventually to a jury.

It was mysterious enough, in fact, that he had to

refresh his memory by looking up everything he could find out about it. He wanted to be able to speak about it with some expertise, although he is the first to say that *expertise* is not the word anybody can easily apply to their knowledge of the pineal.

As he explained at the first press conference:

"Its name comes from the Latin for *pinecone,* because that is what it resembles: a tiny, fleshy pinecone. In the seventeenth century, the French philosopher René Descartes declared it to be the seat of the soul. It was in the human pineal gland, he claimed, which was located deep in the folds of the brain, that a dualist world of matter and spirit converged, it was there where the creative impulses of the invisible world of thought and spirit were magically transformed into the visible world of real things. Only humans had souls, Descartes declared, because only humans had pineal glands. He was wrong about that, as about some other things. Vertebrates have pineal glands. But to this day, science does not know a whole lot more about the purpose or function of the pineal than he did. We know it is part of the endocrine system, which also includes the pituitary, the thyroid, and other glands, and which secrete hormones. We know its function has something to do with light, and sleep, and sexual maturation, but as of the turn of the twenty-first century, we still don't know much else about it."

When his listeners still looked baffled, he continued:

"Picture a tiny, tiny pinecone. Imagine that this object is grayish in color. Like a pinecone, it is vaguely pointed at one end, larger and rounded at the other, and the whole thing is smaller than your littlest fingernail. Now place this thing in the center of your head, got that? Put it right in the middle of your brain, so to speak, although please understand that the pineal is not actually part of your brain, but rather, a part of your endocrine—your hormonal—system."

"You mean, like our sweat glands?" he was asked.

"Exactly. And our pituitary gland, and gonads. Endocrine glands secrete hormones, and in the case of the pineal gland, the hormone it secretes is melatonin."

"The stuff that helps us go to sleep?"

"Yes, although we think it does other things as well. It appears to regulate sexual maturity, for one thing. The pineal gland is larger in a child under the age of six than it is in an adult, and in the small child it secretes more of the hormone melatonin, which seems to have the effect of delaying the onset of sexual maturity. In the rare cases in which a child has a pineal gland that is smaller than normal for his or her age, that child ages faster sexually than their peers. The secretion of the hormone seems to be affected by the seasons, and by the available light. More light, more secretion of melatonin; less light, less melatonin being secreted by the pineal gland."

"What else does it do, Doc?"

He compressed his lips, and shook his head, as if at an unsolvable riddle. He decided not to confuse them by telling them what was known about the functions of the pineal in lower vertebrates, and to stick to human beings. "I wish we knew. Some scientists think it must be an extremely important organ in the body, because otherwise, why would nature have gone to such trouble to protect it? I mean, think of it, hidden way deep in the brain, behind the hard skull, and the tough, tough, dura membrane, and way on down into the midbrain. It's really no wonder that Descartes thought it was the seat of the soul. As our heart is in the protected center of our chest, so the pineal gland is in the very most protected center of our heads."

"How did he do it?" he was asked. "How can you get part of the brain out, without cracking open the skull?"

Dr. Strough hesitated at this point. What he had to say

next was pretty awful, even though the victim hadn't felt it. "I believe he went up through her nose."

His audience seemed to recoil as one, with some people crying out in disgust and horror.

"He probably used a thin probe of some sort that had a small scoop attached to the end of it."

"How could anybody ever even *think* of a thing like that, Doc?"

"Well, it's actually a very ancient method of removing a brain without disturbing the skull. The ancient Egyptians employed it when embalming their mummies. All you have to do is stick the probe up just hard enough to crack through a little bone at the base of the nose."

His audience reacted again, drawing back in dismay.

Eventually, in later interviews, he began to use charts, photographs of brain sections, drawings, even X rays, to educate a morbidly curious world about the one tiny organ that had been stolen from the body of a little girl. But at that first conference, convened by the public information officer of the Bahia Beach Police Department, he kept it simple.

"Was she raped?"

"No."

"Was there any sexual assault on her?"

"I have not found evidence of that."

"Was there anything else done to her body, besides . . ."

"Besides removing the pineal? I find no evidence of it."

"How did she die, exactly?"

"Pressure was applied to her carotid artery, hard enough and long enough to kill her. That cuts off blood flow to the brain, you know. It was quick and, I would say to you, relatively painless. The pressure the killer put on her neck might have hurt her a bit, but she would have lost consciousness quickly. And let me be very clear about the fact that the, uh, surgery on her was performed postmortem. She was dead when the probe entered her brain," he assured them. "She felt none of that."

"Small comfort," somebody muttered

And yet, as the medical examiner seemed to sense, it was an important comfort to her family and to everybody else who cringed at the merest idea that Natalie might have felt any of the physical mutilation that was performed on her body. She didn't. Everybody kept saying that to themselves, she didn't feel it. It didn't make her death less awful, but it made the hideousness of it a little easier to bear.

And then somebody asked the obvious question:

"Doc? Why would somebody want to take a pineal gland?"

The medical examiner had to shake his head and shrug, helplessly.

"Who knows why people do such things?"

But the truth was "people" didn't "do such things." As the Bahia police search on the Internet would turn up, this was apparently a unique crime. Murderers had been stealing body parts for centuries, but there was not on record any report of anybody ever before taking only the pineal gland. It is the most deeply hidden of any organ in the body, so a person would have to know how to get at it in order to take it.

"Was this, like, a surgery?" the medical examiner was asked. "Like, by a doctor?"

"Well, I wouldn't want this person operating on me," he said, grimly. "My guess is that he got what he wanted. I suppose it's even conceivable that he got it intact. But if he was operating on you, when you woke up from the anesthetic, you'd be dead, or a vegetable."

"He made a mess of it?"

The doctor merely nodded, thinking that obvious, and not wishing to dwell on it. Privately, he was thinking that if they'd seen what he had seen, they wouldn't ask questions like that. Did they really think it was possible to do such a thing neatly? "Surgeon do sometimes go in through a patient's nose for certain procedures," he explained, "but not without modern equipment to guide their hands where their eyes can't see." This had been no modern surgery.

The whole thing made people who heard it feel very nervous. They shuddered at the mere idea of it.

At first, the homicide of the little deaf girl had seemed tragic and horrible, but not unique.

Yes, there was the dramatic manner in which her body was suspended from a bridge, waiting to be discovered as soon as somebody noticed the fishing pole or the tide receded. That was unusual, maybe even unique in the annals of such morbid things, but it certainly wasn't the first time a killer left a body for easy public discovery. And yes, there was the fact that the little victim was deaf, but children both hearing and nonhearing have been dying at vicious hands, probably since the dawn of time.

And of course there were the coincidences and the speed by which the suspect was eventually located and apprehended. But that does happen sometimes, cops will tell you. ("On a good day," they may add, with a wry smile.)

In media terms, if not human terms, none of that added up to any more than a brief sensation, since a suspect was arrested so quickly. The crime provided horror for the noon news, and the arrest led the six and eleven o'clock broadcasts. By the next morning, it was already superseded by other "top stories."

But that lasted only until the results of the autopsy became known.

That's when the judgment of the suspect turned from "killer" to "monster."

The Little Mermaid

By Marie Lightfoot

~

CHAPTER SIX

That was certainly the view of the interrogating cops, and it wasn't improved when the suspect refused to take a lie detector test. The detectives had to settle for judging the relative truth of his answers themselves.

"Ray, do you know what a pineal gland is?"

He squinted his left eye. "A what?"

"Come on, Ray, a pineal gland. What is it?"

"Never heard of it." By this time, the suspect had recovered from his initial submissive attitude, and grown increasingly antagonistic. Over time, he would slide into moods and attitudes as different from one another as the various stages of a metamorphosing insect. Sometimes they would have sworn he was mildly retarded, at other times, he sounded intelligent. At first, there was a zombielike acquiescence, then combativeness, which was followed by an expansive attitude that looked suspiciously like enjoyment, and eventually there would come an iron resistance.

Paul Flanck glanced over at Robyn Anschutz, both detectives thinking the same thing: If he didn't know what a pineal gland was, why would he want one? And why would he go to so much gruesome trouble to get it?

"Did you remove the pineal gland from Natalie McCullen's body?"

"Fuck no!"

The very speed and vehemence of his answer seemed to imply that his first answer had been a lie. If he didn't know what the organ was, why was he so quick to deny taking it?

"Did someone else remove the pineal gland from Natalie McCullen's body?"

"How would I know?"

"Who else would know, but you?"

"Is this, like, multiple choice?"

"Yeah, here's your choice, Ray: life in prison, or death in the electric chair. That multiple enough for you? It could depend on how well you cooperate with us. Who put a probe into her skull and took out the pineal gland?"

"Gross! Who would do a thing like that?"

"Is that your answer?"

"Are you deaf?"

"You got a thing about deaf people, Ray?"

The suspect cupped a hand to one ear. "What'd you say?"

Paul Flanck experienced such rage at that moment that he had to leave the interrogation room and go stand outside in the hall and take a few deep breaths.

The detectives attempted to ascertain what Ray had done with the pineal he claimed he hadn't taken. Robyn could hardly believe she was actually sitting in a room listening to somebody ask questions of this nature.

"Did you eat the pineal gland taken from Natalie McCullen's body?"

"No." But he licked his lips when he said it.

Robyn thought she had never seen such an obscene gesture.

"Did you store it somewhere?"

"I don't know what you're talking about."

"Did you throw it away?"

"Waste not, want not."

Robyn said, "Did you feed the pineal gland to the fish, Ray?"

"Are you sick, or something?"

Their suspect actually looked shocked, Paul thought. Amazing what could shock a killer. He knew murderers who acted offended if anyone used the name of God in vain. Paul knew one killer who stabbed a woman because she said "goddammit" after he specifically *told* her not to. Bad guys, Paul thought, far from being truly tough, had about the thinnest skin of anybody. Their egos were not strong enough to withstand much beyond their own narrow limits on other people's behavior. You insulted them to your peril. And you could never predict exactly what would insult a really bad guy, so if you were smart, you avoided them altogether. Natalie McCullen, unfortunately, had been too young to know this, and far too little and vulnerable to be able to avoid a bad guy who really wanted to grab her.

"Did you give it to somebody else?"

"You can't give what you don't have." Ray looked smug.

Out of their suspect's line of vision, Robyn shook her head at Paul. It wasn't hard for him to read the expression on her face: *This is too weird!* He rolled his eyes, in heartfelt agreement with her.

"If you didn't give it away, did you sell it?"

"How, like in the Yellow Pages?"

When he was taken away, and they were all left in the room, Robyn exclaimed in frustration, "What the hell did he want it for?"

"We've forgotten to ask something," Paul said.

"What?"

He shot his partner a waspish look. "If we knew that, we wouldn't be forgetting it."

"He had to do something with it," Robyn said, stating the obvious.

But by the time of the trial, they still had not discovered what that was. And, although the jury would hear the grisly evidence, they wouldn't need to know all of his reasons in order to convict Ray of the murder.

If the marina of the Checker Crab Company looked a mess before the police searched it, that was nothing compared to how it appeared after they went in looking for the site at which Ray had performed his "surgery" on the body of the child. From Donor Miller's ratty desktop to the greasy dark corners of the maintenance sheds, to the interior and deck of every boat that was known to have been docked at the boatyard the night of her murder, it was all gone over with the proverbial fine-tooth comb, but to no avail.

"We left a hell of a mess for Donor to clean up," Paul Flanck says, not even trying to hide how much that pleases him, "but we didn't find what we were looking for. We thought we had something for a little while, but it was just the table where they cleaned their fish."

In fact, in spite of their best efforts to locate the place of surgery, they would come up empty-handed even by the time of the trial. The prosecutor, Franklin DeWeese, would be forced to enter the courtroom without any idea where Ray had taken the child's body between the time he picked her up and killed her, and the time he hung her from the Thirty-second Street bridge. It was frustrating, but, as the prosecutor would aver to the jury in his opening argument, "Let me tell you right off the bat, that we don't know where Ray Raintree went with Natty's body between the time he killed her and the time he abandoned her upon that bridge.

"Somewhere between her death and her hanging," State's Attorney DeWeese went on to say, "he did something terrible to that poor little body, but even as of this day, we don't know exactly where that event took place. The defense will try to tell you it matters. They'll try to tell you that you need to know what he did every minute in order to declare him guilty of these crimes. But I swear to you that's not true. It doesn't matter, not according to the law. It doesn't make any difference to this trial. In order to find him guilty, you don't have to know anything other than the fact that he killed her. Simple as that. While it matters to all of us in our hearts, it doesn't matter from a legal standpoint. He kidnapped and killed that child and mutilated her body. Period. End of statement. That's all you need to know in order to convict him, and to prevent the possibility that this man could ever commit a similar atrocity upon any other innocent child."

Even though the "surgery" was conducted postmortem, there had to have been a quantity of blood and tissue, but they didn't find much. There was some on a tarp, and microscopic examination turned up some in the boat, where they also found strands of her hair. They surmised that afterward he covered her body with the tarp in the bottom of the taxi. Eventually, based on the location of blood evidence, it was surmised that he hung her head over the side of the boat to perform his "surgery." However he did it, he kept most of the blood and tissue from getting on her or the boat, thus hiding the shocking truth inside her skull.

They couldn't point to a spot on a map where he had performed either the murder or the mutilation. They didn't know what he had done with the pineal gland after he had removed it, and they didn't know why he had taken it. And none of that mattered to the prosecutor, nor would it matter to the eventual jury.

As Franklin DeWeese would hammer home to them:

"The question is not, where did he kill her? It is not, how and where did he mutilate her body. It is not even, why did he do it? It is just: Did he do it? Did he kidnap her? Did he kill her? And the simple answer to those simple questions is: Yes, of course, he did! His own words convict him. The evidence in the boat convicts him. The eyewitness living across the canal convicts him. The testimony of the policeman in the helicopter convicts him. The footprint and the ashes on the Hatteras convict him. The footprints going up and down the bank beside the bridge convict him. The fingerprints on the fishing rod convict him, and a little girl's bloody handprint on his shirt convict him."

The prosecutor gazed from juror to juror.

"There is no reasonable doubt. No. Reasonable. Doubt. He did it. Nobody else did it. You will be so convinced of that indisputable fact that you will find it a straightforward matter to come to a straightforward verdict: Ray Raintree is guilty as charged in the first-degree felony kidnapping and murder of six-year-old Natalie Mae McCullen."

"And that's how it really was," individual members of the jury said afterward. "It really was that easy to convict him. We didn't bat an eyelash, not one of us. Guilty, guilty, guilty, twelve times, the first time we took a vote. We knew we didn't have a lot of the facts, and the defense tried to fool us into thinking that was important, but we knew better. Mr. DeWeese told us right, and we made the right decision, based on the law and the evidence."

It would not even matter that Ray's employer, Donor Miller, would not be available to testify at the trial. Three days into the investigation—after Ray had been arrested and arraigned, and following the intensive search of the premises of Miller's company—the chubby, grubby boatyard owner disappeared.

"We called him, and one of his employees answered the phone," Robyn remembers. "They said he hadn't been in that day, and nobody knew where he was, but they'd have him call us as soon as he got there. We didn't hear anything for a couple of hours, so finally we went back out there."

The detectives found everything just as they had left it: in an utter mess, which the young employees were still attempting halfheartedly to clean up. But they were slowing down their labors, as it was payday, and their boss wasn't appearing with their checks in hand. Flanck and Anschutz found Miller's ancient Oldsmobile convertible still parked in the marina lot, and his papers spread on his desk, as usual. Having learned where he lived, they stopped by a little condo where they found dozens of old movies on videotape, and musical instruments that looked even more ancient. The ratty place seemed to suit its owner well, but he wasn't in, and none of his neighbors reported having seen him since the day before.

"We figured he made a bunk," Paul Flanck says.

"A couple of the employees heard him arguing real loud with some man at the marina, and they figured it was a bill collector," Robyn adds, to explain the "bunk."

"Plus, he had made it clear he didn't want anything to do with this business," Paul adds. "He didn't want to get blamed for anything, or sued for anything, and we figured he just said the hell with it, and got himself a new used car, and left town."

Both detectives had been right there in front of Miller when he had seemed surprised to learn that his boat had actually been missing for a time from his boatyard.

They were convinced he had nothing to do with the crime, because why would he call to report his boat missing, if he were involved? Why summon cops to his marina, if he were guilty?

If Donor Miller had just upped and left, it meant that he had apparently abandoned a profitable, if not beautiful, little business. But they didn't spend a whole lot of time attempting to locate him, for the same reason that they didn't pursue the answers to some of the other mysteries of this case: They had their man, and enough evidence to convict him without any help from his employer.

Donor Miller was gone, vanished into thin air—or, rather, the thick, humid air of south Florida—but it didn't matter to anybody except the employees to whom he owed a week's pay. Nobody even bothered to tell Ray Raintree about it. Nobody cared where Donor Miller went, or what he did when he got there.

It just didn't seem to matter.

The furor over the autopsy results had not even begun to die down when the Bahia cops stopped hedging about inquiries and came out in public with the truth and a plea:

"Who is this man?"

It wasn't that their suspect didn't tell them anything. He did, increasingly and at length. Ray talked a lot of people's ears off, before he stopped talking altogether.

When Detectives Flanck and Anschutz asked him where he was from originally, he told them that he was born and raised in Brooklyn, to a family of barbers. He said that from the time he was big enough to sit up by himself in a barber's chair, he went to work with his dad and two of his uncles on Saturdays.

It sounded so normal, they nearly dozed off as they heard it.

"Biggest day of the week for barbers," he said, "'cause all the men were off work. Coming in for the trim they'd put off too long. Their wives were teasing them they looked like hippies. After they came to our barbershop, then they'd go get their cars washed and stop by the hard-

99

ware store. Then they'd go home to watch a sports game on TV. Maybe barbecue for friends in the backyard that night, with their hair cut all nice, so their friends'd say, 'Hey, who's your barber?'"

Saturday sounded like an all-male, all-American day in Brooklyn to hear Ray tell it. He painted a word picture to the detectives of himself as a little boy listening pleasurably to all the man-talk.

"The women came in during the week," he said. "Tuesdays, Wednesdays, Thursdays, with their little boys, after school. Monday's we were closed, of course. Barbershops and beauty salons are always closed on Mondays, you know."

"What was the name of the shop, Ray?"

"Ray's Barbershop," he said, as if that should be obvious. "My dad was Ray, Senior, and he was the oldest of the brothers, so it was only right to name it after him."

But then later, he told them the barbershop went back four generations, which would have placed its origins back around the Civil War, Robyn figured out. This genealogy made a certain gruesome sense to her, given the facts of the case.

Robyn said to Ray, "It seems to me that barbers used to be surgeons. Is that where you came by your interest in . . . surgery . . . Ray? Sort of part of the family history, you might say?"

He laughed, which made her skin crawl.

"Wait a minute. I thought you said it was named after your father," Paul challenged Ray. "How could it be Ray's Barbershop if your grandfather and your great-grandfather owned it, too?"

"Oh, they were named Ray. Raymond. All the men, all the fathers in my family are named that."

"Your dad wouldn't have been a senior then, would he?"

100

The suspect shrugged, as if the complexity of naming the generations was beyond him.

"I hear you used to be a barber," Ray's public defender said to him the first time she met him. This was before Leanne English's law firm appeared on the scene.

"Where'd you hear that?"

"It's here," she said, patting a transcript of his interview with the detectives. "I read it."

"That's not how it was."

"No? How was it, Ray?"

"Sharecroppers. My folks were sharecroppers in Alabama. Near Mobile? We raised cotton." He lifted his hands to show her his palms. "Still calloused, from pickin', all the years I was little. We'd be out in the fields from sunup to night. That's why I never went to school. My parents always made me work beside them in the fields. We needed the money, otherwise they'd never have done that to me. You might think that they were terrible parents for working me like that, but they were great and we had a real good time together. My mom was a great cook and my dad was the strongest man in the county, maybe in the whole state. He made a lot of money, but we never got rich, because he always gave it away to other sharecroppers for their families, so they wouldn't go hungry and their kids'd have shoes to wear in the wintertime.

"My mom always complained when he gave everything we made away, but she didn't mean it, and I could tell, because she was always cooking for other people, taking them sweet potato pies and ham steaks and biscuits, like that.

"They're dead now, my mom and dad, but they were wonderful people."

His public defender sat staring at him.

"Were there any barbers in your family?"

"Nah, I just told them that because I don't like them. My folks were sharecroppers, like I'm telling you."

The lawyer took it hook, line, and sinker until she reported it back to her boss, who looked at her incredulously, and said, "Philanthropic sharecroppers?"

When a young assistant state's attorney came to the jail to interview Ray in the watchful presence of his public defender, the young prosecutor started it all out by saying, "So which is it, Ray? Son of a barber? Son of a sharecropper? Son of Sam?"

"Hey!" objected the public defender.

"All right," the suspect said, as if capitulating to the inevitable. He cast a sly smile toward his own lawyer, whom he had fooled so easily. "Okay, I'm just screwing with you guys. I'm tired of this. I'll tell you how it really was, but then you got to leave me alone about my life. I mean, all that's over, and I don't want to have to talk about it all the time. What I told the detectives and what I told you"—he shot another sly look toward his lawyer, who stared impassively back at him—"was kind of both true. My dad was a doctor."

Ray laughed, so that his teeth showed. They looked more like baby teeth than adult ones, his public defender thought. If he had ever used the toothpaste the cops found among his belongings, she didn't see any evidence of it.

"He was a surgeon, like what barbers used to be. So that wasn't so far-fetched, was it? And he was like a gentleman farmer, too." His sly grin appeared again. "That's where I got the sharecropper. But the truth is, we raised horses, mostly, but there was a few pastures of hay to feed them. You could say that's related to sharecropping, right? And my dad really was a great man, like I said. He saved all kinds of kids' lives. He was a bone doctor, what do you call it?"

"Orthopedic surgeon, Ray," said the assistant prosecutor, with heavy sarcasm.

"Yeah, that. He fixed their bones and birth defects, and stuff."

"And your mother," said the prosecutor, in the same sarcastic tone, "she was a great cook, no doubt. A Pillsbury Bake-Off winner, maybe?"

"Well, if you're not going to believe me," Ray said, looking offended, "I'm not going to tell you anything else."

"Come on, Ray," said the prosecutor. "Tell me another story."

"Where'd you come from, Ray?" they all asked him.

He had other stories, too, to "explain" himself. He spun them out one by one, as each previous one got shot down or the detectives' patience wore thin. As each story grew more elaborate than the one before, they also seemed to move further away from anything resembling the truth.

4
Raymond

I feel my own patience wearing thin, so I put down the manuscript, and look at my watch: almost midnight, and I still don't know anything new, except that I've done a fair job on those four chapters, and I feel okay about them. Unfortunately, a good literary effort doesn't help the search effort. I get up and stretch, and go to my kitchen for a snack to see me through the next batch of pages. With a pot of smoked fish dip, a box of rice crackers, a knife, and a napkin, I return to my office to go through my notes.

Here's a sarcastic quote from Paul Flanck about Ray: "There was the My Father Was a Fireman story. Dad Was a Doctor Who Saved My Life One Time. That was a good one. Then we had, My Mother Was a Doctor and My Father Was a World-Famous History Professor. I kind of liked that one."

When she heard that, Robyn retorted, "No, the best one was, I Come from a Long Line of Attorneys. His great-grandfather was Clarence Darrow in that one, I believe, and the way he told it, you would have thought it was the god's honest truth."

But the truth is apparently what Ray is incapable of telling.

Each story sounds convincing for about the first five minutes of the telling, until it unravels over some obvious boner—like the number of Raymonds in his family. Then the detectives would say again, "Okay, one more time, Ray, whose little boy were you?" And their suspect would shrug and frown and appear to be trying really hard to remember something.

Robyn told me they thought they had a break when she telephoned Paul at home one night, woke him up, and asked him, "Paul? What kind of kid makes up stories about hero dads?"

"What?" And then the sleepy detective got it. "Adopted kids?"

"Yeah. Or kids whose dads have died."

"And kids who hate their dads—"

"I think so. They fantasize about how they're really adopted and their real dad is, like, an astronaut."

"A rich astronaut."

"A rich, handsome, football hero astronaut."

"A rich, handsome, football hero astronaut who is desperately searching for the son who got away by mistake."

"So, Robyn, are we looking for a Raymond Raintree who was adopted about twenty-eight years ago?"

Maybe they were, they agreed, but it was damn little to go on. For one thing, they didn't even know if that was his real name. Or exactly how old he was. And they sure didn't have a clue as to where he'd been born. By the time they hung up their telephones, they were both feeling as discouraged and frustrated as they were before Robyn got her bright idea to begin with.

According to my notes, it was about that time when Ray stopped spinning his tall tales. They kept asking him the same questions, but now he shrugged his skinny shoulders and said with a martyred air, "Nobody believes anything I say, so I'm not even going to try to tell you anything anymore." This was before he stopped talking entirely; at this juncture the only thing he refused to utter was any more stories.

"I think somebody insulted him," Robyn surmised at the time.

Paul disagreed. "Nah, I think he got bored."

"Maybe." For once, Robyn had conceded a point to her partner. "If we aren't going to believe him, maybe it's not fun anymore."

I was there, to see Paul roll his eyes. "And don't we just live to entertain Ray Raintree?"

"One of the problems with the situation involving Raymond," Robyn Anschutz admitted, and I wrote down, "was that sometimes it seemed so absurd that we had a hard time remembering how serious it was, too."

My own eyes are gritty with fatigue, but I think of the searchers who are a lot more weary than I am, and then I think of children all over Florida who will not be safe until Ray is captured.

I pick up my notes again, and read:

What they couldn't get out of their suspect, they attempted to dig out of his meager belongings.

"The contents of those backpacks were intriguing," Robyn said, "but they didn't tell us a thing about who he really was, or where he came from."

The detective wasn't particularly surprised to find the comic books.

"Superheroes," she scoffed. "Typical. These guys, these killers, they have this inflated idea about themselves. I've talked to psychiatrists about it. They call it 'inflation,' it's like blowing a limp balloon full of hot air. These guys—their egos—are limp balloons. Sometimes their peckers are, too, and they can get it up by acting out against weaker people. Low self-esteem doesn't even begin to describe it." She warmed to her theme. "And the way they see other people, that fits a comic book, too. We're not real or three-dimensional to them, we're just these pictures they think they can move around, stomp on, do anything they please."

You're so right, Robyn, I thought. I wouldn't be able to use that wonderful pecker quote for my book, but I could use the rest of it. From Robyn's own reading on the subject, she knew it was unfortunately true that psychopaths—if that's what their suspect was—didn't model themselves on the sterling virtues of comic book superheroes. It was only the power they craved. Psychologists might say it was a power over other people, because

106

sociopaths/psychopaths lack any real power over their own wills, having wholly surrendered to sick compulsions.

I set those notes aside and pick up another pile.

The medicine the detectives found in one backpack had troubled them.

If Ray had been stealing other people's medicine and swallowing it indiscriminately, his lawyers might have a stab at some kind of effective defense, if they could demonstrate diminished capacity.

"He was a regular little pharmacist," Paul Flanck had told me. "There were a lot of over-the-counter pills, like cold medicine, the sort of stuff everybody has in their medicine cabinets, even on a boat. He had NyQuil, Sudafed, Robitussin, zinc lozenges, ibuprofen, you name it. But he also had prescription medicine for high blood pressure and asthma. We found antibiotics and vitamins, there were suppositories and inhalants. Stem to stern. We figured the guy was a galloping hypochondriac. If he wasn't sick before he took all that stuff, he would be if he mixed them up."

They were glad of one thing: The only steroids they found were cortisteroid pills used to treat asthma and allergies.

"At least," Robyn said before the trial, "his lawyers couldn't claim a defense of steroid rage."

They asked Ray, "Why all the pills?"

He had stories for that, too.

"I collect them and give them to poor people," was Robyn's favorite.

Her partner preferred: "People take too much medicine. I'm just helping them clean out their systems."

One day, Paul asked him, "All that medicine you like to take, Ray, which one is the bullshit pill?"

How could Paul have known that this one sarcastic statement—out of all the others uttered by the frustrated cops and lawyers—would so offend the suspect that he would stop talking altogether?

But that was the beginning of Ray's long silence, a campaign he waged for many weeks, against a system that had finally stopped believing his lies. The problem was that without his lies, they didn't have anything, except the bare fact of his part-time employment at a water taxi company and the meager contents of three backpacks.

Immediately after Ray's arrest, the detectives interviewed Donor Miller again, as well as other employees of Checker Crab. I turn next to those notes. Some of my "notes" are copies of the cop's actual interviews and their arrest records. Some are just their best memories of who said what to whom. It turned out that the other employees—mainly young men and women—stayed away from Ray, considering him to be a freak. So they had nothing to contribute to the investigation, except that they hated it when Ray took out a boat for any reason, or slept on one, because he left messes behind him: food wrappers, unflushed "heads," water left running from taps, grimy handprints on pristine fiberglass, and footprints on clean canvas, not to mention cigarette butts and ashes.

"He didn't actually grind out the cigarettes on the decks of the boats," one of the girls said, referring to those boats whose owners rented dock space there. "But he'd smoke on boats where the owners told us not to, and he was real careless about where he flicked his ashes. I heard Mr. Miller yell at him a lot of times about that."

"Why did you put up with him?" Paul and Robyn asked Miller before he disappeared.

"Hell, I got a soft heart."

"Yeah, and you never personally had to clean up after him, right?" retorted Paul Flanck. "Not with other employees to do it."

"Listen, he's a worm, but even a worm's gotta live, is how I look at it."

"You're all heart, Donor."

"Like I said."

They asked how long Ray Raintree had lived and worked in the boatyard.

"Year and a half, maybe two."

That's what the other employees confirmed, although none of them had actually been employed at Checker for as long as that themselves.

"Where'd he say he came from?" the cops asked. "What did he tell you about himself when he showed up here?"

"He said he needed work and a place to bed down," Miller answered. "I told him I couldn't pay him nothin', but he could work for a bunk."

"You're all heart, truly."

"Hey! I gave him money to eat, too. You don't see him starving to death, do you?"

Once they had interviewed everybody at Checker Crab, the detectives had no place else to go.

"Dead end," said Paul.

"I think he spontaneously generated out of thin air," said Robyn. "Like on *X-Files.* He looks like something from that show. Maybe he can turn his skin inside out, or set people on fire without touching then, or maybe he's actually some kind of alien insect, or a slug, or something."

"It's too bad aliens didn't abduct him," her partner joked.

On that, the partners were agreed: It appeared that the earth would be a better place without Raymond Raintree on it.

All of that is in my notes, ready to transform into a chapter.

On my desk, volume nine of the *Encyclopedia Britannica* still lies open to pages 452 and 453, where I have been researching the pineal gland. From the encyclopedia, I have learned what the Howard County chief medical examiner didn't bother to mention, which is that in lower vertebrates the pineal has a structure like an eye, and that it's a light receptor. Human eyes are thought to have evolved from it. Upon reading that, I wondered if it could possibly have anything to do with why Ray had amputated the child's pineal gland. It sounds to me as if the pineal gland—also known as the pineal body, or the epiphysis cerebri—might also be the source of the metaphysical concept of the so-called third eye, which in some spiritual traditions is believed to "open" upon the advent of enlightenment. A spiritual adept whose third eye has opened is said to be the recipient of a pouring in of phenomenal intuitive abilities, of ageless wisdom, and even supernatural powers.

It's just what a superhero needs.

That's what we need, I think, a few supernatural powers to help us figure out Ray.

Unfortunately, I don't expect my own third eye to open, even by so much as a squint, that evening. I prop myself against a pillow. If I can't read Ray's past or his future by supernatural means, I'll keep reviewing my own manuscript instead. Maybe it will trigger some intuition. Sometimes intuition is nothing more arcane than ideas inspired by experience lodged in unconscious memory.

I reread my own words: "The Howard County state's attorney, Franklin DeWeese said, 'Ray can call himself anything he wants to, but if he's the one who murdered that child, I'm going to call him a killer. And that's all anybody needs to know.'

"No, Franklin, it isn't!" I throw the chapter aside, in frustration, before finishing even the first page. "It's not all anybody needs to know!" Or, at least it's not all my readers will want to know, and expect me to tell them. One of the reasons normal people read true crime books is to find out why people turn bad. Are they born that way, or does their family create them? Maybe Franklin could convict a man with no past, but I can't finish a book about such a person.

"Who is he?" I ask in total frustration.

My deadline is zooming up, and I'm trying not to panic.

Shame on me for agonizing about my own fate, when other fates are at stake. If there are clues in the notes and chapters I have just reread, they haven't popped out at me. Maybe they will later. I am so tired, and yet I feel morally obliged to persevere. Maybe if I take a shower, that will revive me. When I feel fresher, I'll reread the strangest interviews of all, the ones I, myself, had with Ray. They were the weirdest interviews of my life, and that is saying something, considering the villains I have known.

Bleary-eyed, I appraise my office before leaving it.

The top of my desk is three inches deep in manuscript pages from many different drafts of *The Little Mermaid*. Square in the middle of them, sits my telephone.

Uncannily, while I am looking at it, it rings.

I reach for it, but check out caller ID before picking it up. The little window says PRIVATE CALL, so there's no name or number.

"Hello?"

There's no response, though I sense somebody still on the line.

I hang on a little longer, in case it isn't a "breather," and then I hang up in disgust. I hate it when that happens. People could at least say, "Sorry, wrong number."

The call punctuates my evening, putting a comma between the last chapter and the next. During the pause, I go take a shower, which is my favorite place for sifting through old information to get new ideas. Unfortunately, nothing comes to me, though I spend a good half hour washing the courtroom off my body and out of my hair. I step out of the shower, grab a towel, and partially dry off, and I'm still half-wet when I open my bathroom door and step back into my bedroom.

I scream bloody murder.

There's a naked man lying on my bed.

"Jesus, Franklin," I exclaim, starting to laugh. "You could have knocked first."

He's the only person to whom I have given carte blanche entrance past the guard house and into the cul-de-sac, and he also has keys to my house. We've been carrying on like this since just before the trial began, and nobody knows but us. It's not as if it's illicit—I'm single, he's divorced—nor is it any particular conflict of interest for either of us. I suppose somebody prissy could make a case that it's a potential conflict for me, because how can I write objectively about somebody I'm sleeping with, but I had already written most of the chapters in which he appears, long before our heads hit the pillows. And I haven't changed a word of it. No, we keep this con-

111

fidential because we hate the idea of the gossip, and it's more fun this way. Secrecy is sexy. We've even agreed that if it ends, it'll be so much easier to quietly slide away from each other without having to say a word about it to anybody else. No explanations. No chatter behind our backs. No sympathy or arched looks toward either of us. Just a good time and then a good-bye, if that's how it plays out.

"You forgot I was coming over," he accuses.

No way I'm going to admit that's true. For one thing, it would be rude, and for another, it speaks poorly of me to say I am such an obsessive worker that I could put this vision out of my mind for a minute.

"You're a vision," I say, neatly avoiding the charge. The problem with dating trial attorneys is that they have a tendency to cross-examine. "You look like a sexy ad for sheets and pillowcases. Brown man on white linens."

"Come here," he suggests, "and let's see if you disappear."

I leap upon him without even stopping to dry off any further, and he laughs, and rolls me over until I am pinned damply against my own white sheets.

"Where'd you go?" he teases. "I can't even see you now."

I work a hand loose, and move it strategically.

"Ah." He closes his eyes, and smiles. "There you are."

As I'm showering for a second time, and he's drying off, I talk to him through the shower door over the sound of the water, telling him what I've been doing for the last several hours. "Captain Giancola wants us to go through our notes on Ray, see if we can get any clues to where he might go."

"Are you hungry?"

"Does that mean you are? Help yourself, silly."

"Want anything from the kitchen?"

I peek my head out the shower door, and with a smug and satisfied smile I say, "I already have everything I need, thanks."

He lands a quick kiss on my lips.

"You're welcome," the man says.

"Franklin?"

He sticks his head back in.

"Why aren't you more upset that Ray got away?"

"Upset?"

"Frustrated, angry, whatever."

He looks puzzled, then smiles at me. "I did my job. If they catch him, it's still done. If they don't, it's not my fault."

"No offense, but you can certainly be cold-blooded when you feel like it."

"That's why I'm the prosecutor." On his way back out the door, he adds, "And no offense taken."

I dress again, and go back into my office while he's fixing himself a late supper in my kitchen. I can hear pots and pans banging, and I know that soon rich aromas will reach me. He's an omelette wizard. While Franklin works culinary magic, I pick up some chapters I think I'm going to have to redo, because they're written in first person. Ordinarily, I don't like to put myself in my books. I know my place: I am the detached observer, invisible behind the searchlight I am shining into the souls of other people.

My stomach growling, I start to read.

The Little Mermaid

By Marie Lightfoot

~

CHAPTER SEVEN

If you ever want to experience the luxurious thrill of freedom, all you need do is take a stroll near the Howard County Jail, adjacent to the courthouse. It is all part of a legal complex that sits in downtown Bahia, only three miles from the Bahia Boardwalk, which runs along the Atlantic Ocean. If you happen to be one of the six million people who visit the area annually, you can hop on a trolley and see it all, from the sight of an accused murderer in a courtroom, to string bikinis on the beach. If the trolley doesn't appeal to you, it's only five minutes by car or a half hour by boat, from ocean to downtown. A free man or woman can even wave up at the slits they call windows in the walls of the county jail, although you'd have no way of knowing if anybody waved back. They can see you from up there in their cells, but you can't see them.

The jail where Ray Raintree resided before and during his trial is a fifteen-story blond building only a short walk away from houseboats on the New River, and park benches and patio cafés. There are probably few places in the world where the juxtaposition of imprisonment and freedom is more startling than there, in downtown Bahia. What could possibly be more free than life on a boat on a river leading to the sea?

Walking to my first appointment with Ray Raintree at the jail, I found myself staring up at those slits and thinking, *Are you guys crazy? To give up all of this, for that? What were you thinking?* There are approximately three thousand hours of sunshine in Bahia every year, and those fellows had managed to land themselves in the one place in town where the sun didn't shine.

Prison cultures are notoriously idiosyncratic. Different wardens, different ways. But as a general rule, the worse the crime the greater a prisoner's "privacy." Crimes against children, particularly, are likely to get prisoners placed in solitary confinement to protect them from the rest of the convicts, all of those sterling, virtuous characters who have so much room to be self-righteous. Heaven knows, someone who murders a middle-aged clerk at a convenience store doesn't want to be seen associating with a child molester. Goodness no.

The "privacy" accorded to the most heinous criminals often means that interviews are conducted in private as well, and not out in the bullpen with everybody and their mother. Literally, their mothers. Sometimes, these more private interviews are held in side rooms that might be otherwise entirely empty except for a table and a couple of chairs. There will be a guard observing, if not actually in the room.

My preference is for the guards to be as close as possible and heavily armed without being so obtrusive that they inhibit the person I am trying to interview. The killers are usually shackled, hands and feet. They can grab a cigarette, but they can't grab me. If they are real-life counterparts to Hannibal Lecter—completely out-of-control psychopaths who will attack anybody at any time with anything including their own bodies—then I won't go in a room with them, not even with a whole armed battalion; instead, I interview them through heavy security.

I had heard that Ray Raintree was not like that.

I decided it was safe to be in the same room with him, provided there was an armed guard seated there, too. If a guard keeps perfectly still during an interview, then the prisoner usually forgets the guard is there. That's when killers really start talking.

The first time I interviewed Ray Raintree, it was that kind of layout: a burly guard in the corner of a big empty room with muddy gray walls, no windows except for one in the door, three gray metal chairs, and a card table set up for Ray and me in the middle of the room.

The card table made me feel uneasy.

It put me too close to Ray, even though we both pushed our chairs back on the cold cement floor, and leaned our bodies back, like a couple of introverts looking for space. It was too casual, that table, especially with my cup of coffee and Ray's can of cola sitting on it.

My tape recorder didn't get much that first time, only the sound of my own voice trying to get a conversation started, and the sound of Ray playing his acoustic guitar in reply.

At my request, he didn't smoke.

The guitar was a battered old thing. The design around the hole was mostly worn away, and the edges looked like somebody gnawed on them. Even so, it was slightly amazing they'd let him have it. Some prisons do lean in a bit for those who are condemned to die, as they believed he would be, and should be. They also make a few small concessions for those who are in solitary and who are tractable, as Ray was reported to be. Evidently, he wasn't giving anybody any trouble.

There was a sour animal scent in the room, from all

116

the men who had sat there sweating into their orange jail jumpsuits.

I had been told that after he was arrested, Ray wouldn't stop talking to the detectives—one story piled atop the next—but the first time I interviewed him he wouldn't say "boo" to me, which was just as well, because I might have jumped out of my skin.

"Hello," I began.

I sounded more confident than I felt.

In response to my greeting, Ray strummed a C-major tonic chord: CEG.

I recognized it only thanks to the enforced piano lessons of my childhood: ten years of lessons and practicing, to turn out a woman who panics if she tries to play for anybody other than herself.

I interpreted that chord to mean, *"Hi, yourself."*

"Thank you for seeing me, Ray."

He strummed a C-major subdominant chord: FAC.

It seemed to say, *"What the hell, I got nothing better to do."*

"How are you doing in here?"

C-Major dominant chord: GBD.

I recognized the chords, all right, but I couldn't translate them into English. That one might have meant, *"Okay,"* or *"What a stupid question,"* or *"The food in here really sucks."* I didn't fool myself into believing we were having an actual conversation.

"I don't know how much you know about me, Ray, or what your lawyers have told you about my work?"

He began to pick out a tune one string at a time, plunk, plunk, plunk. "The Naughty Lady of Shady Lane."

I didn't know how to answer that one.

I'd heard he had a warped sense of humor.

He switched to playing, *"I wish I was in the land of cotton . . ."*

Again, I tried not to let my surprise show. I was born in

117

Birmingham, Alabama, but I couldn't believe he was referring to me. How would he have known that, anyway? There's always a little biographical information about me on the covers of my books, but he couldn't have read them; he was illiterate.

I decided to stop talking, and see what he'd play next.

That gave me a chance to get accustomed to his appearance, which was unexpectedly shocking. I had been warned, but it wasn't enough. I had heard he looked creepy, but I hadn't really understood how unnaturally small he was, or how confusingly young he appeared. It wasn't just that he was short, although he wasn't quite five foot four, but rather that he looked like a strange kind of boy, instead of a man. Skinny, bony. He might not have weighed a hundred pounds.

It was strange that someone so small could seem so terrible.

Ray looked as if he had never "filled out" as we say about grown men. There's a stage with some kids when their joints look too big for the rest of them. Their arms and legs are four sticks hinged in the middle by their knees and elbows and when they take off their shirts, they're all rib cage. He looked like that, not that I could actually see his ribs.

Ray Raintree looked like a kid in a man's outfit.

I had also heard he was a full-blown hypochondriac, constantly requesting medicine they wouldn't give him. Getting a prescription meant going to the prison clinic, and he refused to do that, not seeming to understand the one was a consequence of the other. He just wanted pills, any pills from the sound of it, something to swallow, or apply to his skin, or inhale. It made sense of the cornucopia of other people's prescriptions they had found in one of his backpacks.

When they originally booked him into the jail, and he

got the usual checkup, the doctor noted three distinguishing physical characteristics: a scar on the front, right side of his throat, a second scar right below his rib cage on his left side, and only one testicle. Ray claimed the other one got removed because he got kicked, and it ruptured, but who knew whether to believe him?

When they gave him a transcription of his own words to sign, he claimed he had never learned to read or write, except his name. Then he scribbled a sample of that on a spare piece of paper. Paul Flanck said it looked like "Da Tee," and asked him, "Where'd you go to school, Ray?".

"What's a school?" his suspect had answered, with a smirk.

"Where did you learn to play?" I asked him now, but got no reply at all.

I could see the long, narrow scar on his throat, rising out of his collar, and my gaze fastened on that for a moment, because I would rather look almost anywhere except straight into his eyes.

His face looked both too young and too old, all at the same time. The "youth" was partially in the hairless skin. Ray had probably never shaved, even though he was probably close to thirty years old. The razor and the blades in his backpack were just wishful thinking. The "age" was in the eyes, which were a flat, unpretty grayish blue color, and in the mouth, which he breathed through. He had thin, grayish blue lips, almost the same color as his eyes, very unusual, very strange to see. To me, Ray had the look of a frozen boy; a human Popsicle, shrunken and evaporated, left in the ice box too long.

He gave me the willies.

Ray played "Dixie" one clear note at a time, all the way through to the end of the song.

"Are you originally from the South, Ray?"

In reply, he strummed a G-major tonic chord: GBD,

119

followed again by the subdominant and dominant chords, and even a dominant seventh. To the detectives, when they asked about his origins, he wouldn't stop talking, even if it was all lies. I got chord progressions.

Progressions, hah! The truth was, I got nowhere with him.

I wondered if he had a large repertoire of plucked tunes, or if I was going to hear "Dixie" over and over again.

Uncannily, he began to strum another tune just as I was having that thought. This time, I recognized "Stardust," the old Hoagy Carmichael standard, which I wouldn't have thought Ray was old enough to know. He played it one note at a time. *"Sometimes I wonder why I spend the lonely nights dreaming of a star . . ."*

It's a melancholy song.

If there was anybody anywhere in the world who cared about him, the sound of his playing that song on the tape might have made them cry.

"Pretty song," I said, when he finished.

He twanged out a discordant arpeggio, which I took as a kind of musical snub, along the lines of, "Who cares what you think?"

After that, I had to give up, and say good-bye.

On my tape of that "interview," there is the sound of my chair being pushed back on the concrete. Then my footsteps, a door opening, my polite exchange with the guard who opened it. All the while, my tape was still running, recording everything. It sounds dramatic, Gothic, to hear it, because underneath the sounds of my exit there is Ray picking out on his guitar "Some Enchanted Evening."

"You will meet a stranger . . ."

I played it later for Detectives Flanck and Anschutz, and it even gave them the shivers. I've played it for a few other people since then to show them one of the spookiest interviews of my career.

I didn't know if he would agree to see me again, but my educated guess was that he would. What I suspected was that Ray wanted an audience, and if he couldn't keep it by telling lies, he'd get attention with his silence.

I never choose a case entirely because of its victim; it is usually the killer who really draws me into it. The awful truth is that, by and large, victims are not nearly as interesting, being almost by definition weaker than their killers. Can the average person name any of the eight nurses Richard Speck killed? It is the names of the killers that people remember, and that is not only because of the media's attention to them.

There are exceptions to that general rule. There are victims whose names people remember, while their killers are forgotten. But that is because those victims are the *stronger* ones, either because of their fame, or because of the strength of the outcry and investigation raised on their behalf. John Lennon and Mark . . . what's his name? And what's the name of the fellow who shot Ronald Reagan?

So what is this supposed *strength* that the public perceives in these dreadful men, and how could I possibly detect any of it in skinny, weird, unhealthy-looking Ray Raintree?

It was the strength of his long silence, for one thing, the way he wouldn't talk to anybody for the longest time, and at no apparent advantage to himself, like prisoners of war won't talk to the enemy. What was even more strange, Ray refused even to give anybody so much as the equivalent of his "rank and serial number." Even prisoners of war do that much. As for his name, that strangely poetic, alliterative, haunting moniker, nobody could even swear it was the genuine article either, not after the string of other lies and stories he spun out.

121

"Got a middle name, Ray?" they asked him.

"Steven," he said, and Francis, Quentin, and Federico. Take your pick, he gave them everything but Peter, Paul and Mary. Those first four were evidently stolen from movie directors: Spielberg, Ford Coppola, Tarantino, and Fellini. When he finally said his middle name was Suck My Cock, they quit asking him.

Even before that, there was the absolute, head-shaking, throw-your-hands-up-in-the-air utter frustration of the strength with which the guy continued to maintain black was not black and white was not white. Yes, he gave her a ride in his boat. No, that didn't mean he killed her. Yes, she stopped breathing. No, that didn't mean she was dead! As Robyn Anschutz said, "It makes me crazy, how he does that. I want to shake him until his eyes pop out of his head. I want to pick him up by his ankles and slam his head into the bars of his cell. He makes me crazy."

It was already getting into August when I got my second interview with him. He had already run through one public defender, and he was close to losing his second one, too.

The day I went to see him for a second time, I was not in a good mood. Usually, when interviewing killers, I tried to win them over, but Ray had annoyed me with the little game he played with his guitar, and the longer I had to think about it, the more annoyed I got, and I had decided to let him know it.

"Here we go again," I said, and tossed my tape recorder down.

I was determined to behave in front of him exactly the way I felt about him, which was, essentially, "Talk to me, don't talk to me. I want your story, but it's not like I care about you, or any of my readers will. You are not the hero of this book."

It was a brave attitude, but not quite an honest one.

I very much hoped he would talk his ugly little head off.

I stuck my legs out in front of me and crossed one ankle over the other. I slouched down enough to feel comfortable, and then I crossed my arms over my chest. It was a closed-off, screw-you posture, which some people might have made the mistake of seeing as defensive. It wasn't; it meant, "I can't stand you."

I let all of my dislike appear in my words and voice, too.

"Monologue with musical accompaniment," I said.

He grinned, and I nearly sat bolt upright in the chair.

A response! And one that didn't require any musical knowledge to interpret.

Ray began to pluck notes, apparently aimlessly.

"There are many things I don't know about you, Ray. Most things, I guess. I'd like to know them, not because I would be interested in them for their own sake, although I might be, but because it would give my book a greater feeling of verisimilitude."

I had planned this out, in a rather bratty way.

There was a brief pause in his plucking, and I knew I'd caught him listening to me, and that he was thinking, What is veriwhatever?

"Verisimilitude. As you know, it's very important for any writer, but especially for someone like me who purports to be writing about actual events. It's a funny word, don't you think? Its roots make it sound like an oxymoron. *Veri*—meaning, truth, and *similar*—meaning, like something else. Like the truth. Not *the* truth. Just like the truth. And yet it means, to impart a feeling of accuracy."

I had no idea if he was bright enough to follow this pompous baloney, but I knew one thing for sure: You could never exaggerate a killer's overestimation of his own intelligence. The dullest-witted psychopath was convinced that he could be in Mensa, except that taking the IQ test was beneath him.

I was trying to snag that killer-ego.

"I'd like to write about your life in a way that gives my readers a feeling of verisimilitude, Ray. If I can't do that, I'll make it up. Like you do. I'll retell the stories you've told us, and then I'll get various learned professionals to analyze them and make suppositions about what those stories suggest about the truth of your life. They may hit close to the mark, they may get it all wrong. But whatever other people say about you, that's what I'll write, and that will become the official version of your life, forever."

I stopped talking.

He began to play "Yesterday."

His choice hit me hard, that song always does, but I didn't let him see that. Was he musically joking around again? Giving me a clue?

I took it as a legitimate reply in a real conversation this time, and I listened to it as if he were talking. When the notes died away, I replied, just as if it were my turn to talk, "I don't like to tell much about myself to strangers, either. It's weird, I guess, since I tell so much about other people in my books, but I keep my own life pretty much a secret, like you do yours. When I get interviewed for magazines, I tell them exactly what I want them to know, and nothing else. And when I have to finish a book, or things start closing in, I leave town, and I go away to a place that nobody knows anything about except my attorney. I even use a different name, like I'm a criminal on the run, or something." I laughed a little. I had planned this out, too. "I'll tell you the truth, Ray. I'm not crazy about the idea of having anything in common with you, but apparently, I do."

Then I acted as if I had just had a brainstorm.

"Hey, listen, have you ever heard of hypnotic regression?"

His right hand hovered, motionless, over his strings.

"You could get hypnotized, and go back to when"—I

paraphrased the lyric to the Beatles song, which played right into my scheme—"all your troubles . . ."

He plucks the notes to accompany the next four words: *seemed so far away.*

"I know of a woman who can take you way back, skip you right over Natalie's death, Ray, and all of the years you'd rather forget, and go straight back to any happy time there might have been in your life, even if it was only the first five minutes after you were born."

His hands froze on the strings again.

"You might see your mother's face, or your father's, or maybe just a doctor or a nurse. I don't know. But a hypnotist might be able to take you back to only happy times."

I paused, raised my gaze from his frozen hands to his face.

His mouth looked slack, and he was staring at the floor.

"Think about it. Only happy times."

Our "interview" ended in silence, without any music to accompany my walk to the door this time. Then, for the first time, I heard his voice, just as I had previously heard it on the interview tapes. It was high pitched, thin, more like a boy's.

"You ever done it?"

I turned slowly, trying not to whirl around in excitement.

"Get hypnotized?"

"Yeah."

"No."

"You ever want to?"

I smiled slightly at him. "No."

He strummed the strings, looked down at his guitar, and mumbled, "Somethin' else we've got in common."

I waited a moment, and then exited.

When I went to see him three days later, it was at his request, and he didn't have his guitar with him, and he

125

began to talk. Not easily, not in the flow with which he flamboozled everybody, but slowly and cautiously, like a blind man walking down a pot-holed street.

"Ask me questions."

"Where were you born?"

"Don't know."

"How old are you?"

"Don't know."

"Do you have any memories of your childhood?"

"No."

"None, Ray? Isn't there a wisp of some kind of memory? A feeling you can recall?"

He shook his head from side to side, and frowned.

"What *is* your first memory?"

He took a very long time to answer that. Finally, he said, speaking as if reluctant to tell me, "A dog."

I waited a beat, then said, "Tell me about the dog, okay?"

He looked me full in my eyes, which unnerved me so much that I had to force myself to hold his gaze.

"Like a cocker spaniel."

"Brown and white?"

His brow furrowed again, as if something puzzled him. "No, like orange."

"Yeah, that could be right, Ray. Cockers sometimes have a kind of orange color. What did the dog do?"

He shook his head. "He was just a dog."

"You remember it was a male?" I asked, quickly. "Maybe you remember his name?"

Suddenly he stood up, startling the guard and me.

"I want to go back now."

To his cell, he meant.

He would rather go sit in his cell than sit there talking about these things.

Before he walked out, he turned around and said to

me, "That woman, the one who hypnotizes people. It won't work on me. Nobody can hypnotize me, not if I didn't want them to."

Of course. I had forgotten about the problem of a killer's ego. Of course, he wouldn't want to admit that anybody could exert any power over his own thoughts, except him. He wouldn't want to make himself that vulnerable; only victims were supposed to do that. And yet the fact that he has mentioned it at all meant that he had been thinking about it.

I remained seated until the door snapped shut behind them.

This could take forever, was my thought, and it might not be worth anything when I got it. And yet, it was well known that sociopaths often started their reign of pain with small animals. Dogs and cats were common, easy targets. Did the memory of a cocker spaniel make Ray feel uncomfortable for just that sort of reason?

No, I argued with myself, because if the memory of torturing an animal made him feel uncomfortable, he couldn't be defined as a sociopath, could he? These things could get very circular, and the more books on psychology I read and the more analysts I met, the more round and round I went sometimes. It was a good thing I could quote the "experts" in my books, because my own opinions about these things were as firm as tapioca pudding.

All I knew was that I was going to have a hard time creating a real-sounding life out of, "Dog. Orange and white."

I made a bet with his lawyer that he'd do it.

For the session of hypnotic regression, Ray sat with his legs sprawled on the raised bottom of a reclining chair, with his fingers splayed on the armrests, and his eyes closed.

And what a strange session that was.

After taking Ray through a relaxation exercise, the psy-

127

chologist said, in her literally hypnotic voice, "With your eyes closed, look down at your feet. What do you see?"

Ray laughed. "Little feet. Little white feet. Bare."

"Now move your gaze up your body. What do you see?"

"It's like a dress, only it's not. I don't know why. Does this mean I'm really a girl?" The question was sarcastic.

"Don't worry about what it means." The doctor's voice was relaxed, neutral, resonant. It reverberated in the listener's chest like the low notes from a cello. "Just be there. See what you see. Do you think it's a little girl's dress?"

"No. Feels like a boy. But why's he wearing a dress?"

"I'm going to ask you to look around you now, and see if you can see anybody else who is there. Do that now."

"A lady."

"Try to see her face. Does she look like anybody you know?"

"Yeah, sure, she looks like that movie star. Cool."

"Movie star. Do you know her name?"

"Can't think of it."

"Are you saying anything to each other?"

"She's jabbering about something, I don't know what. Oh, I'm in bed, she's by the side of my bed. Yum."

"How do you feel toward her?"

"Ooh, I want to kiss her. I love her, and she loves me."

"Okay, so you're a little boy in bare feet wearing something that seems like a dress."

"I'm not wearing a fucking dress."

"Just relax into it. It can't do you any harm. Just let it be as it is. You're perfectly safe in this deep place. Now I'm going to jump you forward in time to the next thing that happens. I will count backward from three to one, and when I reach one, you will be there. Three. Two. One. You're there. What is happening?"

"I see her. Through a window. She's leaving. No! Don't leave without me! I want to go, too! Mommy, wait for me!"

128

"She's your mother?"

"I guess."

"And you're standing at the window watching her leave?"

"No, I'm running after her."

"Where is she going?"

"Into some trees."

Ray looked on the verge of saying something else, but then didn't. Even with his eyes closed, his face looked as if he were watching something with great intensity. Again, he appeared about to speak, but then he held his tongue, and looked as if he were fixated on some scene playing inside his eyelids.

"I'm going to jump forward again—"

"Somebody's calling me."

"Yes? Calling your name?"

"Jimmy! Jimmy. Where are you? They're all really worried. Everybody's looking for me. They think I'm lost."

"Are you lost?"

"No, I found her."

"What's happening now that you've found her?"

"She's dead. All dead."

"Your mom? How did she die?"

"Don't know."

"How do you feel when you see she's dead?"

"I don't understand dead."

"Yes, you're a child. Is there sadness?"

"I don't understand why she won't get up. Wet."

"Wet? Is she wet? Your mom? Did she drown?"

"We're in water, not very deep, like a swamp. I have to go get help for her."

"You're leaving her to find help?"

"Yeah."

"Do you find it?"

"No, they find me. My dad cries and gives me a big hug."

"Try to see his face. Does he look like anybody you know?"

"Weird. That other movie star. The dead one. I don't know his name, either."

"What's going on now?"

"Everybody's been real worried and searching for me. They thought I died. The whole town is happy to find me. But my dad feels bad 'cause my crazy mom is dead."

"Crazy? She was insane?"

"Yeah, nuttier than a fruitcake."

"But you're safe now, in your father's arms?"

"Yeah."

The psychologist chose that moment to bring Ray up out of the hypnotic trance. Afterward, while Ray still reclined in the armchair, the doctor complimented him. "You are a very talented trance subject. It's rare for people to do so well the first time. They don't usually go so deep so fast. Only about fifteen percent of my clients do as well as you just did. It was a pleasure to work with you."

"Great," Ray said, in a mocking tone.

"Ray, think back over this experience, if you will. And tell me, do you make any connections with something in your present life?"

"Yeah, I'd like to kiss a movie star."

The consensus in the crime unit immediately after the hypnosis session was that Ray had put one over on them again. The story starred yet another devoted mother, even if she was crazy, and not perfect. One more idealized dad. And the romance of everybody in an entire town concerned over the welfare of poor little Ray.

"Could be worse," Paul Flanck observed. "This time he could be telling us about something he really did. Like, maybe he killed a woman. Maybe his own mother."

"In water," Robyn contributed. "A swampy area."

130

"Someplace on earth," Paul added, sarcastically.

"Big help," his partner said. "Maybe if we'd gotten her name and the so-called dad, maybe we'd have something."

"Right, like they're real," he joked.

"It feels familiar to me," she insisted. "I wonder what movie stars he was thinking of?"

The hypnotherapist—a woman in her fifties— listened to the young detectives debating this and said with an air of amused disbelief, "Haven't you guys ever heard of *Raintree County*?"

They drove to a video sales and rental store, feeling foolish.

There among "The Classics" was their answer, all right: *Raintree County*. Robyn picked up the cardboard cover and handed it over to Paul so he could also see the two young and beautiful faces pictured on it: Elizabeth Taylor and Montgomery Clift, the "actor who died."

When they viewed it, there was the storyline just as Ray had spun it out under hypnosis: The scene of a small boy named Jimmy, in a nightshirt that looked like a dress, which was the sort of thing all children used to wear to bed. He was in bed, as his "crazy" mother told him goodbye, though the child didn't comprehend she meant "forever." There he was running to his bedroom window. Catching a glimpse of her as she vanished into the forest. Running out of his room, out the front door and across the wide lawn, chasing her.

The detectives watched it with their mouths hanging open, shaking their heads in wonder and dismay at their strange, fantasizing suspect.

"There it is!" Robyn pointed at the screen. "Elizabeth Taylor's dead in the swamp! Just like Ray said. And there are all the townspeople out searching for the boy. And here come's Dad."

Montgomery Clift, she meant.

"Jimmy" was a fictional child in a movie recalled by a murder suspect with the same surname as the title of the film.

"Strange days," remarked Paul Flanck.

On the screen, the Montgomery Clift character, who was named "John," said, in a resigned and disillusioned voice, "There is no Rain Tree."

"You said that right, Monty," Paul cracked. He turned toward Robyn and me. "What's that old-timey word for ghost?"

"Haint?" Robyn offered. "Shade? Specter?"

"That's it. Maybe that's what we've got jailed up. Not a man, or a real human being. A specter. Wooo."

Robyn thought of another line of dialogue in the movie they had just watched. At one point, a character said of the little boy who was missing, *"He hasn't been found yet."* And Robyn thought, The real Ray Raintree hasn't been found yet, either.

There were other uncanny quotes from the movie that haunted her, too, such as: *"Another day of corpse-making,"* and *"Tomorrow you're starting a journey to a place called hell."*

They wished they knew what it all meant.

It was right after this that a well-known, local criminal attorney by the name of Leanne English walked into the Howard County Jail one day and announced that she wished to see "my client, Raymond Raintree." When that wish was conveyed to him, "her client" snarled that he'd never heard of her.

"I have been hired to represent him," Leanne shot back.

"Who by?" was Ray's next response.

"None of his business," his new attorney said, and she added for the benefit of the jailer who was carrying these messages back and forth, "or yours, either."

132

She got in to see him, and that put an immediate end to any experimental psychology, or writer interviews, or statements of any kind from the defendant to anybody but her and her minions. Raymond Raintree was now the property of Sounder, McKee, Morrison and English.

5

Raymond

"Normally, I don't enter a murder case until the trial," I tell Franklin over a plateful of the cheese and vegetable omelette he has brought into my office. He takes his own plate and sits down with it on the apricot leather love seat across from my desk. "If I were doing this book my usual way, I wouldn't even have met you until then."

He seems endlessly fascinated in how I work.

Of course, that makes me endlessly fascinated in him.

"That's when I start covering it in person," I continue, "but I start to research the case long before that, and I also start to correspond with the principals. Like you. I write letters to the prosecutor, the defense attorney, and the detectives, as well as to the victim's and murderer's families and friends."

"What do you say?"

"I just introduce myself. I also write to the killer. I have to begin to establish a level of trust that will convince all of those people to let me into their lives."

"You seem to have established it quite well with me."

We smile at each other, coconspirators.

"You're the best omelette maker in the whole world."

"That's why I trust you, because you have exquisite taste."

He wants to know why I haven't done this book my usual way.

"Because it happened in my own hometown," I say. "I knew you by reputation. I'd met Paul and Robyn previously when I did some research at the police department. Judge Flasschoen was a familiar name to me, just from reading the newspaper, and so was Leanne. So it didn't seem necessary to wait for the trial when all I had to do was drive downtown to interview most of you. The only people I didn't know anything about were the McCullens and Ray. Plus, I thought that if I started the interviews early, I would get the book done faster.

"Greed," I now confess. "That's why I did it."

He knows how worried I am now about meeting my deadline.

I broke my own rules, and got intimately involved with the case much sooner than I normally do. And much more intimately, obviously. In spite of that, the whole process seemed much like any other book, until I got to the defense attorneys, but I don't feel that I can tell the state's attorney about that without betraying Ray's lawyers.

Instead of writing to Leanne English, I had just picked up the phone.

"Sounder, McKee, Morrison and English."

"Hello. I'd like to speak to Leanne English, or to her secretary, please."

"Just a moment . . ."

"I'm Ms. English's secretary, may I help you?"

"Hello. Yes, I hope so. My name is Marie Lightfoot, and I am writing a book about the Natalie Mae McCullen murder case. I would like to set up an appointment to speak with Ms. English about the case."

"I'm sorry but Ms. English is not doing interviews."

"Do you mean, about that case, or about anything at all?"

"I really can't say."

"I don't want to ask her to reveal anything that might compromise her case, I just want to—"

"I'm sorry, but I've been instructed to say, no interviews."

I didn't want to antagonize the secretary. "All right. I understand. Thank you—"

"Ms. Lightfoot? Are you *the* Marie Lightfoot?"

I smiled at the phone. "I guess I am."

"Oh, this is so exciting! I've read all your books. Are you really going to write a book about this case?"

"Well, thank you. Yes, I am. That's why I need to interview your boss."

"Oh, I wish I could help you, but I can't."

The woman sounded genuinely sorry.

"I understand. Do you think there's any flexibility in their position? If you told them I'm trustworthy as Fort Knox, would that help?"

"No, I'm really sorry."

"It's okay. Thanks anyway."

"If they changed their minds, would you put me in the book?"

My hope lifted again. "I'd even spell your name right."

The secretary laughed, and sounded pleased as she said, "Well, I'll try, I'll really try to get them to change their minds."

"Do you know who hired them?"

"No." Suddenly the friendly secretary turned to stone. The word came abruptly, and was just as quickly followed by, "Goodbye."

Sitting in my office with a dial tone in my hand, I shrugged and thought, wryly, I had to ask.

I didn't understand their attitude at all. When Sounder, McKee appeared on the case, I expected them to do what defense attorneys do these days: use the media to win sympathy for their client before they ever set foot in a courtroom to defend him. But nobody from the firm appeared on television to do that, nor were they interviewed for stories about the crime.

"I should have written to her," I reproved myself.

136

My next move was a carefully composed letter in which I presented my own bona fides, and then went to pains to emphasize that I never betrayed a trust or a secret, from either side of the aisle. In the blandest terms, I asked Leanne English for an appointment, "for general background for my book."

The attorney did not reply to my letter.

I called Robyn Anschutz at the police department and asked, "Robyn, where'd they come from? If Ray didn't hire them, who did? I'll bet Leanne costs three hundred and fifty dollars an hour, don't you?"

"At least. I don't know, Marie, but I'd like to."

"Do you think it could be that man Ray worked for?"

"Donor Miller, you mean?"

"Yes, him."

"I suppose. But even if he had that kind of money, which I doubt, he didn't strike me as somebody who would dish it out for another person. Especially not for a loser like Ray."

"But he did offer to get Ray a lawyer, didn't he?"

"Well, yeah, but at three hundred and fifty dollars an hour?"

"Do you know where Miller is these days?"

"Not a clue."

"Well, if he isn't paying for Ray's defense, have you got any ideas how I could find out who is?"

"Not unless you can hack into the billing system of Sounder, McKee."

We laughed at that felonious suggestion.

"You probably know some of the other defense attorneys over there," I suggested to Robyn.

"Yeah, but nobody's sayin' nothin'."

"Don't you think this is very strange?"

"Tellin' me?"

But there the matter stood, up to and including the trial.

Raymond Raintree, who didn't have two pennies to rub together, had for his defense team one of the most expensive lawyers in Bahia Beach. And nobody knew who was paying her.

137

                    *   *   *

I swipe my finger along the edge of the plate to swab the last bit
of buttery goodness from the omelette, and decide it would be
okay to get Franklin's opinion of this.

"Do you know who's paying Ray's legal bills?"

"I don't, and I sure have wondered. Do you know?"

"I was hoping you did. I'll tell you one thing—whatever she's
being paid, it can't be enough to compensate her for what she
went through today."

Franklin visibly shudders as he reaches for my empty plate.

"You're going to wash them, too?"

"I want to make sure of my welcome."

I could learn to like this. The man sure knows how to work his
will with juries, and with me. But I have my doubts about a serious involvement with a prosecutor. While I know many whom I
admire, as a breed I think they tend to be tough, demanding, argu-
mentative, and unforgiving. While those may be requisite qualities
for seeking a death penalty, they aren't the best ones for love.
Tonight, I'm seeing the softer, more winning side of Franklin
DeWeese, but he's got another personality, the one that wants to
run thousands of volts of electricity through defendants, and I'm
not forgetting that for a minute.

I stop him before he leaves the room with the dishes.

"What's going on with the judge, Franklin?"

"Self-defense. An administrative hearing. No charges. This is
just a nice little vacation for her. She'll be back on the bench soon."

"What's your opinion of that?"

"On the record?"

"To start with, yes."

"Judge Edyth Flasschoen is an outstanding representative of
Florida jurisprudence," he pronounces glibly. "Her quick return to
the bench will be bad news to the criminals of this state."

"Very nice. And off the record?"

He laughs, and says in a tone of mock injury, "What? You sus-

                              138

pect me of saying the politic thing? What do I really think? I think she should have shot him with a bigger pistol."

"Yeah," I agree.

It's 1 A.M. on the morning after the day that Ray escaped, and the state's attorney is in my kitchen cleaning up, and I'm finished with what Robyn asked me to do. I've reread everything I've ever written about this case, and I don't know anything I didn't already know before.

Just as I'm walking out of my office, the phone rings again.

Again, the caller ID says PRIVATE CALL, and again I grab it, say, "Hello," and get no response.

But I've been reading all of those interviews, and so maybe that's why this time a feeling hits me, and I sink down into my chair, and I say, "Ray?"

"How'd you know?"

That weird, high-pitched voice is his, all right.

My heart stops, and my mind screams out to Franklin who is only a few yards away from me: *Franklin! Come in here!* Jeeze Louise, what do I do about this? I can't get Franklin's attention from in here, I can't call the cops while Ray's on the line, I can't alert 911, I can't get anybody to trace this call. I don't dare ask Ray, "Will you hold on a minute?" For a crazy instant I am tempted to start pounding on the wall with my fist so Franklin will come running, but if I do anything like that, Ray will hear me.

Immediately, I do the only thing I can do: I switch on a recording device that I use when I interview people over the phone, with their permission. I don't ask this caller's permission.

"I just knew," I say, getting my nerves under control.

There's no sound for what seems a long time.

I am way out of my league here.

Please, Franklin, *please* finish up in there, and come back.

I'm afraid to ask Ray a direct question, because they tend to scare him off, or launch him into stories, lies, and fables. I want to ask him, "Why are you calling me?" I want to say, "What do you want? Where are you? Why did you hurt those people so bad?"

I don't say any of that, because it would be a mistake.

Finally, I say, carefully, "So . . ."

"They're lookin' for me."

"Yeah." I pause, treading carefully like somebody on the edge of a crumbling volcano. "Are you . . . okay?"

"Tell them to leave me alone."

"I don't think they will, Ray."

"I can take care of myself."

This is so absurd that I just remain silent.

"There are five principles of survival in the wilderness."

I blink, unprepared for what's coming out of his mouth now.

"Protect yourself, be able to signal for help, know how to provide food and water, have a goal, and stay healthy."

He sounds as if he's parroting what he has learned from somebody else.

"Where'd you learn that?" Damn, a direct question! I didn't mean to do that! This is hard, second-guessing every word before I say it.

As if I haven't spoken, he says, still in that odd lecturing kind of voice, "Protecting yourself, that's the first priority, and that means clothing and shelter. You don't need much clothing in Florida, but you need some for camouflage, if you're hiding."

I take a chance and say, "So where do you get the clothes?"

"That's what beaches are for."

I try to think what he means. "You mean, for stealing stuff?"

"Yeah, or you can find a soccer field and grab some kid's soccer bag, and get clothes out of there."

"So clothes aren't a problem."

I'm careful to turn it into a declarative sentence, not a question. The second "principle" he listed, if I recall it correctly, was "signal for help in an emergency." He's in an emergency, all right. And then it hits me: I'm the one he is signaling. Does he seriously think I can tell the police to lay off, and they will?

140

"Don't go hungry, and don't go thirsty," he says, breaking the silence, "'cause they're killers, they'll sap your strength when you need it. A person could live a long time without food, but he wouldn't think straight, he'd get nervous and angry and start making mistakes. He could find little bits of money, and buy stuff, but he'd have to be so careful, going into convenience stores. Better to steal it, if you can, although that's risky, 'cause you can get caught."

"Yeah," I say, agreeably, feeling completely lost with this.

"You don't ever want to get caught. Do anything you gotta do, but don't get caught. And if you get caught, keep quiet and tell lies. Don't ever tell anybody the truth about anything."

I am fascinated by what I am hearing, horrified by who's saying it.

"About food? Like I was saying? You're better off hunting, fishing, eating seaweed if you have to. The stems, roots, and leaves of most grasses can be eaten raw, cattails are a great source of food, pine trees are full of edible shit, and green seaweed is good, as long as you get it out of the ocean or off of rocks, and don't pick it up from the beach."

I feel an hysterical urge to laugh.

"Why not the beach, Ray?"

"It gets all moldy."

"Oh."

"Some berries are okay, just not the white or red ones. Bugs, slugs, maggots, ants, earthworms, grasshoppers. Any snake, as long as you've got a blade to skin and gut it, and a fire to cook it. You got to know how to test a plant for edibility, how to snare a bird, improvise a club, or a slingshot, build a box trap for small game."

He is using words—*improvise, snare, edibility*—that I would not have thought he knew. I'm guessing that somebody's taught him this, and told him over and over again, and made him memorize it.

"And water?" he says, as if I have asked about it. "Look for lawn spigots, and public fountains. Or, you can build a beach well, or vegetation bags to trap the dew on the leaves of trees. And people are always leaving half-empty bottles of mineral water all over the place."

I nod, and then feel ridiculous.

"What's the next one?" he asks me.

"The next—"

"Principle of survival."

"I don't remember what you said."

"It's, you got to move toward something, not just run away."

Oh, boy, do I ever want to ask, "Where are you going?"

"Remember the last one?"

"No, I'm sorry, this is all new to me."

"You have to stay healthy, so stay away from doctors and hospitals. And that means fight if you have to, but not if that would get you so injured you couldn't take care of yourself. It's almost always better to run than to fight. Remember that. Don't be a fighter, unless you have to. Don't fight 'cause it's usually not worth it, and you're only going to get hurt if you do."

"You fought today."

"Couldn't go back."

"To prison."

"Yeah."

Suddenly I get it, it's clear. "You'd rather die first, and if you didn't die, then you'd fight to get away."

There's silence, and I think it means yes.

This is so strange, and I want to ask him so much else.

"You didn't fight when they arrested you."

"Fuck, I didn't know they'd make me stay there forever!"

He sounds agitated, and I feel scared. Immediately, I attempt to calm us both down again. "You didn't know they were going to put you in jail for so long." I am trying so hard not to phrase things as questions, but more as agreements with what he is saying. With each silence, I sense his own agreement, and he's silent now.

"Ray?"

"Yeah."

"Do you mind if I ask . . . I mean . . . all these things you know about how to survive . . ." I don't know how to say this any way but as a question. "How'd you learn all that? Did somebody teach you?"

He doesn't answer, and the silence grows very long.

"Fuck," he says, sounding agitated again, only worse this time. "It's happening again. I hate it when this fucking happens."

"What, Ray?"

"It's like I get all stupid, like my brain goes all numb, and I can't think or remember anything. Shit, it's like I'm going to pass out, and I hate it, I hate this!"

And then he hangs up, just like that.

"Franklin!" I shout, and keep shouting until he appears in the doorway. "Ray just called me! What do I do? What should I do?" Without even waiting for him to answer, I pick up my telephone receiver again, and press the star button then six and nine to activate call return. If I don't do it now, it won't work. Call return only works on the last incoming call. Ray might still be there, if I can get him back on the line . . .

But the phone rings and rings and nobody answers.

Franklin is shouting, "Call Anschutz or Flanck!"

I look up Robyn Anschutz's home number. The detective picks up before the second ring.

"Robin? It's Marie Lightfoot. Ray called me."

I tell her what just happened. Her response is jubilant.

"Hot damn! Why would he call you?"

I tell her about killers sometimes mistaking me for a friend.

"How nice for you," she jokes. "Can I ask a favor? Would you put on some coffee? We'll be right over."

I hang up and say to Franklin, "You've got to leave."

We can think of no good reason for him to be there, waiting for the cops to arrive. If they want to call him, and bring him into this, they will. But that's not my decision to make. For the first time, I wonder if we have made a mistake, and maybe there is a potential conflict of interest here, even if I can't quite work out

143

what it might be. He gives me a quick kiss, and he's gone, and he even leaves the kitchen sparkling behind him.

"Hi, Robyn," I say as I open my front door.

It is at exactly this moment that I realize that I'm not going to be able to keep myself out of this book. Ray's life is now intersecting with mine. This is an odd sensation for someone who prides herself on being a detached observer of crime, but never a participant in its effects. Like it or not, I'm part of his story now.

"Cell phone," are the first, triumphant words out of the detective's mouth. "In this county. North and west of here. We've got him now. We'll have that location under surveillance and that whole area cordoned off before he can call you back."

"Cell phone? Where would Ray get a cell phone?"

And I wonder: Can it really be this easy?

"Come on in," I invite, only to discover that means admitting half a dozen uniformed and plainclothes officers into my home.

I haven't made nearly enough coffee.

6

Raymond

It doesn't matter how much coffee I prepare, or how much the cops drink, because Ray Raintree never calls me back. The calls are tracked to a cell phone on board a residential trawler on a branch of the New River. The owner of the boat, an elderly hippie with a private number, is missing and presumed murdered. Ray's fingerprints are all over the place.

And he is long gone.

I am sickened by the thought that he may have killed the man to get the phone to call me. Hurting people in a desperate attempt to escape a death penalty is one thing, horrible, but understandable in a sick way. But killing a man to steal his cell phone?

My comprehension of Ray's psyche stops at that barrier.

One day later, the local newspaper accusingly trumpets, "One lone suspect, wounded, unarmed, and allegedly not even very bright, has thus far managed to humiliate three counties' worth of law enforcement by slipping through the noose they futilely tightened around the northern neck of Howard County. Unfortunately, they are the ones who choked on it."

Considering the nature of the murder case that started all this, I find that an appalling choice of metaphors.

It isn't clear how Ray has evaded capture all this time. It is possible, says Detective Paul Flanck, "that Ray swam out to sea and did us all a favor and drowned himself."

"I wish," says his partner, Robyn Anschutz.

On the third day, having been deluged by frightened and furious phone calls from the mothers and fathers of Florida, the governor calls out the Army National Guard. They are assigned to assist in the search for the escaped convict, who is "considered extremely dangerous." A one-million-dollar reward is posted by a coalition of private donors and nonprofit organizations devoted to helping missing children. Internet sites spring up overnight, rife with feverish and morbid speculation. One of them, called Sightings, posts an average of one hundred new "Ray sightings" per hour. Cranks and other people genuinely wanting to help swamp 911 and the other police phone lines.

News of the developments in the case goes out over the national wires, and networks and CNN, spreading a far wider net of communication than the abduction and murder case have produced up until this time. On the popular television show *Entertainment Tonight,* they even report that Ray Raintree is a main character in "a true crime story soon to be published by best-selling author Marie Lightfoot."

Almost as soon as *ET* goes off the air, readers begin posting computer E-mail messages to me about the book-in-progress. I answer them in clumps, trying to keep up with them as they come in. There are always a few to which the only appropriate reply is no reply at all, but most of them are from fans, and I am grateful for the chance to express my appreciation to them. Scrolling down a dozen of them, I am unprepared for the surprise that awaits me, eleven messages down the line.

Dear Ms. Lightfoot, I am a retired sheriff's deputy who investigated a missing child case many years ago. I have good reason to believe it is connected to the case of the man you know as Raymond Raintree. Please call me collect as soon as possible. Yours truly, Jack L. Lawrence, Olathe, KS.

That one gives me pause. I read it twice, looking for clues to what it means, but find none. The fact that he suggests I call "collect" is a good sign that at least he means well, even if his information's no good. Still, I hate to get stuck on the phone with kooks, so I E-mail my message, rather than calling as he asks me to.

"Dear Mr. Lawrence," I type, "I'm intrigued by your message. What is the connection between your case and Ray Raintree? Sincerely, Marie Lightfoot."

The response reaches me within minutes, as if he is sitting at his computer waiting to hear from me. And this time, what I read on the computer screen makes my pulse race. He writes:

> Twenty-two years ago, I investigated a tragic case of a little boy named John Kepler who went missing from his parents' front yard. We never found any trace of him. But Johnnie Kepler had an imaginary playmate, as children do, and his imaginary friend's name was Raymond Raintree. Please contact me as soon as possible. Yours truly, Jack Lawrence.

This time, I call him, and not collect, either.

"I'm just a retired old codger from Kansas."

I hear a gravelly, authoritative voice, and I can well believe that Jack Lawrence was a law enforcement officer.

"I'm nobody important," he tells me over the phone. "What big city cop down there where you are is going to listen to a retired deputy from a county they never heard of? I called their TIPS line, but they just wrote down my information like anybody else's, and I suppose they must have gotten a thousand different calls. It could be weeks before they get far enough down the list to call me. I imagine you know how it is. I used to know a couple of Florida cops, one over in Sarasota and another up in Naples, but they're as old as I am, nobody knows them now."

He says he got his local sheriff to contact the Howard County sheriff, who hasn't been available to talk to him personally but whose secretary has promised to get somebody on it right away.

"I recognized the runaround when I heard it," he says.

Forty-eight hours later, he still hasn't heard anything back.

"I got our sheriff to call again, and I've tried to make a pest of myself."

But it appears that law enforcement in Florida is otherwise occupied this week with the search for the escapee.

"You're kind of our last-ditch hope," the retired deputy tells me. "Kimmie got your name off the TV show, and she's read your books, and she's a big fan of yours."

"Kimmie?"

"Kim Kepler. Sister of the missing boy. She seems to think you'll pay some attention to us."

"I certainly will."

"Now listen," he says in a way that sounds stern and kind at the same time, "these people, the Keplers, they've been through a hell of a lot, and they don't want a big fuss, if they can help it."

"I gather they're hoping that Ray Raintree can lead them to information about their boy? I'd hate to get their hopes up, Mr. Lawrence. Maybe Ray just heard the name somewhere, and he can't help them at all. I've got to tell you, it's next to impossible to get information out of him. Or, at least truthful information. Sometimes he'll talk your ear off, but you can't believe a word he says."

There is a silence on the other end, in Kansas.

Then the retired deputy says, "I don't think I've made myself clear. When I said there might be a connection between John Kepler and Raymond Raintree?"

"Yes?"

"What did you think I meant?"

"Well, that maybe he knew the kidnapper. Or maybe he saw the boy sometime, and picked up the name to use for himself."

148

"No. Hell, maybe this is why nobody paid any attention to me down there. My wife—I'm a widower—always used to tell me nobody can understand a thing I say when I try to explain something. What we're saying is, Ray *is* John. It's not that he may have seen Johnnie, or heard about him. He is Johnnie Kepler."

A shock of electricity runs through me, leaving me literally gasping.

"Ray is the boy you're looking for?" I can hardly take this in. I am flabbergasted. This is the miracle I have been looking for, and it might never have happened if the judge hadn't shot Ray, and Ray hadn't escaped. "My god, Mr. Lawrence. You're saying you think that this man who abducted a child was himself abducted when he was a child?"

"Yes, that's what I'm saying."

"How many years ago?"

"Twenty-two."

"That would make him—"

"Twenty-eight."

That was right for Ray, who said he was twenty-eight, but never seemed sure of it. Ray Raintree was a missing child? My mind is bouncing off its own walls at the cruel twist of this. Can it be true? It would make sense of so many things about Ray that don't make sense. "Oh, my god," I say again, feeling breathless. "But what is there, besides the name? Is that all you're basing this on?"

"No, ma'am, this isn't wishful thinking, and it isn't a coincidence, and it isn't a guess. We know. We *know.* That's why the Keplers want to talk to somebody, and if the cops won't talk to me, we'll talk to you. We've got to get connected to this business down in Florida, just as soon as we can. They're scared to death he's going to get electrocuted, and they'll never get to see him alive, now that they've finally found him. You understand?"

"Oh, yes." I'm trying to think fast, to come up with solutions for him. "I can get through to the prosecuting attorney for you, Mr. Lawrence, shall I do that? Or, how about the two detectives who arrested Ray?"

"No, Katherine's changed her mind—"

"Katherine?"

"Johnnie's mother."

His mother. My mouth drops open at the idea of meeting Ray Raintree's mother.

"Changed her mind about what?"

"She doesn't want to talk to them yet. Soon, real soon, just not yet. They're going to have to wait a little while before they get hold of her. You can imagine, this is very emotional for the Keplers, it's just difficult as hell, and they've decided they don't want cops and reporters crawling all over them. They just want to make absolutely sure he's really their boy, and they want to see him again."

I can't find words to reply to that amazing wish.

"But I thought you said you know he's their child."

"I do know it, but there's nothing like actually seeing him. It's like they know, but they can't let themselves really believe it until they see him with their own eyes."

I think that's a futile hope, given the current manhunt.

"Hell, he may be dead already," the retired deputy says, echoing my thoughts. "Katherine's worried about the death penalty. I'm more worried about some trigger-happy bounty hunter. If they capture him, and put him in prison, the Keplers will have plenty of time to get to know him. But that's my point—the Keplers want to see him if they can, but they also want to try to keep this quiet for as long as they can. It's not like they want to end up on *Entertainment Tonight* themselves."

"Deputy Lawrence—"

"Not anymore. I'm just Jack."

"Thank you. And I'm Marie. Jack, may I meet them?"

"Yeah, they want to tell somebody their story."

"The cops are going to have to hear it, Jack. It might help them find Ray, or even bring him in, if he thought he was going to get to see his family."

"We'll cross that bridge real soon, but they want to talk to you."

"Why?"

"That's easy. Because you're writing a book about him. You're the one who's telling his story, whether he lives or dies, and his mother wants to make sure somebody tells it true. You've met him, right?"

"Yes, a few times."

"She wants to talk to somebody who knows him."

I want to tell him that nobody "knows" Ray Raintree.

"We figure if Katherine talks to you, she won't have to talk to any other newspaper people, or other journalists."

I can't even begin to tell him how naive that hope is.

"Plus," he adds, sounding forceful and upbeat, "you've got all those contacts, when we're ready."

"Do they want to talk to me over the phone?"

"They want to meet you."

"Are they coming to Bahia?"

"Could you come here?"

"You bet! How soon?"

"Sooner the better."

"I'll get the first flight I can, Jack. Tonight, if I can do it, or is that sooner than you meant?"

"No, that's great. We were hoping."

"Good. Well, tell me where I'm going, and how to get there."

"You'll fly in to Kansas City International Airport. I'll pick you up, and we'll drive right over to Katherine's house. She told me to tell you that she'd really like it if you'd stay in Johnnie's room."

I wouldn't miss this chance for anything.

"Please tell her that I gratefully accept her kind invitation."

"She'll like you," he says, with a sudden smile in his gravelly voice.

"How do you know that?"

"You're polite, not like some big shot."

I have not felt quite so flattered in a long time, but I know that now I have to risk losing his good will.

"Jack?"

151

"Yes, ma'am."

"Listen, I have really got to let the authorities down here know about this. I can't just go flying off to Kansas like a private eye, without telling the cops about this."

"Well," he says, doubtfully. "Katherine says—"

"She doesn't have to talk to them, Jack, not until she wants to."

He finally agrees to let me do it, because I make it clear that ethically I can't do otherwise. I'm not going to Kansas without informing Anschutz and Flanck about this revolution in their case. I can just imagine how they would react if they found out later that I had kept this amazing news from them.

As soon as we hang up, I call a series of people, starting with my travel agent. Then I call the detectives, and Franklin, and Leanne English. I have to be evenhanded, or I'll lose my sources in my own hometown. It's policy with me to be honest with everybody I interview. I never attempt to play one against another, either. I never lie to the cops, to the victim's families, or to the murderers—especially never to them, on the theory that it takes one to know one, and I'd get caught at it. In fact, if one of the other principals in this case were to ask me, "Are you having an affair with the prosecutor?" I'd have to say yes, and I've told him I would. Apart from that, I keep all of their secrets, unless given permission to publish them. My career depends on earning and keeping the trust of dozens of people. Many of these people are suspicious of journalists, and all of them are vulnerable, in their own ways. With a careless phrase, I could humiliate an innocent person, or ruin a lawman's or a lawyer's reputation. I prevent that from happening by checking my facts, and by choosing to err on the side of kindness if I have to choose between that and printing a gratuitous cruelty. That's why—except for the villains—nobody is "ugly" in my books; they are "interesting-looking." Nobody is fat or skinny, either; they are "attractively robust" or "fashionably slim." By now, I have a reputation for being both diplomatic and a straight shooter, which is a high-wire act at times. It also helps to be famous, because total strangers are more likely to take my phone calls.

I have no problem getting through to the detectives with this stunning news from the Midwest.

"You believe these people?" Robyn Anschutz asks me.

"I think . . . that they believe it," is my careful reply.

"If it's true, it's damned amazing."

"It sure is."

"It would explain a lot."

"Yeah."

"But not everything, like where he's been all these years."

"And who took him," Paul Flanck interrupts, on an extension.

"Who abducted the abductor?" Robyn says, wonderingly. "Wow."

The detectives promise me they will contact Jack Lawrence before attempting to call the Kepler family.

This time, even Leanne English takes my call.

"How are you?" I ask her, sympathetically.

She is speaking through a wired jaw and is hard to understand. "I've been better," she slurs. "Give me these people's phone number."

"I'll give them your number," I counter. Briefly, I consider offering her a deal: You tell me who's paying Ray's legal bills, and I'll tell you how to reach his mother. But I can't do that.

She has to be satisfied with my other offer.

Then I call Franklin, and we spend several minutes expressing our mutual astonishment at this turn of events. Finally, I say to him, "Okay, give me an official quote for my book, sweetie."

He thinks a moment, and then says:

"If this turns out to be true, it is a terrible twist of fate." He puts on his "prosecutor" voice and gives me plenty of time to write this down. "As far as I know, this is the first case on record of a kidnapped child growing up to become a kidnapper. The principle of abuse begetting abuse is familiar to most people, but this variation is unknown to me."

"Great," I murmur as I scribble. "Anything else?"

"We should have seen it coming," he gives me. "Think of all

153

the kids who get snatched. It's mostly parental kidnappings, but it's still kidnapping. I think we could start seeing second- and third-generation snatchers." Suddenly he really does sound like a prosecutor, angry, and ready to charge into battle against anonymous legions of kidnappers, be they biological parents, or total strangers. "If abuse is all you know, then maybe abuse is what you do. If kidnapping is what you know, then maybe kidnapping is what you do."

"Yeah, but Franklin, what about children who grow up with cruel parents, and turn out fine?"

I know what he's going to say, but I need it in quotes.

"Then abuse is *not* all they knew."

"Well, then, what about the first six years of Ray's life, Franklin? What if it turns out that he was loved and treated kindly then?"

"What about it?"

"Well, shouldn't that have saved him from this?"

"Not necessarily. You put the best adjusted rat in the world in a box, and you subject it to random torture, and it will give up hope, and die. The most loving rat mother in the world could give birth to it, and nurture it for the rat equivalent of six years of a child's life, and you turn that sweet, beloved little rat over to an experimental psychologist, and you'll have a psychotic rat, and then a dead one, in a matter of days."

"But rats aren't human beings, Franklin."

"Yes," he agrees, with a steely edge to his voice. "But a lot of human beings are rats."

That is exactly what I hoped he'd say. It will look great on the page.

I think he's finished speaking, and I put my pen down, only to have to pick it up again quickly, when he bursts out furiously, "That is why it is so important for adults to be nice to kids. Every damn, annoying one of 'em. Smile at every kid, I tell people, because that may be the only smile they get from any adult all week long. If I catch any of my assistants being rude to children, I tell them, congratulations, you just helped create another alienated, miserable human being."

"If this is true about Ray," I say, "and they bring him in again, will you still want to go for the death penalty?"

"Absolutely! The fact that he may have been abducted, or even abused, doesn't bring Natty back, does it? You try telling her parents to feel sorry for poor little Ray Raintree, and see how far you get. I don't care where these cycles start, we've got to stop them somewhere, Marie, and if that means I have to put Ray in the electric chair, I will."

"But what if he's one of those miserable alienated human beings that other miserable alienated human beings created?"

"Well, then, let's put him out of his misery," says Franklin, in a tone of wry, grim humor.

It's easier to agree with him before I meet Ray's mother.

Twenty-four hours after those conversations I find myself feeling simply astonished to be sitting on Ray's childhood bed, in Kansas. The wallpaper is from the 1970s. His toys surround me, and I see some that would be considered collector's items now. His mother is awake in the living room, because she says she doesn't know how she can ever sleep until she sees him again.

I open my laptop and begin writing a new chapter for a book that is suddenly not just about one abduction, but two.

Part 2

JOHNNIE

The Little Mermaid

By Marie Lightfoot

~

CHAPTER EIGHT

*W*hile *Florida searched for Ray Raintree, the solution to the* mystery of his identity began to unfold in a place most of the cops had never heard of, in the home of a woman they didn't know anything about.

The place was Olathe, Kansas, thirty miles south of Kansas City.

The woman was Kim Kepler, thirty years old and unmarried, with no children. At the exact moment the mystery dissolved, Kim was eating take-out Chinese food off a TV tray and watching *Entertainment Tonight.* The food was moo shoo pork, shredded meat rolled in thin pancakes, which she dipped in soy sauce. It was her favorite oriental food, a little bland for some people's taste, perhaps, but tasty to her, and she ordered it every time she ate Chinese. She had definite habits like that, sticking to her tried-and-true favorites whether that meant cheese enchiladas at Mexican restaurants, or a quarter pounder with cheese at McDonald's, or fettucine Alfredo at Italian places. There was comfort in those familiar dishes, no surprises, no disappointments, and nothing to throw away if she didn't like it.

159

The fluffy show, which came on every night at 6:30 P.M. on local channels, was the closest she could stand to watching or reading or listening to anything that might possibly be construed as "news." Kim Kepler, like her mother, Katherine Kepler, avoided the news. The two women couldn't bear to hear of little children being abducted from their families. It hurt too much, and brought back too many memories, because Kim's own youngest brother had disappeared when he was only six years old. She just never knew when a horrible story like that might get broadcast, or put in the newspapers or magazines, and bring it all back, and make her cry, and ruin her day. There seemed to be an epidemic of child abductions in the United States, especially by parents, so those stories were commonplace. But she tried very hard to avoid them, without being conspicuous about it. If anybody where Kim worked ever tried to talk about a story like that, she made excuses and quietly walked away from the conversation.

It was too personal, too painful, even after twenty-three years.

But *Entertainment Tonight* always seemed pretty safe to Kim.

It was all about movie stars, TV stars, gossip, and no missing children.

It helped her relax to watch it while she ate supper by herself. Not that she was a lonely person. She was gregarious, in fact, with lots of friends, and she was especially close to her mom, and to her younger sister and to a lesser degree, to their other brother.

Kim just didn't want to hear or see any bad news, that was all.

Lots of people felt that way, and she didn't apologize for it.

Neither did she apologize for being a midwesterner, although she knew it wasn't many people's idea of sophisti-

160

cation. Those same people might think of the Midwest—particularly Kansas—as safe. But to Kim's way of thinking, that was an illusion. Just look at what had happened to her own brother. And then to her father, who just walked away one day, and never came back. Even so, she had never seen any reason to move away. If Kansas wasn't safe, then probably no place was. Besides, her mother would never leave, and Kim would not leave her mom.

So there she was, eating off a tray and watching *Entertainment Tonight,* smack in the middle of the city of Olathe, in Johnson County, Kansas, which was a very long way away from the city of Bahia Beach, Howard County, Florida.

Olathe, the county seat of Johnson County, is the fastest-growing city in Kansas. From the air, or passing by on Interstate 35, it looks like a bedroom suburb of Kansas City, but up close it maintains pockets of its original small-town charm, with little white frame houses with front porches and swings, and large gardens in the yards. The city's name is pronounced O-LAY-tha, at least by the white people who incorporated it, with the accent on the second syllable. Wild Bill Hickock once lived down the road apiece.

Kim lived in one of those little white houses.

Her mother lived in another one, two blocks away.

Her sister and her sister's family lived one suburb over, in Lenexa, and their remaining brother and his family lived only a twenty-minute drive away in Prairie Village.

Kim listened as Mary Hart said on the television, "In Florida, a plot thickens! A massive manhunt is under way for an escaped killer who is the main character in a real-life crime story soon to be published by best-selling author Marie Lightfoot. Just when Lightfoot thought she already knew the ending of her book, the killer escaped from the Bahia Beach courthouse two days ago. He had just been convicted for the abduction and—"

Kim reached for her remote control.

"—murder of—"

She fumbled with greasy fingers to find the off button.

"—a six-year-old girl, Natalie Mae McCullen. Her killer—"

Frantically, Kim pressed the button, but nothing happened. Sometimes it didn't work the first time.

"— who is known only by the name Raymond Raintree—"

When Kim Kepler heard that name, she felt as if somebody had swung a mallet at the center of her chest. She gasped, and jerked in her seat, and cried out as if she had been hit with ferocious force by an invisible enemy. She clutched her chest, and couldn't breathe. Her head filled with a loud ringing. She felt dizzy, and her vision darkened at the edges, as if she were suddenly going blind. The remote control device dropped from her fingers, bounced onto the wooden TV tray, and then onto the carpet. The back of it broke open, spilling out both of the AA batteries. Kim's mouth opened and closed, opened and closed, but no sound came out.

Frantically, she tried to listen to what the TV announcer was saying, but the pounding of the blood in her ears made it hard to hear. The sound of her own breathing deafened her. All she heard was a tag line, "—a movie deal already signed, but now nobody knows how this story will end." When she saw them move on to other stories, Kim brought her hands to her mouth and stood up so fast that the TV tray tottered on two legs and then dipped over, spilling her dinner.

"Raymond Raintree," she whispered in a shaky voice.

And then Kim screamed, and screamed again. She began to cry, and then to run like a wild woman from room to room of her little house, wringing her hands, beating her fists and her palms against the walls and the

162

door frames. "Oh, my god, oh my god!" Had she heard it, had she really heard that name? "What should I do, what should I do?" She screamed it over and over, feeling as if she were falling down a well with no handholds, falling, falling, with no end in sight.

"Mama!" she screamed, inside the empty house, and then, falling to her knees on the floor beside the telephone, she whimpered, "Johnnie!"

Raymond Raintree was the name that her little brother Johnnie Kepler had given to an imaginary playmate when he was six years old. She had never forgotten that name, and she had never heard it again from anybody except her own mother, until now. Did this terrible man, the one who had escaped in Florida, have something to do with the abduction of her brother twenty-three years ago?

Should she call her mother, and tell her what she'd just heard?

But what if this man with the unique name had absolutely nothing to do with her long-lost brother? If he did, or if he didn't, mightn't this just bring more heartbreak for Katherine Kepler?

"I don't know what to do," Kim sobbed, feeling desperately alone.

She picked up the phone to call her sister, and then put it back down again. Then she picked it up to call her brother, but changed her mind. She wanted to check it out with them, and ask them what they thought she should do.

"No." Suddenly, Kim knew she had no choice. Her mom would never forgive her if she didn't call her right away, no matter how it turned out. If anybody had a right to know first, it was Katherine Kepler. "I have to call her."

Kim picked up the phone again, and held it while she attempted to get her crying and her voice under control. But when her mother's gentle voice said, "Hello?" she lost it again, and started sobbing like a little girl, scaring her mother half to death, even before she heard the news.

The last time they had seen John Michael Kepler, he was six years old, on the day he was abducted from the front yard of his home. But unlike Natalie Mae McCullen, little Johnnie Kepler was not seen again, either dead or alive.

"Raymond Raintree. That was the name Johnnie gave his imaginary friend," his mother and Kim would explain later, to all the people who asked her about it. The police. The reporters. The FBI. The lawyers. "We never knew where he got it. Nobody we knew had the name Raymond. We'd never even heard the name Raintree, except in that old movie with Elizabeth Taylor. We never knew if he'd heard those names somewhere, or what."

But, like many children, John Kepler developed a fantasy friend, and when his brother and sisters, mother and father asked him who he was talking to, he answered forthrightly, "Raymond Raintree." He said it, his family recalled, in four quite distinct syllables, possibly because it was quite a mouthful for a little fellow to pronounce. Ray. Mund. Rain. Tree. And, just like other kids with imaginary playmates, Johnnie took his invisible friend with him almost everywhere.

When Kim first heard the name of the escaped convict in Florida, she only thought he must have some indirect connection to the disappearance of her brother. Her family had always thought of it as an abduction, but the truth was that they didn't know what had happened to Johnnie. One minute he was playing in the front yard, and the next minute he wasn't. It seemed impossible that he could have wandered off, fallen in a well, or entered an empty house somewhere and *never* been found. But they didn't know.

Amazingly, it didn't even occur to Kim that the man calling himself by that long-ago name might *be* her brother.

164

If there was any connection at all, she merely thought this might be the fiend who had wrecked their lives. Later, she realized the man they showed on the television was too young to be the kidnapper. But it still didn't penetrate into her heart or mind that it might be Johnnie himself, because the man looked far younger than the twenty-eight years of age that John would be by now.

"The truth," she admitted later, "was terribly hard for me to grasp. I don't know why, exactly. I just think maybe there was a part of my mind that refused to take in the possibility that the strange-looking man I saw, this awful person who had maybe murdered a little girl, that he could be my brother. No. I just . . . no."

It was not so difficult for her mother to comprehend.

"I knew," Katherine Kepler would say later. "It was my son." She knew it the minute she heard Kim say that name. "There wasn't any logic to it. I just knew. I felt the strangest surge of hope and at the same time this sickening dread, like I was going to throw up. It felt like going up on a roller coaster and coming down, all at once. I was overwhelmed. Actually, I did throw up, if you want to know. I was shaking and crying. But I knew!"

Kim literally ran to her mother's house, from where she called her siblings. She also called Jack Lawrence, a deputy now retired from the Johnson County Sheriff's Department. He had kept in touch with the Keplers all those years, never entirely giving up on finding Johnnie. The Keplers loved Jack, and knew his wife and kids, and they treated him like family.

Kim told the retired deputy what she had just heard on TV. He promised to get hold of the Bahia Beach P.D. immediately and find out everything he could, and then he'd get right back to them.

"How's your mother?" he asked Kim, and she could hear the excitement and concern mixed in his deep voice.

165

Kim told him that Katherine was, at that moment, a mess—throwing up in the bathroom and weeping when she came out of it—and that the only thing that would help her now was to get more information.

He promised he would do that immediately.

Unfortunately, that would prove to be impossible at that time, because he couldn't get anybody official in Florida to pay any attention to him.

How could the Keplers be sure?

In the two days that passed before anybody in Florida paid any attention to them, the family worked frantically on their own trying to find out if Raymond Raintree was their lost boy.

Kim Kepler had heard of a video-imaging laboratory at the National Center for Missing and Exploited Children in Arlington, Virginia. The NCMEC, as it is known internationally, hadn't even existed when her brother disappeared. Eventually, the organization made it possible for anyone to search their database, at no charge, simply by logging on to the NCMEC Web site and entering descriptive information about a missing child or an abductor. Johnnie Kepler had been listed with NCMEC for many years. Now technicians there were using a poignant, powerful collaboration between technology and family photographs to age-progress pictures of missing children.

When Kim called there, they told her to put together full-frontal photographs of Johnnie, along with photos of family members at the same age Johnnie would be now if he were still alive.

"Do you have videotapes of him?" they asked her, gently.

"No," she had to tell them.

The very Christmas before Johnnie disappeared, their father had thought about giving their mother a video camera as a Christmas gift. He finally decided not to do it, because he was the one who really wanted it. It wouldn't be right, Fred Kepler had told the older children. It would be like their mother giving him the waffle iron that she wanted. Later, everybody in the family wished he had been as selfish as he usually was. But because Fred Kepler had an uncharacteristic burst of thoughtfulness that Christmas, there were no videotapes of Johnnie, no moving pictures of the little boy running, playing, eating, laughing, being held, taking a bath, sleeping. There were only still photos. One of them was a big, clear studio shot, an eight-by-ten picture in full color, showing Johnnie's little grin, his gray-blue eyes, his wild shock of brown hair.

"Bring it," Kim was told, for her plan was to go there.

Within less than a day, Kim was in Arlington, and she added to the photos as thorough a description of her brother as she could. She also took with her every other good picture of her brother she could find, as well as a studio picture of herself at twenty-eight and several snapshots of her older brother and even their parents at the same approximate age. In addition, she copied off the Internet some newspaper and magazine photographs of the suspect in Florida.

"I have to go myself," she explained to her siblings. "I can't put this precious material in a FedEx box and send it away. I have to keep my hands or my eyes on it, because if anything happened to it, it would kill Mom."

Over the years, many well-intentioned people had volunteered to get copies made of those precious photos, but Katherine Kepler would never give permission. She was too afraid that something would happen to damage or destroy them. She wouldn't take the chance. Except for a lock of hair from his first cut, and a baby tooth and his toys, they were all she had of her youngest child.

But she let her daughter hand carry them to Virginia.

167

Katherine Kepler didn't let Kim know at the time, that she burst into sobs the minute the pictures left her possession for the first time. Nor did Katherine admit to her other daughter and her son that she was in a lather of anxiety until Kim returned and placed them whole and undamaged in her hands again.

"If I had known that," Kim said, "I might not have had the heart or the courage to go away with them."

At the lab, the first time they tried the enhancement, Kim and the technician saw a man's face emerge. It looked a lot like her older brother, but not at all like Ray Raintree. This man in the enhancement was too full-faced, too healthy-looking, and he looked all of twenty-eight, which Ray didn't.

In a moment of tragic inspiration, Kim blurted to the technician at the keyboard, "What if nobody had loved him in all this time? What if he'd been neglected and underfed? Would he look any different than that?"

The technician tapped his keys again.

The photograph on the monitor began to melt and shift and change. The face became thinner and somehow smaller. The whole figure seemed to shrink. And there, suddenly, was a picture of a man who was the spitting image of "Raymond Raintree."

Kim cried on the plane, all the way back home, with old and new photographs in the padded envelope on her lap. She half-dreaded showing her mom.

Katherine's child was alive.

But her child was a monster.

Katherine Kepler was the exact same weight she had been on the day her son disappeared: 135 pounds on a small-boned five foot five inches. It was, on that day as it was to this, ten pounds more than she would like to have weighed. She also had the exact same hair style and color as she'd had back then in 1976: a streaked blond Dorothy Hamill "wedge" cut that was all the rage back then. Fortunately, it was a classic style that looked good anytime, but that's not why Katherine kept her hair fixed that way, or why she maintained her body weight at ten pounds over her personal limit.

"I wanted John to be able to recognize me," she explained. "If he had any memories of me, it would be when I was thirty-two years old, with this haircut." She touched the neat "do." "And with this body." She indicated the figure she kept looking youthful by exercising. With middle age had come the struggle to keep those extra ten pounds from becoming twenty. But with dieting and aerobic classes, she had managed to do it.

"And this face," she said.

At the relatively young age of fifty-four, Katherine had already had two partial face-lifts, which were her desperate attempt to keep the face her vanished child had known and loved. It was a good, open midwestern face with lips that naturally lifted up in a pleasant expression, and with a narrow nose and blue eyes, and dainty chin and ears and a wide brow. As a result of the surgeries, Katherine Kepler still looked remarkably like the younger woman in photographs with her youngest son.

If Johnnie Kepler, who would now be twenty-eight years old, ever saw her again, she hoped the sight would trigger memories of the first and most loving face he had ever seen.

"When he was born," Katherine remembered, "he had his eyes all squinched up and he was crying. Until they gave him to me. Instantly, like a miracle, he stopped crying. He popped open his eyes and I looked at him and he looked back at me. I was literally the very first person he ever saw on this earth."

Twenty-seven years later, his mother was determined

also to be the last person her son would ever see, if that was how fate played itself out. He had come into this world seeing love in her eyes, and he would leave it, seeing the love that was still there for him.

In her heart of hearts, she knew that he might stare at her then as he had first gazed at her when he was born: as a stranger who looked nice, and somehow familiar.

When Kim showed her mother the age-progression of Johnnie's picture, Katherine Kepler didn't hesitate for one moment. She took one look, and pressed it to her breast. "This is my beloved son, and I would give my life for him."

Kim's brother said sarcastically, where their mother couldn't hear, that they probably wouldn't have to give their lives, just nearly everything else they owned, if they had to pay his legal fees. "I want to see more evidence than this photo," he told his sisters. "DNA. Fingerprints."

Hearing that, Kim thought that even with all that, Johnnie might never know them, never recognize them, or call them his own. And even if he did, did they really want him back now? For her mother the answer to that was easy, a natural yes. But for his angry brother, who didn't want to have to claim a killer, and for his confused sisters, the answers weren't easy at all.

Once they had the photo confirmation, Katherine Kepler told herself and warned her children that Johnnie probably wouldn't remember her, or any of them. He had been so young and it had been so long ago and so many terrible things must have happened to him in the intervening years. Or else, why would he have turned out this way?

She told them this to protect them, and herself.

There exists scientific research that suggests physiological support for the validity of Katherine's ideas. Both long- and short-term memory are associated with twin organs in the brain called hypocampi. The normal human brain has a left hypocampus and a right hypocampus. Certain studies have shown a dramatic shrinkage of the hypocampi in Vietnam veterans suffering from the syndrome known as post-traumatic stress. In those vets, the shrinkage has been demonstrated to be as much as twenty-six percent of the total volume of the hypocampi, resulting in long-term amnesia and difficulty with short-term memory. Shrinkage has also been observed in victims of severe child abuse. It is suggested this phenomenon might account for the fact that many victims of child abuse cannot seem to recall large chunks of their childhood. Those blocks of memories are just gone, the victims claim; and now science is saying that might be literally true, that years might be lost in the shrinkage of a sensitive and important organ of the brain. It appears that severe stress of any sort can affect memory.

If those studies are accurate, there could be a real, physiological reason why the escaped murderer in Florida might not ever be able to recall a former identity. Ray Raintree truly might not remember being Johnnie Kepler. Katherine fully expected to be proven to be correct; her son, if this was her son, might never remember or acknowledge her. That's what her brain said. Her heart spoke a different language, and it said, "Remember me."

But even if "Raymond Raintree" claimed to recall an identity as Johnnie Kepler, how were they to prove whether or not he was?

"Thank God for modern science," Jack Lawrence commented to the grown Kepler children. "And for sentimental mothers who save their children's baby teeth, and locks of their babies' hair."

Thank God, in other words, for DNA typing.

The shortest path to the point of establishing a person's identity through so-called DNA typing, or profiling, is to take DNA from his mother and DNA from his father, and compare them to his DNA. If there are certain similarities between his DNA and theirs, then he is probably the child of those two people. (There is no such thing as a perfect "match" in DNA profiling, there are only statistical probabilities. It is not like fingerprinting, where prints can be exactly matched. There is not, in fact, a standard definition of what is a "match" in DNA typing. As the O. J. Simpson case suggested, it is not yet the precise science many people think it is, and much depends on the reliability of the lab and the technicians performing the work.) In this case, obtaining DNA from the mother would be easy, but nobody knew if Johnnie's dad was even still alive, much less where he was.

It would probably be enough, however, to find out if the man named Ray Raintree was linked to Katherine Kepler through DNA. In addition, Katherine had saved a lock of John's hair from his first trim, when he accompanied his father to a barbershop when he was only eleven months old. She also had one of his baby teeth, so there was, at least in theory, plenty of biological material available for DNA testing. If Ray Raintree carried her DNA and if his own DNA "matched" that of the teeth and the hair, then he would certainly be identified as Johnnie Kepler.

"If dinosaur DNA can keep in amber for millions of years," Katherine said to Jack Lawrence, "surely my son's DNA can keep in a plastic Baggie for only twenty-two years." At least, she prayed that it could, although anybody who knew anything about DNA could have warned her that she shouldn't absolutely count on it. DNA "keeps" in amber because no oxygen can reach it. Over the years, not realizing it might ruin her chances of ever knowing, Katherine had many times removed the precious lock of soft hair from the plastic and held it, caressed it, pressed it to her cheek, to her lips to kiss it, and she had also han-

172

dled the tiny tooth, crying over it, remembering the pillow under which it had lain, the dime she had substituted for it, and the excitement of the little boy when he found the shiny treasure left by the tooth fairy while he slept. In so doing, she might have destroyed the DNA, or irretrievably mixed it with her own.

"I'm not hopeful about the tooth and hair DNA," Jack Lawrence admitted to Kim, but not in such direct words to Katherine. He couldn't bring himself to tell her that the artifacts were probably useless by now. It wasn't as if they had been kept in laboratory conditions; hell, back in 1976 when Johnnie disappeared, deoxyribonucleic acid was still a relatively new toy for crime labs. Rapists were languishing in prison who might one day be freed, based on the DNA evidence of their semen. And as far as comparing the DNA of mother and son, Jack wasn't even sure whether the courts could—or would—require Ray to submit to DNA testing, in order to establish his identity, if he refused to cooperate. Did he have a constitutional right to refuse? Back in Kansas, Jack Lawrence set himself the task of calling judges to find out.

DNA testing takes awhile, sometimes weeks, and naturally the family wanted to know sooner than that. They wanted to know immediately. They wanted to know right *now*. But it seemed nothing, not even Kim's trip to Arlington, could give them irrefutable proof beyond a shadow of a doubt.

Kim Kepler jokes that she puts on all of the weight that her mother takes off. While it's true that thirty-year-old Kim is one inch shorter and thirty pounds heavier than her mother, she looks great. With her wide brown eyes—like her father's, she says—and her dark brown hair curled around her face, she is a dead ringer for the former movie star and U.S. diplomat, Shirley Temple. She also has the

173

same intelligent look in her eyes that Katherine has, and the same merry lift to her frequent smile. There's definitely an intensity about her, too, that reminds the rest of the family of Katherine. Both of them appear nice, even soft, but give them some purpose to hold to—such as doing everything you can to look exactly the same for twenty-two years!—and you soon sense the determination within. "A goer and a doer" is how Kim, known as Kimmie to her family, describes herself, and everyone who knows her seems to agree with that assessment. When Kimmie Kepler's around, things get *done*.

Kim dresses beautifully—lovely suits and blouses every day to work—and carries herself with a head-high dignity that would put a diplomat to shame. Her emotions, nonetheless, are almost always close to the surface.

"I cry at movies," she says. "But I'll also laugh at any excuse."

Likable is the word to use in summing up Kimmie Kepler's appearance to other people. That, along with *sincere*. And *responsible*. And *brave*.

"Oh, I'm just a Girl Scout at heart," she says, with a laugh. "Just don't ask me to light a fire by rubbing sticks together."

That would seem a highly impractical request to Kim, who always carries a little Swiss Army knife and a packet of matches in her purse, because you never know what you might need or be called upon to use in the campground of life.

And don't ask her to talk about her father, either.

"Dad left," she says succinctly.

They are two little words of one syllable each, spoken with clipped efficiency. *Dad left*.

Her mother doesn't say much more on the subject, adding only a few extra, careful, one-syllable words. "It was too hard for him," Katherine says, if asked . . . *why*.

174

Her other remaining children, Kim's older brother and younger sister, are not so reticent on the subject.

"When Johnnie disappeared, it destroyed our family at the time," says Christie Kepler Warneke, herself now the mother of three. At twenty-five, she's the baby of the Kepler family. "I guess you could say we've rebuilt it, Mom, Kimmie, Cal, and me, but it took a long time and we had to do it without Dad."

So, where is Frederick James Kepler, now sixty-three years old?

Where did he go?

Why did he leave them?"

"I used to fantasize," says Christie, "that Dad took Johnnie. That this was just a custody case, where Mom and Dad couldn't get along and so he left and took one of the boys with him."

For years, little Christie had herself convinced of that, that Johnnie was safe and loved somewhere with Daddy. It didn't keep her from missing her father desperately, but it kept her fear down quite a bit. A psychologist would probably call it a "coping mechanism." And quite an effective one, at that.

"If my brother was with my father, then the world wasn't such a scary place," Christie says, remembering the hopeful, impossible dream of her childhood. "If Dad took him, then the worst that could happen was that he was fine—even if he missed us—and we'd probably get to see them both again someday. And the world wasn't full of evil cruel strangers who could snatch *me* and take me away forever."

The factual problem with that clever theory, unfortunately, was that her brother disappeared in 1976 and her dad left home in 1979.

To this day, Christie still has a favorite fantasy.

In the current one, the reason Fred Kepler left in 1979

was to spend his life, if need be, searching for his lost son.

"It could be true," she says, defensively, heatedly, although everybody else in her family scoffs at her ideas. "I mean, it could! It's not like Dad ever told us exactly why he left us!"

Her mother's eyes mist over when she hears that. Fred's leaving may not have been accompanied by a torrent of explanatory words or even letters after the fact, but it was not exactly mysterious either. At least, it wasn't a mystery to his wife. She says that Fred withdrew more and more from interactions with her and the children he had left. He refused counseling. He dropped out of their church. Finally, he quit his job and began drinking heavily nearly every day with people Katherine didn't know, in parts of town she'd never been.

Then he asked for a divorce. Nothing else. No division of property, no custody, no visitation rights, nothing but the divorce. She gave it to him without contest. By then, she was fed up with him, he was "more trouble than he was worth," as his remaining son now describes him.

"Dad was a mess after Johnnie left," says Calvin, who goes by Cal. "I guess anybody would be, but he never was a particularly strong character. Kind of a weak man, I guess. Mom has always been our pillar of strength."

He thinks that over, this thirty-four-year-old, handsome man whose little brother was his mirror image. One wonders, seeing Cal now, if—all things being different—the two of them might have grown up to look nearly like twins. Having thought over his last words, which he seems to recognize as a cliché, a superficial response, Cal corrects himself, with a slight air of surprise. "Or, maybe Kimmie was. I don't want to take anything away from Mom, but maybe it was all she could do to keep herself standing. Kim kept the rest of us going, I'd have to say."

Cal is known for being plainspoken. "Rude," his

youngest sister calls it; "blunt," his other sister says. "Truthful," is what he says he always aims to be. He follows up many of his statements with the phrase "I'd have to say."

Fred Kepler never again surfaced in their lives, not even during all of the publicity attendant to their reunion with John/Ray. Searches were newly made for him. Nothing was found, and nothing in the media brought him forth again.

"He could be dead," his firstborn son says, and then Cal adds firmly, "That's how I think of him. Of both of them. Those people I knew—my little brother and my dad—they're dead. They died a long time ago. I'll never get them back again. I've adjusted. That's how I see it."

And that's why Cal refused to go along with his mother's and his sisters' idea to fly to Bahia Beach to try to get in to see "Raymond Raintree" once he was captured, and in custody again.

"That's not my brother," he says, almost angrily. "I don't want anything to do with that person, and he doesn't have any claims on me. I have to say I'll be ashamed if it turns out we actually share the same blood."

Kim tried to change Cal's mind about it, but their mother spoke up, saying, "Let Cal be, Kim. Let it be."

People, Katherine Kepler believes, have different limits, and we reach those limits at different times from one another. "Maybe it's easier," she says, "for a mother to love all of her children, exactly as they are, than for them to love each other."

They were four siblings, on the eve of possible reunion. And what were they . . . "exactly" . . . at that moment? Well, Kim was excited, hopeful, tearful, full of nervous energy to go there and meet him and help him. Christie was apprehensive of the reunion, scared of what she'd heard about her brother, and she was having nightmares. Cal was embarrassed and angry and rejecting. And John was . . .

evil. At least, that's how Katherine saw her kids, at that moment. "You have the children you have," she says, simply, "not necessarily the ones you thought you were going to have. You've just got to accept them as they really are, and love them any way you can."

It was a noble aim, born of never-flagging love and hope, and it would prove extremely difficult to achieve, for how can even the most loving, longing mother accept the Devil as her child?

7
Raymond

On my way to the Bahia Beach airport, I stop at the home of Susan and Anthony McCullen. I don't want to forget them or their daughter in my pursuit of this story. Sure, I may be on my way to meet Ray's mother, but what about Natty's mom? I'm worried about how the McCullens are enduring this second search for her killer.

Tony opens the door to me, and says, "Why the hell didn't she kill him, Marie?"

"It sure would have made things easier," I agree. "How are you, Tony? How's Susan?"

"Come on in." He steps aside so I can enter the foyer of their beautiful, and now tragic home.

"I don't want to bother you, Tony. I just came by to say hello."

"Susan!" He yells toward the back of the house. "It's Marie Lightfoot!"

In a moment, Susan McCullen rushes toward us, wiping her hands on a dish towel. "I'll be so glad when he's dead," are her first words, which are identical to what I've heard the families of other victims say. "It's unbearable to think of him walking around out there like any other person. I can't stand it if I had to think of him . . . alive . . . for the rest of my life."

179

"The only thing that would make me happier," Tony chimes in, "would be to kill him myself." He is dressed in black boxer swimming trunks that hang loosely on his six-foot frame, which has visibly dropped quite a few pounds over the past few harrowing months. It is no longer so easy for people to look at him and think, "ex-fighter." But at the moment he says that, I think that he looks pugilistic right down to the balled fists at his sides. "They oughta give us families the choice. Let us flip the switch. Or drop the pellet."

"Or inject," Susan says fiercely. "I'd do that."

"You would?" I ask her.

Natalie's mother nods her head until her hair bounces. When I saw Susan in the courtroom hallway on the first day of the trial, I thought the bereaved young mother looked as pretty as the beauty queen she used to be. She has blue eyes, like Natalie, and streaked blond over brown hair, cut blunt at the shoulders and worn with bangs just like her daughter. Back then, I thought Susan was already way too thin for good health; since then, grief has wasted her away. Now it appears that the only thing that keeps her standing is fury, and I wonder how long that will last. Until Ray is dead? If I were to make a prediction based on the experience of other families I've known, Susan will feel a little relief at Ray's death, and then she'll collapse.

And only then may come the long, long healing.

"You bet I would," Susan answers me while Tony stands, swaying like an old fighter, exhausted but ready to fight somebody. "In a minute. Let me fill the syringe. Show me the vein to hit." She makes a furious jabbing motion with her right hand, as if poking a needle into Ray Raintree. Her lips thin and tighten into a grimace as she does it.

With a shock, I realize that Susan is not beautiful anymore. Her skin is grayish now, like a cancer victim, and her complexion is blemished. Every day she went to the courthouse her physical appearance seemed to slip a little more, until it was obvious to anyone who was looking at her daily. And everyone was. Not just

180

looking, either, but staring. They were staring discreetly—the kind ones—but all eyes were on "the parents," all the same.

Susan and Tony experience those stares as accusing.

To Susan, those staring eyes say: *There she is, the mother who wasn't watching her child.* And to Tony, they shout: *There he is, the father who didn't lock the back door before he went to bed.*

I believe that most of the people who look at Susan and Anthony are feeling horror and sympathy. *There they are, the ones whose little girl got killed. Oh, poor things!* That's what they say in quiet, sympathetic tones behind the parents' backs. There is a universe of sympathy available to Natalie's parents, but the young couple is having a hard time believing it, or accepting it, because their own sense of guilt is so enormous. They simply can't believe that other people don't hate them as much as they hate themselves.

Tony is constantly in agony, thinking, *Why didn't I lock the door!*

And Susan's obsession is, *I should have known something was wrong, I should have dreamed it, or heard a sound when she went outside, I should have known and gone to check on her! I'm her mother, I should have known!*

There is no talking them out of it, either.

We all hope that time persuades them otherwise.

I've seen Natalie's inflatable life preserver ring still floating in their swimming pool. I know that Susan swims slow laps, clinging to it and crying. It breaks people's hearts to see the child's belongings still scattered around the house all those months later. But Susan gets furious if anybody suggests moving them out of sight, or giving them away.

"You'd feel better," people tell her.

"I don't want to feel better!" she explodes at them.

The McCullens cling to their anger and their guilt as hard as Susan clings to the plastic life ring in the swimming pool.

"We've got the TV on," Tony tells me. "We're always waiting for the bulletin, to tell us they've caught him. I'm hoping he bleeds to death on the run. Either that, or when they find him, he tries to get away and they shoot him, and they do a better job of it than the judge did. I don't think I can ever sleep again until I know the bastard's dead."

Suddenly I feel overwhelmed in that small space with them.

"Where are the twins?" I inquire.

Susan looks puzzled, as if she has temporarily forgotten she has other children. Then she says, almost dismissively, "We took them over to a neighbor's house, to spend the night with their kids."

My heart sinks. I've seen this happen before: parents who lose one child to murder becoming so obsessed by grief and revenge that they can barely recognize the existence, much less meet the needs, of their other children. Equally painful is the opposite reaction, when grieving parents cling to their remaining children like fallen climbers to a lifeline. Either way, it's hell for the surviving children.

"Have dinner with us, Marie?"

"Yeah, come on," Tony echoes. "We need to talk to you anyway."

"Thanks, but I've got a plane to catch. I just wanted to tell you I was thinking about you. What did you want to talk to me about? Can it wait? I could call you from where I'm going."

The couple exchange glances. Suddenly, I feel wary.

"We don't want to be in your book," Tony says, gruffly.

The marble under my feet starts to crack.

"It's nothing against you," Susan assures me.

"We read those pages you sent us, and we just decided we don't want to be in the book," Tony says. Although most journalists never let the subjects of their articles read them before publication, I do, especially where the victim's family is concerned. I don't want to hurt them, and I do want to get things right. I had sent to the McCullens the sections of my manuscript that are written specifically about Natty and them.

It's a gamble, and this is the risk I take.

"Why?" I ask, through numb lips.

"It's all that stuff about this house," Tony says, looking embarrassed but obstinate. "I don't want people knowing all that, how it's free and all. It makes us look like moochers."

"I don't think it does," I say.

"All that stuff about spending too much money," Susan says. "I don't want people reading all that about us. You understand, don't you, Marie?"

I want to say to them, Do you understand that I don't need your permission for any of my book? Do you get it that you're news? I can write anything I want to as long as it's true, and I can prove it? But I can't say that to these suffering people, no way.

"I do understand," I say, because I certainly do understand the concept of having second thoughts about things. If they only realized to what lengths I have gone to protect them, even as it is written now! But I have to let it go. Later, I'll try to persuade them, or maybe I can rewrite those scenes in a way that appeases them without sacrificing my own integrity. I want and need their cooperation. Without it, the promotion of the book could be a disaster. I can just see the headlines and interviews: "Victim's Family Sues Writer." And there would be Susan on television, saying, "We pleaded with her not to write it."

Tony looks marginally more relaxed now.

"You take care of yourselves," I tell them as I start to leave.

Susan replies bitterly, "Why should we?"

"Because of the boys!" I urge her.

She gives me a quick hug. "Thank you for being so nice to us."

Naturally, I feel like the world's biggest hypocrite as I get back into my car, take out a pen and writing pad, and begin to scribble notes. I will change their minds about those scenes in the book. I have to, that's all there is to it. But what will they say if it turns out that the man who murdered their child was himself abducted when he was Natty's age? Will they hate him any less? I recall Franklin's words, and I doubt it. Ray will still be the killer, and Natty would still be dead. With a sigh for the McCullen family and

183

every family like them I have ever known, I drive on to catch my flight to Kansas.

Once in the air, I accept a cup of coffee from the flight attendant, and think about the truths I know, but won't publish, about the death of Natalie Mae McCullen.

Some things I will never tell anybody.

The way I wrote the story of how Tony McCullen went to bed the night his daughter died wasn't quite the way it happened. I won't be telling my readers the real reason why he didn't even think of looking in on his children. And I'm not about to divulge the probable truth about why Natalie woke up.

Tony didn't check on the kids, because he was horny.

"I don't know," he told me, trying to explain something that probably didn't require explaining. This is why ordinary people have to be protected by the journalists who "cover" them; they don't have any experience being "news," and they don't begin to understand how vulnerable they are to being quoted correctly, but embarrassingly. If they're plainspoken people like Tony and Susan, they're likely to blurt out truths they would never want millions of people to read. "It had been—God—I'll bet a week since Susan and I had done it. One thing and another, either the kids interrupted us, or one or the other of us was too tired, or some damn thing. And I was watching Leno, but he had a hog caller on, so I was switching over to HBO, and they were showing these episodes from foreign sex shows. French. English. I can't remember what all, but I remember there was even one from some Arab country, if you can believe that. All it was, was a belly dancer though.

"Anyway, they were showing everything, practically porno flicks, right there on HBO. Lots of huge boobs and dirty jokes and people humping each other, and sexy stuff, and I was just sitting there getting horny as hell. But I thought Sue was already asleep, and she hates it if I wake her up to screw."

But then he heard the toilet in their bathroom flush.

"I knew she was up. Hot damn. I flicked the tube off and hustled my young butt down the hall. God, I never gave the kids a thought, you know?"

Or the door locks, either.

"I just wanted to get there before she fell back to sleep."

If the security of their home passed through Tony's mind at all that night, he only thought he'd get to it later, afterward. Only, Tony fell asleep right after they made love.

Their front door was locked. Susan had seen to that earlier when she had looked outside to make sure the kids had driven their assorted rolling toys into the garage.

"Everything was in," Susan remembered, and I wrote down. "So I closed our front door and bolted it. I went into the family room and saw that Tony was watching Leno—he loves the opening monologue—so I kissed the top of his head, and he gave me a pat on my hair. I told him I was pooped, and I was going to bed."

They said good night to each other.

There was no talk of lovemaking.

"The twins had woken everybody up at dawn that morning," Susan said. "I don't recall why, just sheer energy, I think. It's like they're only wired to sleep a few hours at a time. Anyway, we'd had a few nights in a row of that, and I'd had it. I really needed some rest."

But she didn't get to sleep right away.

"I don't know what it was, but I couldn't fall asleep. I think I was worrying about all our bills and should I get a job and how much would child care cost, or should we just get out of this house, rent a little place where we could live more cheaply." Susan tossed and turned a bit. Then she got up to use the bathroom.

"It wasn't all that late. Eleven-twenty. I looked at our clock that glows in the dark. I got out of the bathroom and here came Tony slipping in the door. He took off his pants and I could see right away what he had in mind." Susan smiled faintly, but it didn't last. Her mouth began to tremble as she told what happened next. "I thought, what the heck, I can't sleep anyway, and it's been awhile."

She said, "We tried to be quiet, but there was a point where we got to laughing about some dumb thing and I swung my leg out and managed to knock into my bedside table."

Susan had several books piled there, novels she was hoping to get to. Her romance-loving sister had pressed them on her, saying she'd love them. The accidental kick jarred the table, which was all it took to topple the precarious pile of books.

"They really crashed," Susan said. "We held our breath, to see if it woke anybody up." Her eyes filled, overflowed, as she told the story. "We didn't think it did. We didn't hear any of the kids make a noise."

Within moments, she estimated, Susan and Tony were sound asleep, nestled in their favorite sleeping posture, with her head on his left shoulder and her right arm across his chest. They both thought that what probably happened was that the vibration of the books falling woke Natalie in the next room. Her bed lay up against the very wall the books had crashed into. She couldn't hear the noise, but the little girl was almost as attuned to vibrations and subtle movements as hearing people are to sound. To her, vibration *was* sound.

I would never divulge that truth in a book.

They hadn't been shy about telling me, but how would that be for them? To have everyone picturing them horny, laughing, careless, making the noise that may have awakened their daughter in the next room? I know that Susan can't stop putting cause and effect together. Her thinking goes: If she and Tony hadn't moved into that house, they never would have fallen into the temptation of living beyond themselves, and if they hadn't gotten into so much debt, she wouldn't have been awake that night worrying about money.

Tony wouldn't have heard her moving around.

They wouldn't have had sex.

The books would have stayed on the table.

Natalie would have continued sleeping in her bed.

Ray would have motored right on past their dock.

186

It could very well be that something else had awakened Natalie that night, but there was no convincing her mother or father of that. Susan and Tony hated Ray, but they blamed themselves.

No, I won't write that, I think again as the airplane flies me to the Midwest. Who needs to know that? I don't think anybody does. So, they're human. He wanted to make love with his pretty wife. They enjoyed it enough to get a little carried away. So, every couple should be so lucky to have a robust sex life.

Both of the McCullens implied to me that was the last time they ever made love. And I'll never write that, either. Besides, it might not be true. I can't always trust the people I interview to tell me the whole truth even when they think that's what they're doing. People forget, they gloss over, they get things wrong. And people do lie to me. Sometimes they know it's a lie, and sometimes they don't. Sometimes I recognize it as a lie, or I get lucky and uncover the truth, and sometimes I don't. I hate to find out later, after a book is published, and then have readers, reviewers, or cops correct my mistakes.

If I'm going to publish this story about Raymond Raintree being Johnnie Kepler, it had better be ironclad true, is my thought as the plane descends toward the runway. If it isn't, I will have no ending, no identity for the killer, no motive, no scene of the crime, no idea where Ray is, and the victim's parents don't want to be in the book.

Apart from that, Mrs. Lincoln, how was the play?

I feel panic rise, and try to calm myself by remembering there are worse things in life than missing a deadline. And I am just about to hear of one of them. I reach for my lipstick and hairbrush, and mentally prepare to meet a retired deputy sheriff by the name of Jack Lawrence.

8

Raymond

"I can't get my brain wrapped around the new facts."

The retired deputy drives me south from Kansas City International Airport in a two-door green Ford pickup truck. He's got the air-conditioning going full blast at first, so we have to raise our voices to hear each other talk. Outside the truck windows, it's still eighty-seven degrees at nine o'clock in the evening, and even the inside of the truck door is warm to my touch.

"For so many years, I have been thinking of Johnnie Kepler as an innocent little boy," he tells me. "I felt so bad for him, and for his family. They're such good people, especially his mom and that older sister of his, Kimmie. I won't speak of his father, because we don't know what it would have been like to walk in that man's shoes. But now here we are with this news that the little boy we all mourned is still alive. Only he is a grown man who is supposed to have abducted another child, like somebody did to him. It is very confusing, and upsetting, very."

"I'm sure it is, Jack."

Around us, I can see nothing except highway, dark open fields, and well-lighted strip malls. The man himself is tall, lean, courtly. He carried my overnight bag for me, opened the passenger door, and helped me up with a firm hand on my elbow. He has a superb posture that pulls my own spine up straighter, but his face sags comfortably into bags and jowls, and his thinning gray and brown hair looks as if it could use a patting down. I'm guessing his age to be near seventy, which would put him in his late forties when the boy disappeared.

By the time I have been in his company for fifteen minutes, I feel as if I have known him for fifteen years. As I often do when I meet a nice man of his age, I wonder what my own life might have been like if I had been adopted by someone like this, instead of by my mother's sister and husband. I shake off the sentimental daydream in order to pay attention to the words of this man who, after all, I don't really know at all.

"You probably want to know all about it, right?" he asks me.

"About how Johnnie disappeared, you mean?"

"Yeah. I'll let Katherine tell you, herself."

"It's late, will she still want to talk tonight?"

He gives me a quick look. "Kimmie told me they would stay up all night, if that's what it takes. You're the first link they've ever had to him since 1976. They want to know everything you can tell them about him."

I wince. "None of it's good."

"Well, let's just think of the boy as a prisoner of war for right now, how about that?" the retired deputy advises me. "He was taken, he may have been tortured, he was brainwashed, and now he's coming home. Is it any wonder if he's not the same man he would have been?"

"That's a very humane way to look at it, but I doubt that his victim's family will agree with you. They could say, he still had choices. They could say, not every prisoner of war becomes a murderer."

"I wouldn't expect them to see it any other way."

"You know that he's never coming home, Jack."

"I know, but the Keplers don't. You're going to have to tell them."

I turn and look out the window, feeling my heart sink again.

"Before I left home," I say, "I stopped by to visit the parents of the little girl Ray killed. Of course, they hate him. They wish the judge had killed him when she shot him, and since she didn't, they hope some bounty hunter gets him, and if that doesn't work, they'd like to kill him themselves. Natty's mother told me she would be happy to flip the switch on the electric chair, or inject him with chemicals to kill him."

"If I were them, I would, too. Did you tell them about the Keplers?"

"No. I'm not sure why I didn't, except that it seemed too much to expect any sympathy out of them." I look over at him, and when I see that he is nodding in agreement, I add, "It's difficult to put Natty's mom and Ray's mom in the same picture."

"Like I said, I can't get my brain wrapped around it."

When he pulls into a driveway beside a small frame house, I ask, "Is this where it happened, Jack?"

"Yep. She's never moved. He disappeared from this very front yard."

"How can she stand to keep living here?"

"She wants everything to be the same, if he tries to find her."

"But didn't she think he was dead?"

"I guess mothers don't think that way."

"And she was right, all along."

He makes a move to open his door, but I stop him. "Can we wait just a minute? I need to absorb this." When he looks puzzled, I say, "So I can report what it's like here, for my readers. I know this sounds weird, and I don't want to keep them waiting, but I need to soak up the atmosphere. I need to do things like estimate how much the trees have grown in twenty-two years, and compare the way the house looks today with photographs of how it looked back then."

What I don't tell him is that I need to try to feel the sensation of tragedy rise in my own body, to attempt to get a hint of what it must have felt like in this house, on that day.

190

"I know, this must seem like a very strange way to make a living."

"I like your books," he says, surprising me. "You do a good job getting things right about law enforcement. If this is what it takes for you to do that, that's fine with me. My job was pretty strange, too, when you get right down to it."

After a few moments, I am able to say, "Thanks, let's go."

I have never met three more nervous women than Katherine Kepler and her daughters. Kim and Christie sit protectively on either side of Katherine on a couch in their mother's living room. Their brother Cal hangs back, standing in the doorway between that room and the dining room with his hands in his pockets and an angry frown on his face. The youngest of the siblings, Christie, looks scared to death, as if she's afraid that her murderous missing brother may come bursting into the house at any moment and kill us all.

We sit on furniture and are surrounded by decorations that have literally not been altered for twenty-two years. She has covered up worn places with doilies, patched scratches with dye, and repainted the walls the same colors over and over.

All three women are dressed in blue jeans and T-shirts, and the family resemblance is strong. At first glance, they look like three sisters, and it's a little eerie to realize that's because the real sisters have aged naturally, while their mother has tried to hold age at bay. Cal is tall and thin, with dark hair and dark, hollowed eyes, and a stiff, reserved air about him when he shook my hand in greeting. He wears black trousers and a white, short-sleeved shirt, and looks as if he came directly here from the telecommunications office where he works.

Kim keeps an arm around her mother's shoulders.

Katherine weeps off and on through the telling of her story.

"It was a beautiful day. November twenty-second, thirteen years after President Kennedy died. It had snowed, but the sun was shining. Johnnie was so excited about the snow, and he couldn't wait to go out to play in it. I had him enrolled in afternoon kindergarten, so we could have nice mornings together after he got up. You know, without all that tension of trying to get a small child awake and fed and dressed when he's still half-asleep. Do you have children, Ms. Lightfoot?"

"Please, call me Marie. No, I don't."

I'm recording the conversation, with their permission.

"Oh, well, I put all my children into afternoon kindergarten, except for Cal, who was an early riser."

"So, John wanted to play in the snow?"

"Yes, and Cal wanted to stay home, of course, and play in the snow, too. But I put them all in the car and took him to school, and Johnnie and Christie and I drove back home. And since we still had on our boots and coats and everything, I stayed outside with them for a little while, and we made snowballs, and even started a snowman. But it was still early, so it was kind of cold, and I made them come in to get warm again." Her face crumples, and I feel as if I can see twenty-two years of suffering in it as Katherine weeps, and her daughters hand her tissues. "He was just getting over an ear infection, and he still couldn't hear very well out of one ear. It has always bothered me terribly that I couldn't recall which ear it was, isn't that crazy?"

I feel such a shock on hearing this woman say that her son had an ear infection that had left him temporarily unable to hear.

The parallel with Natalie Mae McCullen is eerie.

"And then," Katherine goes on, "after he disappeared, all I could think about was, who was going to take care of him, if he was sick? I couldn't bear the idea of him being sick, or hurting, and I wasn't there to comfort him."

She takes a shaky breath, before continuing.

"After breakfast, Johnnie wanted so badly to go back outside again and play, and I thought that was all right."

Katherine looks first at Jack, then at me.

I get the feeling that even after all this time, she's still looking for someone to convince her that she didn't do anything wrong, and I am painfully reminded of Susan McCullen. Twenty-two years from now, will Susan still be blaming herself because she wanted to love her husband on the night her daughter died? Speaking up so quickly that it sounds as if he has said similar things many times before, Jack Lawrence assures her, kindly, "You can't keep a little boy inside when it snows, Katherine."

"No, I suppose not," she says, drying her eyes again.

It is heartbreakingly sweet, I think, how the retired deputy plays his part in a chorus whose purpose is solely to comfort a mother of a missing child. He's a widower, he told me, and I suspect he's half—or more—in love with Katherine Kepler.

The end of her story comes with horrifying speed.

"So I dressed him up warmly again, and sent him outside to play."

I wait for the next sentence, but there isn't one.

A silence grows in the room, filled with implication.

"You mean, that was . . ." I can't bring myself to say it.

"I went to put my own coat and boots back on," Katherine says, "and when I went outside, Johnnie wasn't there. The tracks of his boots went out to the curb, and then they stopped, and that's all there ever was. He had a little plastic snow shovel that he took with him."

I feel grief rise in my own throat.

"Mrs. Kepler—"

"Katherine, please."

"Katherine." I take a breath, then say it all in a rush. "When the Florida cops went through Ray Raintree's belongings, they found a toy shovel."

"Oh, my Lord, was it red?"

My eyes sting with tears. "Yes."

"It's Johnnie!" Katherine springs up from the couch, sobbing and staring about wildly, as if he might suddenly appear in front of her. "I know it's my boy."

While her daughters embrace and comfort her, Katherine's other son, Cal, turns and disappears into the back of the house. He doesn't return until I begin, hesitatingly, to tell them about the man I know as Raymond Raintree. They don't ask about Natty McCullen, and I can't bring myself to mention her. When I finish, holding back little else, because the women beg me not to, Katherine Kepler says, "It doesn't matter what he's like now."

But standing in the dining room doorway, Calvin looks as if it matters to him a great deal. As if sensing his hostility, Kim looks back over her shoulder to glare warningly at him. Even with that, he bursts out with his first words since I arrived. "Mom, how can you say it doesn't matter? He killed somebody. He's a terrible person now. He isn't the sweet little boy you remember, he's a pervert, a murderer, and we ought to stay as far away from him as we can get."

"You just don't want to spend the money to defend him!" Kim accuses.

"Nobody can defend him," Cal shoots back. "He's guilty. He's going to die in the electric chair, if some cop doesn't shoot him first. She didn't tell you that, did she? These guys, they don't make it back alive. Just forget it, if you think you're ever going to see him again. I don't know why you'd want to, anyway."

"Cal, shut up," his youngest sister pleads, looking frightened.

His mother goes to him, and attempts to enfold his tall, stiff body into an embrace. I watch Katherine whisper something to her son, but it doesn't calm him. He gently pushes away from her, and rushes toward the back of the house again. In a moment, we hear a back door open, and slam, and then a car starting in the driveway.

His mother, who is crying again, says to her daughters, "Please don't be mad at your brother. Give him time. It's very hard for him."

I think it is unbearable for all of them, and that it is only going to get worse. They sit back down, and now I interview the women at length. We look at dozens of photographs of all of the kids when they were children. When I see pictures of Johnnie Kepler, I can hardly fathom the tragedy that is going to happen to the smiling little boy. I see pictures of his father, Fred Kepler, who was an ordinary-looking man, not very tall, and a bit pudgy. Several photographs show members of the family with an orange-and-white cocker spaniel dog.

"This dog!" I exclaim, excited. "He remembers this dog."

Katherine's eyes widen. "He does? He remembers Daisy?"

For a moment, I am almost sorry I said it, because of what I have to say with it. "He told me that he doesn't have any memories from his childhood, except he recalls an orange and white dog."

"He doesn't remember anything else . . . me?"

Tears come to my eyes again on behalf of the pretty woman seated beside me, looking through the albums. "Maybe he remembers more than he told me he did." I don't want to offer false hope, but given Ray's talent for lying, it could be true.

When I compare their age-enhanced photo to my own memories of Ray's appearance, I see no difference between them at all.

"It's him," I confirm to Katherine, feeling a kind of dreadful awe. "It really is him."

His mother nods, as if she's always known.

Very late, I walk Jack back to his truck in the driveway, on the pretext of having left a notebook in it. There are tall gangly trees around the property, and their leaves are clapping together in the warm wind with a sound like soft applause.

"Cottonwood trees," he says, when I ask about them.

We stand together for a moment in a meditative silence while the cottonwood trees applaud our thoughts. It looks so different here, from Florida. I am acutely, claustrophobically aware of being in the very center of the country, equidistant from oceans. Even the grass beneath my feet is remarkably different from the saw grass I'm used to. This is thinner, more delicate, softer under my shoes. There's more wind out here in Kansas, just as Dorothy found out in *The Wizard of Oz*, and it never seems to stop blowing. But when it brushes my skin, it's not all that different from home:

as humid as walking into a bathroom after somebody has taken a hot shower.

"I could never live in Florida," Jack remarks. "Too darn hot."

"What do you call this?" I retort as I stand there sweating beside him. "Florida's not any warmer than this, and we've got the water close by."

"Yeah, I guess that would help some."

There's something I still have to say.

"There's one thing I didn't tell them, Jack. I didn't say how Ray looks now. Photos of him now don't even begin to tell the whole story. You'd better prepare her, if she ever gets a chance to see him in person. It's not like he's maimed, or deformed, or anything. It's . . . it's hard to explain to people about Ray's appearance. How do you say to a mother, here's your grown son who still has all of his fingers and toes, he hasn't had his face blown off, nothing like that, but nobody can stand to look at him?"

I take a deep breath, remembering my own impressions.

"What you ought to tell her is, if the Devil had a son, this is what he'd look like, like some kind of strange, slimy evil creature." I shake my head. "No, that's not true, either. I make him sound like the creature from the black lagoon. He's just a normal-looking human being, only . . . he's not."

As he waits patiently, I try again.

"I think I'd tell her that Ray has a kind of odd appearance that you can't tell from the pictures you've seen on television. It's like there's something wrong with him, but you can't exactly say what." And then I finally blurt out the truth. "Ray is repulsive, Jack. He's one of the most repulsive human beings I ever saw."

Even in the darkness, I can see that he looks shocked.

After a moment's thought, he says, "To you and me, maybe. But not to his mother."

But I wonder if even a mother's love can be that strong.

He has told me that he retired to ten acres of woody, uncultivated Kansas grassland, with a retinue of greyhound racing dogs.

That's where he's going now, he says, as we walk around to his side of the truck.

"They're retired," he explains. "Like me."

"I'm ready to retire for the night," I admit, wearily. "But I still have some writing I want to do."

He holds out his hand for me to shake.

Surprised, I take it and find it firmly grasped.

"This has been good for them, Marie. I'm awful glad you came."

"Thank you. I'm glad they've had you all these years."

He releases my hand, and says with painful regret in his gruff voice, "Not that I did a darn bit of good."

"That's not true, Jack. You've given comfort. And you never stopped looking for him. That's got to have meant a lot to them."

"I guess I can stop now," he says, sadly.

I wave him off, after he promises to come back early in the morning.

The sisters could talk all night, but Katherine won't let them, saying that their guest needs to get some sleep. Their guest agrees with her. She sweeps the "girls" out the door to their own homes, and then Katherine graciously installs me in a little bedroom, handing me my own fresh towel and bar of soap.

"This was Johnnie and Cal's room," she tells me.

"Oh, Katherine, are you sure you want me in it?"

She nods. "Nobody's slept in it since then, so you'll be the first." A wave of sadness crosses her face. "Well, except for me. I've slept in here a lot, although I'd just as soon the girls didn't know. But it's time for all that to change now."

"You're sure? I'd be glad to sleep on the couch."

"No, you wouldn't." She smiles, gently. "It's all broken down. Cal wouldn't sleep in his room after Johnnie left, so I let him sleep on the couch. He slept there clear through high school, if you can believe that, and piled up his clothes against the wall in the dining room." She pauses, and sadness creases her face again. "I imagine

Cal resents Johnnie in ways I don't know anything about, but that's just the way life is for this family." Her eyes are clear, their expression brave. "That's just the way life is."

I am without words in the face of her kindness and courage.

It is a very small house, with two other small bedrooms, so closing up one whole room meant quite a lot in terms of space. She has used the girls' bedroom for storage, as if it wouldn't matter if she changed that one room before Johnnie came home.

When she leaves me alone, and quietly closes the door behind her, I feel as if I have been given permission to spend the night in a shrine. It is dusted, it is clean, and except for the fact that everything in it looks thirty years old, it might have been lived in yesterday.

Yesterday, all my troubles seemed so far away . . .

I have forgotten to tell her about Ray's guitar.

A note to myself: Tell them in the morning.

Her central air-conditioning system is blowing cool air through wall vents, so I can't open a window in Ray and Cal's bedroom. I wish I could, because even as hot as it is, I'd like to go to sleep to the sound of the wind blowing through those cotton-wood trees.

On the other hand, I can't afford to fall asleep yet.

I work until 3 A.M., and when I am finished, I have a whole new chapter that I could never have predicted:

While Florida searched for Ray Raintree, the solution to the mystery of his identity began to unfold in a place most of the cops had never heard of . . .

9
Raymond

An aroma of sausage wakes me up at 7 A.M.

After I shower and get dressed in shorts, T-shirt, and sandals, I follow my nose into the kitchen where I find Katherine watching television as she fries potatoes and onions in a cast-iron skillet. She's bare legged and barefoot, in a denim skirt that falls to just above her knees and a plain, sleeveless white cotton shirt worn loose over her waistband. From the back, she could pass for sixteen, and even when she turns around, she still looks younger than I feel on two hours of sleep: When I write late, I'm always too wired to fall right to sleep, and last night was even worse than usual. A TV weatherman tells us, "Our humidity is an exact match for our temperature today, folks. Ninety percent humidity, ninety degrees of temperature, which makes our heat index—"

"I wish they'd never invented those heat and wind chill indexes," Katherine remarks, with a smile of greeting for me. She reaches over to turn down the sound on the TV. "Weren't we already miserable enough without that? Does it make you feel any better, Marie, to know that it's actually more like a hundred degrees outside, instead of just ninety?"

"No, it does not. Good morning, Katherine."

She nods me toward a coffee pot, and I help myself. Then I go lean my back against a counter near to her, so we can talk while she cooks.

"Scrambled, all right?"

"Scrambled is wonderful. You don't have to go to so much trouble—"

She laughs a little. "Yes, I do. If I don't keep busy every second until I get to see Johnnie again, I will go insane, and my children will have to commit me."

I smile sympathetically. "Then cook away."

She lifts sausage patties out of the skillet with a spatula, then pours an egg mixture in and starts to stir it. I can't recall the last time I fixed more than cereal and grapefruit for myself for breakfast. There's a curtained window at my back, but when I turn around to look, all I see is her backyard and the house and backyard of her neighbor behind her. I feel claustrophobic again at the thought of all the houses and all the land that radiate in every direction away from here. Kansas feels too much like the core of the universe to someone like me who is used to living on the edge of it.

We share a silence for a moment until I notice she is looking uneasy. I wait, and finally she says a fragment of a sentence, "The little girl that Johnnie killed."

I start to feel too queasy to eat the food she's fixing.

She doesn't look up as she stirs the eggs with a fork. "Jack won't tell me what he did to her, so I think it must be something really bad. What did he do?"

"It is bad. Are you sure you want me to tell you?"

Katherine picks up a block of orange cheese and begins to scrap it over a grater, so flakes fall on top of the eggs. "I want to know."

"He took her from her home, in a boat." I take a breath, then get it over with quickly. "He killed her by putting pressure on the carotid artery in her neck. That's what he did to her."

She compresses her lips, not looking at me.

"That's the worst of it," I say, "but the next thing I'm going to say sounds worse. Are you sure you want to hear this?"

"Did he rape that child?"

"No, no he didn't, there wasn't any sexual assault."

She begins crumbling one of the sausages into the egg mixture, and hiccups a sob, and then makes a heroic effort not to keep sobbing. I reach over and touch her back.

"What did he do?" she asks me, her voice breaking.

Oh, Jesus, I don't want to tell her this! "He used some kind of thin probe, which he inserted into her nose after she was dead, to scoop out a portion of her brain."

Finally, she gives up all pretense of cooking.

"Our medical examiner believes that Ray stole her pineal gland."

"Her what?" Her mixing fork clatters into the skillet. She turns toward me, and I move her gently aside, and quickly grab a pot holder to remove the eggs from the heat so they won't burn. She lets me take over. "For heaven's sake, why would he do something like that?"

"I don't know. Nobody knows."

"What in the world's a—what did you call it?"

"Pineal gland. It's the smallest endocrine gland in our bodies." I point to my own temple. "It only weighs about a gram. It's up here, in the middle. To be perfectly precise, it's between our cerebral hemispheres, and right above the third ventricle of our spinal column."

"What's it for, for heaven's sake?"

"It secrets melatonin which is a derivative of an amino acid called tryptophan." I haul out the facts, hoping that if I pile on enough of them they will defuse the terror. "Some people think it has something to do with the onset of puberty." I try to remember what the medical examiner has said, and what else I've learned in my own reading. "At one time, people thought it was like a valve in the brain that controlled our memories."

"What do you mean?"

"Well, like a gate, that lets us remember some things, but not others."

"Is that what it does?"

"I guess not." I shrug apologetically. "I wish I knew more. If we understood more about the pineal gland, we might have a better idea of why Ray took it."

"There can't be any reason for anything like that," she whispers, in a shocked voice. "Oh, that poor child!" She stares at me in horror. I don't know which child she means, but she could well mean both of them. With a cry dragged from her heart, she exclaims, "Oh, her poor mother!"

The only one of us who can truly understand how Susan McCullen must feel is Katherine Kepler, the mother of the man who killed her daughter.

Jack Lawrence arrives in time to sit down with us to a breakfast neither Katherine nor I are able to enjoy. He's wearing a yellow short-sleeved shirt, pressed blue jeans, and brown cowboy boots, and his hair sticks up in a couple of places as if he slept on it wrong. His face looks fresh and moist, and recently shaved. Katherine appears glad to load up his plate, and he appears grateful to be fed by her.

"So he got away," Jack comments to me.

"Yes," I say, fiddling with my coffee cup.

"They shouldn't have let that happen."

"I couldn't agree more, Jack."

"How did it happen?" Katherine wants to know. I thought I'd emptied my memories of everything about her son last night, but there was still the murder to discuss, and now this.

Jack said, "I heard that he played unconscious, and the medical attendants let their guard down, that's when he made a run for it."

"More or less." I glance at Katherine, and then decide it is condescending to think of protecting this woman who has already survived so much trouble. "He went for a deputy's gun, and wounded the deputy, and his own lawyer, and a couple of paramedics."

202

"Johnny was a bright little boy," Jack observes, "wasn't he, Katherine?"

"Yes," she says, softly.

Somehow, I'm not surprised to hear this. There were moments of sharpness to Ray, even intelligence and canniness, mixed in with the strange fugue states he got in sometimes when he seemed almost retarded. We sit silently for a moment while Jack eats, and they seem to be lost in thought about the child and the man.

"Are those people okay?" she asks me.

"Ray hurt them pretty bad, but they're recovering."

"I'm sorry," she whispers.

"Where do you think he's gone, Marie?" Jack asks.

"I don't know, because I don't really know anything about him, except that the last place he worked was the Checker Crab Company." After a moment, I say, "I don't have a real clear story in my mind about Johnnie's father. Would you mind telling me a little more about him?"

"Fred?" she says, looking surprised. "I don't think much about Fred anymore, it's been so long ago. What can I tell you? He was a decent husband and father, I guess, until Johnnie disappeared, then Fred just kind of went to pieces. He started drinking, and wasn't any use to anybody."

"I couldn't stand the man."

She stares over at Jack. "You couldn't?"

"No, I thought he was spineless, and he didn't offer any kind of support to you, when you were suffering so much."

Katherine looks touched, and reaches over to pat his hand.

"I never knew you felt that way about Fred, Jack."

He nods. "I'm afraid I carry grudges, especially against him."

"And you don't have any idea where he went?" I ask them.

"I never heard from him again," she says.

"I didn't look real hard," Jack says.

Katherine looks at him as if she's seeing him for the first time, and then she laughs a little. "You didn't?"

"I thought it was good riddance, Katherine."

203

She shakes her head at me, and smiles, and I'm happy that she is not offended by this admission of his. "The things I don't know."

But the phrase "good riddance" is exactly what Jaime Suarez said when the paramedics loaded Ray onto the courtroom elevator. It's an unpleasant connection between a father and a son, and this one I decide not to share with her. I want to give her something—anything—good to know about Ray, instead, and so I remember my note to myself.

"Did I tell you he plays the guitar well?"

Her face melts. "He does? How do you know that, Marie?"

"He played for me when I interviewed him."

"Really? He plays well?"

"Yes, and more than just your basic rock and roll chords, too. Somebody has taught him chord progressions, and—"

I cut off my own words, because she's staring into space as if at a dawning awareness of something hideous.

"Katherine?" Jack asks. "You look like you saw a ghost."

I leaned toward her. "What? What did I say, Katherine?"

"Who taught him?"

"To play the guitar? I don't know. The guy he worked for was a part-time musician, and we thought maybe he taught Ray."

"What's his name?"

"Ray's employer? Uh, Miller. Donor Miller."

Katherine utters a strangled scream, and Jack and I both leap to our feet, scared at the sound of it. He gets to her first, and bends over her, saying urgently, "What is it, Katherine?"

"Mr. Miller!" she says, looking stunned, and frightened. "Cal's music teacher. That was his name. A funny name. Donor Miller."

Jack looks as if he could have a heart attack.

"Donor Miller?" I am practically shouting it.

"I never heard of the man!" Jack exclaims.

Katherine is shaking her head, and soon her whole body is shaking. She grabs onto Jack's two hands to steady herself, and stares up at him. "You wouldn't have. We wouldn't have mentioned him. He was supposed to have moved away before Johnny disappeared. He quit giving lessons. They said he moved to"—she looks up at me with even greater horror—"Florida."

"Oh, my god," is all I can say.

"We didn't investigate him," Jack tells me, looking ill.

He kneels beside her while she still clings to him.

"Mr. Miller," Katherine says, in a deadened voice. "Cal quit taking lessons, after Mr. Miller left. We tried to get him to take more, from a different teacher, but he threw a fit, and just refused. It was really hard to get him to practice, and to go to lessons—"

Again, that look of dawning, awful comprehension.

She breaks off, and gets up stiffly and walks to the telephone, looking suddenly like an elderly woman. We hear her punch in a number, then hear her say in a shaky, loving voice, "Cal, honey? Could you come over this morning, please? I know, honey, you have to go to work, but can you call in late? You know I wouldn't ask this if it weren't terribly important. I really have to ask you something."

She comes back to the table.

"Katherine—" Jack begins.

She holds up her hands, as if warding off evil. "Please, I don't want to talk now. We'll wait for Cal to get here."

In worried silence, Jack and I sit with her.

When her elder son arrives, and sees us waiting for him, he looks immediately wary, and sinks slowly down into the fourth chair at the kitchen table. He's wearing a fresh white shirt, but the trousers look like yesterday's. Katherine has told me he does something arcane in data processing that he has tried to explain to her but which she doesn't understand. Now she takes both of his hands in both of hers so that he cannot run away, and she says gently, and in a tremulous voice that brings tears to my own eyes, "Cal, dearest, do you remember anything about your old music teacher?"

"No," he says, so quickly that we know it's a lie.

"Please, Cal." His mother is begging. "Please, tell me."

"No! I don't have anything to say. I don't even remember him."

205

"You were twelve years old, Cal. You hated those music lessons. Why, Cal?" She is persistent, stubborn, but her face is suffused in love and pity. "Why did you hate them so much?"

"Oh, Mom!" He looks trapped, furious. "Don't ask me."

"Cal, listen to me. The man your brother was working for down in Florida when he killed that child? That man's name is Donor Miller."

Her son flinches, begins to breathe hard, but still he fights it. "So? What's that supposed to mean, Mom? That name doesn't mean anything to me. I never heard it before."

"Yes, you have, Cal. I know you remember Mr. Miller."

He shoots me a hostile look, and I immediately stand up, and say, "You need some privacy. I'll go outside." Before Katherine can object, I hurry out the kitchen door. In a few moments, I am joined by Jack, who says, "Cal doesn't want me there."

He sounds hurt, and I pat his arm, to comfort him.

"What do you think that's all about?" he asks me.

I am astonished that he has to ask, but maybe sometimes even retired deputy sheriffs don't want to know. In a few words, I tell him what I think that Cal is telling his mother.

It finally came out, angrily and tearfully from a grown man with painful and guilty memories: How Mr. Miller shut the door to the little music room in the basement of the instrument store, and how he sexually abused the little boys while their mothers waited on chairs outside in the hallway.

"I didn't know what to do, Mom," Cal told her while she wept for him. He sounded more like a child, telling it, than the grown man he is. "Mr. Miller told me he would hurt my little brother if I told anybody." His mouth trembled, but he controlled that, setting it again in an angry line. "I was glad when they said he had moved out of town and couldn't give lessons anymore. I knew we were all safe then."

At that moment, the truth finally hit Cal Kepler.

His mother saw it in his face, but she also saw that he would not break, not even now. "It's not my fault!" he cried out. "I didn't tell! It's not my fault!"

His mother tried to comfort him, saying, "Oh, my child, of course, it isn't—"

But he flung himself away from her, and fled the house, brushing past Jack and me in the yard as if we were shrubbery. Jack called out Cal's name, but got no response. Cal got in his car, and drove away too fast for safety. I said a quick prayer for his well-being, and I thought: *This is a healing that's going to take long, hard work.*

Katherine told us the rest of the story:

Once a week, she drove Cal to his guitar lessons, and she took his younger brother with her. Cal often came out of the little room in tears, but the music teacher, Mr. Miller, was reassuring. Cal was doing well; kids often found lessons frustrating; she shouldn't be worried by a few tears, "*should she, Cal, because you really love your guitar lessons, don't you, Cal?*" Mr. Miller was kind of a grubby man, Katherine thought, but he was always so nice to the boys, and especially to Cal's little brother, always pausing to say "*what a cute kid. Cal, you're lucky to have such a nice little brother, aren't you?*"

"Where is he?" she demands of me. "Can he be arrested now?"

I have to tell her that Donor Miller is also missing.

She throws her hands up in the air, as if the world is a hopeless place, and gets up and leaves the table. In a moment, we hear the door to the bathroom close.

The old deputy looks stricken to his soul, and a decade older.

"We should have found her boy," he says miserably, taking the blame. "Maybe we weren't good enough. I wasn't good enough. Well, I guess that's pretty clear. I failed Katherine."

"How could you know about a name they didn't give you, Jack?"

"We should have known."

"Jack, how could you? We didn't have the awareness then that we do now. And law enforcement agencies didn't have the tools. You didn't have DNA. There wasn't any FBI profiling. I'll bet you didn't have fiber analysis or lie detectors. There weren't any networks set up to find missing people, or perpetrators."

"We had plain old-fashioned police work."

"It wouldn't be enough now, much less then."

"We didn't have much to go on," he tells me, not as if he's making excuses, more as if he's reminding himself. "No witnesses. No motives. No evidence. And none of those things you just said. We were so desperate that we even thought maybe Nathan Leopold did it." He looks at me. "Remember him?"

"Loeb and Leopold?"

"Yep."

I recall that they were wealthy, brilliant Chicago teenagers who kidnapped and murdered a boy just for the experience of killing someone, and to see if they could get away with it.

"Richard Loeb got killed in prison," Jack tells me, "but Leopold was released a few months before Johnnie disappeared. There was this rumor that Leopold took him. I half-believed it myself, until he showed up working at a hospital in Puerto Rico. Lived there all the rest of his life, and didn't get into any more trouble. But that just goes to show how desperate we got."

"I know you did everything you could do."

"You know, I heard a private investigator one time say he could find anybody. What's more, all he had to do was search the Internet. Well, I'm here to tell you it's not that easy to find somebody—like a child—who gets taken. Some people are just never going to get found. And their bodies aren't going to get found, either."

"I know."

He cocks his head, and appraises me. "You do, don't you? I suppose the research you do—?"

I start to agree, to let it go at that. But this man's deepest feelings are being revealed to me. It might be a kindness to balance the emotional scales a bit. "My parents disappeared, Jack, a long time ago. Ten years before Johnnie did. I wasn't quite a year old. So I know quite a bit about how some people never turn up again."

208

"I'll be damned," he says, looking amazed. "What happened?"

I really don't want to tell him, but then I never do want to talk about it. Getting any words out of me about my parents is like forcing bricks through cement, except when I am actively searching for them. Then I'll ask questions all over the world about them, as if they were just another couple of people in one of my true crime books. At those times I can be quite the objective, efficient researcher. It's different if I have to talk about them as their daughter. "I don't know what happened." That's the easy answer, and true as far as it goes. "One day they were there, and the three of us were living at home together, and the next day they weren't, and I was found in a crib in a motel room at the edge of town."

"Where was this?"

It seems that I'm distracting him, and he's letting me do it. This has an air of unreality to it, but I don't fight it.

"Birmingham, Alabama."

"Ten years before Johnnie, did you say?"

"Sixty-six."

"Were they civil rights workers?"

That's quick of him, but of course almost everybody associates the name Birmingham with the phrase civil rights.

"They were—associated with what was happening down there." I feel myself getting anxious. I really, really don't want this conversation to continue. "Anyway, they never turned up, and I keep looking. Like you kept looking for Johnnie. Maybe they're like him, and they're living under another identity somewhere, and they've forgotten I exist. Or, maybe they're dead at the bottom of an ocean. I'll probably never know."

"Johnnie finally turned up."

"Yes," I agree, a little wryly, "he did."

"Against all odds."

"And sometimes lightning does strike twice."

"Could I have heard about your parents? Was it in the news?"

"Yes."

"I don't remember it."

"Lightfoot isn't my real name, it's a pseudonym for my books."

"Oh. What were your parents' names?"

Like a deer in the headlights, I stare at him. "Folletino. Daniel and Angela Folletino."

"Doesn't ring a bell, I'm sorry."

I'm not sorry, I'm relieved. All the years of my life, I have never reconciled my desire to find them with my fear of finding out *about* them. They were a controversial, even notorious couple where they came from, and I know a few people who still get riled up at the mention of those names.

Jack says, sheepishly, "I guess I was hoping I could produce a miracle for you, on the spot. If I couldn't find Johnnie for Katherine, maybe I could tell you that I recognized your parents' names from some old case I worked on a long time ago."

I'm touched. "You're a nice man, Jack Lawrence." I reach over to grasp one of his hands. "I'm honored to have made your acquaintance."

"Don't see why," he mutters, with his head down.

Katherine comes back into the kitchen, and sinks back down into her chair. She looks as if she has been crying and then washed her face, and she looks defeated. "We have to help Cal," she says in a whispery voice that doesn't even sound like her. This latest revelation seems to have punctured her in a place that allowed her resilience and her courage to leak out. Her words are brave, but the tone in which she says them speaks more of depression than of courage. "We have to do everything we can to help him now."

Not knowing what else to do, I start picking up dirty dishes and taking them to the sink. I turn on the water and start rinsing them and placing them in the dishwater, glad for something to do with my hands at a moment when I might otherwise only wring them helplessly.

It isn't long before Jack inquires of me, "Hadn't we better get you to the airport?"

210

It's true that I do have reservations out in a couple of hours.

Before I go, I urge Katherine, "Come to Florida, and stay with me. There will be tremendous media interest in your story, and maybe Ray will see it. If he knows he has a family, and you're looking for him, maybe he'll turn himself in, Katherine. It's worth a try, don't you think?"

I think this is a good idea, and I'm guessing she will, too.

At first, she looks caught in despair, and taken aback. "I don't know, Marie."

"What if it lured Johnnie into coming in?"

Her eyes light up as if I've given her hope again. "Oh! Yes, I would do that, yes!"

I tell her I'll start working on it the minute I get back home, and she promises to arrange to go to Florida as soon as possible. "Maybe Kim can come with me."

"My guest room has twin beds."

She grabs my hands. "Thank you, Marie."

But as Jack drives me away from the house in his truck, and I twist around to wave at Katherine standing on her front porch, I can't escape the feeling that I've flown through like a tornado, leaving these nice people to pick up the jagged pieces of devastation I've left behind. I didn't mean to do it, and it surely had to happen. But for somebody who claims she doesn't want to do any harm, I seem to be leaving a lot of pain in my path. If Katherine ever gets to see her youngest son again, that will bring more pain, too. The memory of Johnnie Kepler is one thing, but the living reality of Ray Raintree—that's another thing entirely.

Forty-five minutes later, I suggest to Jack that he drop me off at the curb, but he won't hear of it. Again, he lifts my overnight bag for me. On the way in through the automatic doors, he says, "You tell those Florida cops, they can have any information they need from me, and I'm going to go back and see if I can find out more about this Miller fellow."

"I will, Jack."

I thank him, and then stand on my tiptoes to give him an impulsive hug and a kiss on his cheek.

"Nobody could have found him, Jack."

"Maybe not, but it's still going to haunt me to my grave."

I believe it, and I know there isn't anything but the grace of god that will ever ease his heart, or Katherine Kepler's.

After Jack leaves me, I locate a pay phone and call the Bahia Beach Police Department, where I'm lucky enough to catch Robyn Anschutz at her desk. I tell her everything I have learned, but when I finish, she says, "Yeah, but it doesn't help us find Ray."

That's right, I think. He's still Raymond Raintree to everybody down there. He has become Johnnie Kepler to me, at least for a little while, although as I get away from his family, it's harder to hang on to that earlier identity of his. My knowledge of Ray comes pouring back, polluting the memory of the little boy he was.

"I hate it when I end up feeling sorry for perps," Robyn says. "There's that moment in their lives, you know the one I mean? Where they go from being victims to being perpetrators of their own crimes. That's a very confusing moment for me. On one side of that moment, I feel sorry for them. On the other side of it, I step in and arrest them."

"It's like the moment just before an abused child hurts an animal."

"What do you mean?"

"One minute he's an innocent, the next minute he's a monster."

"Yeah. That's the line."

"All of our pity's on one side of it and all of our hate's on the other side of it."

"Once they cross that line, it's all over for them."

"No more pity."

"Yeah, we just have to catch them and put them out of commission. At least, that's what I think we have to do, but it bothers

212

me sometimes. If anything about my job keeps me awake, that does."

"Maybe it should keep us all awake."

"Maybe so."

"It's the moment I try to define in my books."

"Is that right?"

"It's also the moment when somebody turns into a victim. One minute they're alive and safe, the next minute they're not."

"Yeah! It's the same moment, isn't it?"

"Yes, it's very mysterious."

"Well," she says, awkwardly.

"Are you going to look for Donor Miller, Robyn?"

"Yeah, I guess we'd better do that."

After some reflection on the protocol of the thing, I put in a call to the state attorney's office, too.

"Where are you?" he wants to know, and the mere sound of his voice sends a tingling through me. "I hear roaring."

"I'm about thirty thousand feet above Missouri."

I have plucked a telephone from the back of the middle front seat. I am in the window seat, and now I turn my face, my body, and the telephone toward the sky, creating a little private, intimate space in which to converse with Franklin.

"You're calling me from the plane?" He sounds tickled to hear it. "Is this an emergency, or a compliment?"

When I tell him what I've been doing, Franklin's viewpoint turns out to be very different from the cop's. "I don't give a damn if Ray was sold into white slavery as a baby. He killed somebody else's baby, and that's all I need to know."

It sounds like a quote from his closing argument to the jury.

"You'll still seek the death penalty then?"

"You bet, I will."

There appears to be no question in his prosecutorial mind, but there sure is in my own mind now. Of course, he hasn't met Katherine.

"If you're calling from a plane, you must be coming home?"

"Getting closer every second."

"I miss you. Your place, or mine tonight?"

I hesitate, start to say "yours," but then say, "I wish I could, Franklin, but I just can't tonight."

"What's the matter?"

"It's been an exhausting trip."

He's understanding and says we'll get together tomorrow, instead.

I'm not so sure. It jars me, after being with Ray's mother, to think of sleeping with a man who wants to put her son to death. Wouldn't life in prison be enough to punish a human being whose life has already been one long punishment? I think of the McCullens, and feel nothing but sympathy, and yet . . .

By the time the plane dips a wing over Bahia Beach, I am admitting to myself that Franklin and I seem to have developed a conflict of interest, after all. I spot Bahia Bridge far below, and from that I can follow the line of sparkling water to my six towering cypress trees. And there it is, a dot of apricot: home again, home again. I feel a twinge of sudden loneliness at the sight of it, where usually I would feel only relief and happiness.

Among the messages I find at home are five to which I pay particular attention, starting with one from Franklin: "Hey, cutie. Thanks for calling me, but that wasn't enough. I'll be at the office until late tonight, so call me if you change your mind, okay? Don't you think a tired woman deserves a back rub?"

It's tempting enough to make me smile at the phone.

But I erase it anyway, and go on to the next one:

"Marie? This is Kim Kepler? Mom and I have got airline reservations to come to Florida tomorrow, is that okay? She says you said we could stay with you, but we don't want to impose. We could sure stay in a motel. Could you call me back, please?"

I stop the other messages, to take care of this one.

"Does your mom want publicity?" I ask Kim.

214

"We want anything that might bring Johnnie home."

"It's likely to be a madhouse," I warn her.

"It already is," she tells me. "Mom got calls from your police down there today. They were very nice, she said, although they asked a lot of questions. And we also got some calls from some newspapers and TV stations, but Mom just wasn't up to talking to them yet."

"Will she be by tomorrow?"

I don't want to push her, and yet I know that I should.

"She'll do what she has to do," Kim says, simply.

By the time I get off the phone with Kimmie, it is arranged that I will pick them up at the airport tomorrow, and they will stay with me. I promise to help them navigate the shoals of publicity. When we get off the phone, I don't even feel hypocritical: It isn't only that I'm a greedy writer who wants them around to hear what they say, but also that motels and hotels are expensive in Bahia. My home is the cheapest place they can stay, and I'll be a driver for them, too.

I call the detectives and the prosecutor, to tell them the Kepler women are coming to Florida. Everybody wants to meet them.

"Bring them to my office," Franklin urges me, and then pauses as if he's waiting for me to invite him over, after all. When I don't, we exchange awkward good-byes.

And then I return to my messages.

"Hi, Marie," says a sweet voice I recognize as my editor calling from New York City. Immediately, guilt sets in. "How are you? How's the book? This is not pressure. Do not interpret this call as pressuring you in any way, okay? I'm just so excited to see it, that's all. Haven't heard from you since before the trial, and the art direc- tor just showed me your new cover proofs, so I want you to know I think the revised cover looks great. I'll overnight a copy to you, so you can see what you think of it. Let me know tomorrow, okay? Presales are fabulous, by the way. All we need now is the book, but don't think I'm putting any pressure on you, at all. I know we don't have anything to worry about in that regard. Sorry

I missed you! Can't wait to hear how things are going. Let me know about the cover!"

I love my editor, but that was exceedingly clever of her.

Now I have to call her back tomorrow with my opinion of the cover, and what am I going to tell her? "I've got the beginning and the end, but no middle. Now I know about the first six years of Ray's life, and the last couple, so I'm only missing about nineteen in between. And I still don't know why he killed her, or where he did it, and how can we publish a book about him when we don't know if he's going to live or die, and oh, by the way, Natalie's parents want out of the book."

I feel as if my career is careening out of my control.

If the cops could find Donor Miller . . . if they could catch Ray . . .

Going back to my messages, I get one that makes my scalp tingle:

"I'm looking for a woman named Marie Folletino. I knew her parents, and I really need to talk to her. I'll call back."

"When?" I demand of the anonymous female voice. "When will you call me back?"

No name, no number, just that ambiguous message.

And caller ID doesn't provide any clues, either. It says OUT OF AREA, with no phone number. I just love modern communications devices—they give me so many new ways to feel *frustrated!* At this moment, I want to scream, and stamp my feet like a kid in a tantrum. Between my book, and this . . .

She "knew" my parents, so I can't take that to mean they're still alive and she knows them now. Well, a lot of people "knew" my parents, and that hasn't helped me find out where they went after they abandoned me. But there's an urgency to this woman's voice that gives me a nervous feeling. I hate this, this waiting to find out. Why couldn't she just give her name and number like a normal person, so I could call her back?

You know why, a little voice whispers to me.

But I don't, exactly. I know that all my life people have acted

216

loath to discuss my mother and father in any detail. A lot of what they won't say, I have picked up from old newspaper articles. But there's so much that remains unsaid and untold about them, and most of what I've heard or read conflicts with other things I read or hear. They were this. No, they were that. They went there, no they were never there. They said this. No way, they never said that. And everybody always speaks with such authority. Like they know. Nobody knows, is what I suspect. Nobody still living knows the truth about them, and I'll never find out either.

But now this damned phone call from this woman.

It's weird, it's as if by bringing their names to the surface in my conversation with Jack Lawrence, I have stirred up something new.

Well, there's nothing I can do about it unless she calls back.

But how am I going to concentrate on anything else until she does?

The fifth important message focuses my attention beautifully:

"Hey, Marie! It's Robyn. Listen, when we put our minds to something, it happens. Guess who we found already? Donor Miller! You might say he's been waiting for us. Give me a call, I'll tell you all about it."

The Little Mermaid

By Marie Lightfoot

~

CHAPTER NINE

*D*eep *in the Everglades, the earth belched up a secret: the body* of a human being. The remains surfaced, literally, in a particularly isolated section of the Everglades, fifty-six miles to the southwest of Bahia Beach. The unlucky fishermen who made the discovery reported seeing part of a human torso snagged in the dried saw grass, reeds, and mud at the edge of a 'gator hole.

Under natural conditions, the water level in the Everglades is not constant; it periodically rises and falls. In the wet seasons, all manner of creatures thrive in it: otters, turtles, 'gators, snakes, and a cornucopia of fish and bird life. But when the water dries up, sometimes the only fauna that survive are the ones that get trapped in alligator nesting holes. That supplies a feast for the alligator, but it also insures there will be some animals left to repopulate the swamps when the waters rise again. Biologists recognize it as an evolutionary safeguard.

Fishermen recognize it as easy pickin's.

That evening, two good ol' boys were out in their tinpot rowboat in water so shallow they were practically walking their boat across the swamp on its oars. They were looking for exactly what they found: a high round hummock surrounded by water, with alligator tracks leading to and from it.

It was hard damned work.

If either of them could have afforded an airboat, they would have scuttled that old rowboat in an instant and skimmed across the shallow water, "like a swamp chicken with a fan up its ass," as one of them said later. But even together, they hardly had two fishhooks to rub together, much less enough money to purchase any flying power. They were hunting the hard way, rowing when they could, pushing and pulling when they had to, with rifles at their feet and their eyes on the skies as well as the 'glades.

They were also on the lookout for the owner of the nest.

Although alligators have a popular image as man-eaters, the truth is they are a species that doesn't have much of a taste for people. This is not a theory any fisherman wants to test on himself. Alligators can crush their own teeth with the force of their powerful jaws, and their respiratory system allows them to hold a struggling victim under water until the battle is over.

The two fishermen moved warily closer to the hummock.

If the 'gator was absent, and they could get near enough with their nets and their spears, they might snatch themselves a jubilee of good eating, and plenty more to sell. It wasn't legal, taking that much for themselves, but the 'glades are a huge area, and the wildlife officers can't patrol everywhere at once.

From a distance, they spied something large and bloated, appearing to be beached on the slope of the nest. If it was a large fish, they wouldn't want it in that condition. As they floated closer, the fishy, decaying stench from the nest grew overwhelming in the swampy heat, even though the men wore bandanas over their noses.

It was the huge dead fish, they decided, that was raising the stink.

And then, getting closer, they saw it was no fish.

"Goddammit," exclaimed one of the men, "it's a dead man."

"What are we gonna do now?" asked the other one.

Furious at the "Joe" who'd ruined their catch by dying there, the two friends struggled to turn their boat around. They gave it all up for a bad trip, and rowed back on home. They debated whether or not to report what they'd seen to the cops, and finally decided to do it, because they could both use some brownie points with the local law.

They weren't sure, and neither were the police they reported it to, that the remains would still be there when the cops went out in their motorboats, airboat, and helicopter to look for it.

But amazingly, it was still there.

Perhaps the neighborhood 'gator had turned up its snout at it, and the other local predators had already eaten that morning. The two good citizens subsequently declined to give their names when interviewed about their unfortunate discovery.

Fairly early on in the autopsy, it was determined that the remains were that of a Caucasian male, overweight, probably late middle-aged. But even with so substantial a portion of the corpse to work on, it would be a while before that county's medical examiner could make a positive identification of the victim, still longer before he would determine whether this death had been a natural one, an accident, suicide, or homicide, and a bit longer than that before any connection was made between the Everglades victim and a missing marina owner in Bahia Beach.

220

When they finally did make that connection, it would be a wallet and scorpion necklace that did it for them. The two fishermen plucked those treasures in their net, but failed to turn them over to the authorities at first. When the wallet, with Donor Miller's driver's license and credit cards, was handed to the police, strangely, it had no money in it.

One of the fishermen buddies had a helpful suggestion for what might have happened to any cash: "Musta dissolved," he said.

10
Raymond

"I have to tell you some news," I say almost the minute Katherine and her daughter step off the airplane and we quickly embrace. I feel such a desire to protect these women, and yet I blunder right off the bat. When I draw them over to a secluded corner of the terminal, I see to my dismay that Katherine thinks I'm going to tell her something else.

"They found Johnnie?" she asks, with a hand to her mouth.

"No, no, I'm sorry, they found Donor." I feel terrible about getting her hopes —or her dread—up. Now I pause, to look at her and try to evaluate her state of mind. "Katherine, he's dead. They found his body in the Everglades, and they say he's been dead for several weeks already. They don't know yet how he died, but it may have been something like a boating accident."

"He's dead?" Katherine's blue eyes have widened, and I see that it's difficult for her to take in this news. She shakes her head, as if to clear it. "He can't be dead, Marie. He has to be arrested and tried for what he did to us, he has to be punished and put in prison. I thought he could be executed. I thought—"

Kim and I exchange looks, and an unspoken agreement to get her mother out of here.

"I'll get my car," I tell them.

"And I'll stay with Mom and get the luggage."

I tell Kim what kind of car to look for, and within twenty minutes we're driving away from the airport together.

"I'm so angry about this!" Katherine tells us.

That's not hard for me to imagine.

"At least he's gone, Mom," Kim says, trying to give solace. "He can't hurt us anymore. He can't hurt Johnnie, or Cal. He can't hurt any other children. This is a good thing, Mom."

But she will not be distracted from a rage that is visibly building inside her, a rage that only yesterday found its focus in Donor Miller, and now can't even be spent in the normal way.

"I wanted to sit at his trial in a courtroom," she says, fiercely. "I wanted to testify against him. I wanted to hear a jury pronounce him guilty, and I wanted to hear a judge sentence him, and I wanted all of us to get a chance to get up and tell the world what a horrible person he is! I feel so cheated! It isn't fair."

She makes me think of Natty's parents.

I called Susan and Tony McCullen this morning, to warn them what was coming: Ray's mom and sister on television, pleading for his surrender and his life. They seemed stunned by the story, not quite able to take in all at once what I was telling them. From their responses, I couldn't really judge how they felt about it.

I could tell Katherine what I've learned from the families of other victims: That the "satisfactions" of a trial and punishment don't last long, and that they don't dispel the fury and sorrow. I don't say that, however, because it would be presumptuous.

I just drive, and listen, and try to answer her questions.

"I don't understand, Marie," she says, "how the police down here can find the dead body of my son's abductor, but they can't find my son. It's almost two weeks since Johnnie got away! Why can't they find him?"

"Escapees often remain at large for a long time, Katherine, especially in states where there are vast, wild areas, like here in Florida. He could be in the Everglades. He could have gone down

223

into the caverns of central Florida. He could be hiding in someplace like Ocala National Park." I don't tell her that Ocala is a huge forest where black bears and panthers still roam to this day. "There was an escapee in your area who stayed loose for three months in the Ozarks, and there's a man who's been hiding in mine shafts in North Carolina for years."

This is true. Until he was shot and killed, the Missouri fugitive survived by breaking into empty cabins and stealing supplies. The North Carolina fugitive, wanted for bombing abortion clinics, eluded two hundred state and federal agents for three years, and he's still on the loose.

"Ray could stay out for a long time," I warn the women.

"Well, maybe he's safer that way," Katherine says, and then an anguished expression crosses her face, as if she has only that moment recalled the reason he is fleeing. "Oh, but I think of that little girl, and of her parents, and I feel so guilty. I know what they're going through. If only we could have gotten Johnnie back, then their daughter wouldn't have died. This is a terrible thing."

I have nothing but agreement for that.

"It's beautiful here," Kim says, from the backseat, and I sense that she's trying to do what she has tried to do for twenty-two years: make her mother feel better. Her voice sounds brittle, as if she's forcing herself to be cheerful as she says, "Are we very far from the ocean? Is there any chance we could drive by the beach?"

Over a seafood lunch, in a booth by a window overlooking a beach and the Atlantic Ocean, I try to calm them down a little. They both look charming, Kim in a cotton suit that suits her large frame perfectly, and Katherine in a belted, shirtwaist dress. Kim's in red, Katherine's in black, which is probably hot on her. But whether they know it or not, they've dressed perfectly for being interviewed on television.

"Here's what we've done so far," I tell them, talking slowly so they can take it all in. We have sweating glasses of ice water in front of us, and a platter of stone crabs they haven't touched. I have a lot of information to dump on them all at once.

"I've talked to Detectives Anschutz and Flank—" I examine their faces to see if they recognize those names, and they do. "They told me they have talked to you, to bring you up-to-date on their investigation and their search. Is that true?"

Both women nod at me, looking pale and wide-eyed.

"That's great, and did they tell you what their public information officer has done? He called the major local newspaper, which is the *Bahia Sun,* and every television station, including cable, and told them about your story. They're all extremely eager and willing to put you on the air. He went ahead and set up some taping and live news times, and he hopes that's all right with you?"

Looking bewildered, they nod their heads.

The detectives and the public information officer have turned this job over to me, because I'm the first one to see Katherine and Kim today. I don't actually need that excuse for getting involved, however, because this all counts as research for my book. Plus, I can't bear the thought of releasing these innocents into the wilds of south Florida without a native to guide them. Since this was all my idea, the least I can do is to drive them around to their appointments.

"You didn't arrive in time for any of the noon news shows, but he's got you live on one of the six o'clock shows, and you'll be taped for the other ones."

Ordinarily, the public information officer of the Bahia Police Department would never get involved in this, but since the police are hoping these women can lure Ray back into custody, he wanted to help. This is a lot to ask of these rather shy women, but it's one of the reasons they came, and by now I think so highly of them, I'm pretty sure they can pull it off.

"A couple of the stations wanted to interview you someplace else, and I thought you might be more comfortable doing that at my house, so they'll come over in time for the late news tonight. It might seem as if a single press conference would be more efficient, but there's a reason for this madness."

They look eager to grasp any hope I give them.

"This way, every interview will be unique. If you were to be seen on every station saying the same thing over and over people might get bored, and switch channels."

"Bored," Kim says, as if that's unbelievable.

"Marie's right," her mother says. "I should try to say a little something different each time, don't you think? And can Kim do some of these interviews, too?"

Her daughter looks immediately terrified.

I assure Kim, "It's easy, I swear, and it'll be over so fast you won't even know you've been on camera. They'll be very kind to you, I promise, and they'll help you get through it. Yes, you can both do them, I think that's fine, although it will probably have the most impact when you do, Katherine. As for what you ought to say—"

I study the attractive, tense women across the table from me.

"Say what happened to him. Say it will break your heart if you don't ever get to see him alive again. Plead with people to capture him, but not to hurt him. And plead with Ray to turn himself in. Just tell the truth."

"How long before our first interview?" Kim asks, nervously.

"They start at five o'clock," I tell her. "Four hours."

"Oh, gosh," she says.

Her mother grasps her wrist. "We can do it for your brother."

"I can," Kim says, squeezing her eyes shut. "I can, I can, I can."

I decide it is better not to mention this will be good experience for the *Today* show, *Good Morning America,* and the *CBS Morning News,* in case they come calling, too.

"The state's attorney wants to meet you," I tell them next, as our entrées arrive. They have ordered fried shrimp, which I doubt they will eat, either. I can carry it all home in case they get hungry for it later. I give them another choice: "Do you want to meet him?"

"Why?" Kim asks, and I see that she understands I am talking about the man who got her brother convicted. "Why does he want to meet us?"

226

"I don't know," I say, honestly.

He wouldn't tell me when he requested it, after I told him they were coming to visit me.

"Do you want to, Mom?" she asks Katherine.

"If it will help," her mother says.

How can it? I wonder.

The interview with Franklin in his office goes surprisingly well.

He drops everything when I arrive with them unannounced. He is at his compassionate, considerate best, and they are completely charmed by this man who wants to kill their son and brother. Watching them all together, I am not convinced the women quite understand the direct connection between the prosecutor and the electric chair.

"If you can get him to come in, we'll let you see him."

That's Franklin's pronouncement, on the spot.

"What do you mean?" Kim asks him, speaking for both of them.

The women and I are seated in chairs in front of Franklin's big wooden desk, and he is leaning on it directly in front of us. There's a piece of white lint on the left arm of his black suit coat, and it's all I can do not to reach over and pluck it off.

He says, "I mean that we will make it possible for you to see him, under guard, as soon as possible. I'm sure this is extremely difficult for you, and I don't want to make it any harder than it has to be. I don't want to make you wait to go through normal channels before you can see him again."

It strikes me there is no real reason for this meeting.

He doesn't meet my eyes, and that, combined with the fact that he wouldn't tell me what he was up to, suggests a political motive to me. The state's attorney doesn't want to look like a bad guy in this story as it unfolds; he wants to be seen as tough on Ray, but sympathetic to his family. It's cynical, but if it enables Katherine to see her son any faster than might otherwise happen, I'm all for it.

When we leave, Katherine remarks, "What a lovely man."

"I don't know why he insisted on seeing us," I say.

"You don't?" There's a mischievous twinkle in her eyes, the first hint of real lightness I've seen since I met her. "I think I know why, and it wasn't for me, or Kim."

"It wasn't?"

She twinkles at me until I catch on, and blush.

"Me?" I am completely caught out by her. Busted.

"Of course, you, it was plain as day that he likes you."

"Me?" I say, completely caught out by her.

Kim sighs, good-naturedly. "I wish he liked me."

No you don't, I think as we hurry away. They're going to end up hating Franklin, and I only hope that I don't, too.

I have totally forgotten to pass on Leanne English's phone number to them, as I promised her I would do. To make up for that, I tell them who she is, and ask them if they want to meet her, too.

"I think we should, don't you?" Katherine asks me.

If we weren't on such grim errands, I'd feel a sense of power, because even Leanne English drops everything to meet with us.

The Kepler women seem to bring out the best in everybody, and even crisp little Leanne is gracious to them, especially considering the fact that it was Katherine's son who broke her jaw and dislocated her shoulder. Leanne is so nice, in fact, that I am just about to decide she must be on tranquilizing pain pills, when I find out the real reason for her finesse.

"Will you be taking over Ray's legal bills?" she inquires sweetly.

It isn't easy to understand her, and now and then she has to scribble notes to us. This message comes through loud and clear, however.

"His bills?" Kim asks. "Who's been paying them?"

I hold my breath, thinking, *please, please, please tell us.*

Leanne narrows her eyes, and I can practically see her debating whether to tell us. Please don't make me leave the room, I beg silently, like a small child in a roomful of adults who are about to discuss something forbidden. But luckily, avarice appears to overcome scruples, for she slides a manila folder in front of her, and opens it.

I see her pick up what appears to be a check.

"This has been the strangest thing," she says as we struggle to understand her through her wired jaw. "Ordinarily, I would never tell you this, but circumstances leave me no alternative." She gets up with the check in her hand, and comes around to our side of her desk, and props herself against it so that she is standing between Katherine and Kim in two chairs to her left, and me in a chair to her right. It's a mirror image of the scene in the prosecutor's office.

"I need to tell you a story . . ."

Lord, the woman knows how to build up suspense. I could use some of her talent. Did they teach her this in law school? I'm annoyed that she's stringing it out like this, making these poor women wait for her punchline, whatever it is.

"About three weeks after your son was arrested, Mrs. Kepler, I received a phone call from a man who asked me if I would represent Ray Raintree."

"Who was it?" Kim asks.

"I'll get to that," the attorney says. "At the time, I said that I did have an opening, and I could take the case. I asked him what his connection was to Ray Raintree, and if he wished to come in to talk to me about my representation. He didn't answer the first question, and his answer to my second question was to say that he didn't want to come in, but he would send me a retainer."

She waves the check in her hand.

"This is it. The reason I have it, is that it bounced. I didn't know it bounced until I had already started preparing my case, and when I called this man to complain, he wasn't there. In fact, I haven't been able to locate him since then."

"Leanne," I say, "why did you continue with the case?"

She levels me with a hard stare, as if defying me in some way.

"Let me tell you the rest of the story." She's going to tell it her way, with no interruption from us. "When this man called that single time, he set certain conditions on my representation of Ray Raintree. I was never to tell anyone who was paying. I was never to mention his name to Ray, or to anyone else. I was to avoid publicity, if I could, and if it wouldn't get in the way of my defense. I didn't think it would, because the more publicity Ray got, the more people hated him, and I certainly didn't have this kind of story to tell them then."

She gazes at Katherine for a moment.

"I asked the man why he didn't want me to get Ray any pretrial publicity, and he said that he didn't want Ray's mother to find out about her son."

Katherine gasps and looks as if she's been stabbed in the heart.

But Leanne holds up a hand, as if to halt that reaction.

"I don't think he meant to be cruel, Mrs. Kepler. What he said was, that it would break Ray's mother's heart if she ever found out that her son had killed a little girl. I gather he was wrong to withhold this information. But I think he meant well."

"How dare he!" Katherine exclaims, in a fury. "Who is this man?"

Leanne continues inexorably, as if Katherine hasn't asked.

"I was to bill him at the address on this check, as expenses mounted, and he would continue to pay me. He did not want to meet the man for whose defense he was paying, although he said he might ask me to take him to the prison sometime to get a look at Ray. I agreed to do that, if that's what he wanted. But I was never, under any circumstances, to reveal who was paying Ray's bills."

With a dramatic little flourish, she hands the check to Kim, who says, "Oh, my god!" and puts her hand to her heart, before passing it to her mother. Katherine's mouth drops open, and she looks as if she wants to say something, but can't get any words out.

She passes the check over to me.

I actually gasp when I see the signature, which must be gratifying to Leanne English.

It is very clearly signed, *Frederick Kepler.*

"I didn't know he was Ray's father," she tells us, "until Marie, here, called me to tell me about you people. Even then, I didn't know that was their relationship, only that this man had your surname. Now that you've told me your story, I realize who he is. The only thing is, I don't know where he is now."

"And the check bounced," I say. "Why *did* you continue, Leanne?"

She looks angrily at me, as if daring me to debate her reasons. "I continued because I'm a defense lawyer! That's who I am, that's what I do. I defend people that other people hate, and everybody hated Ray Raintree. Nobody wanted to stay with his case, he couldn't even keep the damned public defenders on his side. He needed a lawyer. I'd already done so much preparation, and I knew nobody could save him from a guilty verdict. I figured, it wouldn't take very long to try it . . ."

It's almost as if she's trying to make herself look bad by saying that, but the truth underlying her explanation is that hard-bitten little Leanne English is a woman of ideals and principles, and she was willing to work for Ray for free, if she had to, to provide a defense for an indefensible man.

Katherine stands up, goes to Leanne, and gently embraces her. While the attorney shrinks from the touch, and then stoically endures it, Katherine begins to cry, and to murmur, again and again, "Thank you." When she finally releases Leanne, the lawyer's face is as red as her hair, and she glares at me as if defying me ever to write this in my book.

Tough, Leanne.

You're just going to have to put up with looking like a hero.

Now I understand the antipathy the rest of her legal team expressed toward their client: He wasn't paying any bills! No wonder Manny Meade spoke of him dismissively, and Jaime Suarez was so open in his contempt. Law firms are money-making enterprises, after all. The whole firm must have fought Leanne on this one; if she weren't a full partner and a tough cookie, to boot, she'd surely have dropped the case to please them.

Then she does another courageous thing, by offering an opinion that none of us wants to hear.

"Look, I don't want to hurt your feelings, Mrs. Kepler, but I don't think Ray will come in just to meet you. He may not remember you. Even if he does, he's one strange young man, Mrs. Kepler. I'm sorry, but he is. And if he comes in at all, it means he's going to prison, and then we've got a damned hard fight to keep him out of the electric chair."

Katherine meets that courage, like a bet, and raises it.

"What should we do?" she asks, firmly.

"I don't know what to do about bringing him in. But if they get him alive, I'll try to get the prosecutor to give us a break," Leanne says. "He's got to take the circumstances of Ray's life into account, and agree not to press for a death penalty."

Franklin won't do it, I'm thinking, and even if he did, Ray won't allow himself to be locked up for life. He has already proved that he would rather die first. I recall his "survival instructions," which he probably got from his captor, Donor Miller: *Do whatever you have to do to keep from getting caught.* Ray has already wounded people, and probably killed someone, to stay free.

But Katherine and Kim look hopeful now.

"We'll pay your bills," Kim tells the lawyer. "All of them, won't we Mom?"

Her mother is nodding vigorously, while I am trying to catch Leanne's eye to get across the message: *They can't. This will ruin them financially, just as Katherine's other son has predicted it will. They're not rich people, they—*

"Forget that," Leanne says, harshly. "I'll find Fred."

I feel honored to shake her hand when we leave her office.

Next, with only a little more time to kill, we stop by the Bahia P.D.

Robyn Anschutz and Paul Flanck look completely nonplused to be meeting Ray Raintree's mother and sister. They say "ma'am," a lot to Katherine, and keep glancing at me, as if I have produced rabbits out of my magic hat.

"You're sure it's Mr. Miller who's dead?" Katherine wants to know.

"Pretty sure," they tell her, and go on to explain about the scorpion necklace and the wallet with the driver's license and credit cards. "The only thing left of the body is the torso, ma'am, so there's no fingerprints." They apologize for being gruesome, but they say that there wasn't a head, so they can't identify him that way.

"I remember that necklace," she tells them.

I feel a little shocked to hear her say it. It reaches so far back into a painful history for her. Can she really remember it, or is this just the power of suggestion at work?

"It's not something you're likely to forget," Robyn agrees, with a shudder. It reassures me that Katherine really might be able to recall a detail like that. "I couldn't imagine wearing that against my skin all the time."

"Where was the necklace?" I ask Paul.

"It came up with some other junk in a fisherman's net."

"Along with the wallet," Robyn adds.

"Look, Mrs. Kepler," Paul says, bluntly, "we all feel really bad for you, but we've still got a killer loose out there, even if he is your son. You see what I'm saying? I've got to tell you that Ray is dangerous, and we can't be taking any chances that he's going to harm you, or police, or innocent people. We can hope he comes in alive, on his own, but I'm not going to guarantee that I think that's the way it's going to happen. I think you need to be prepared for bad news, ma'am."

Katherine looks at him squarely. "I have prepared myself for bad news for twenty-two years, Detective."

On our way out, I say privately to Paul and Robyn, "Could you guys check up on the whereabouts of a man named Frederick James Kepler? He may be living around here someplace, but I don't know for sure. He's Katherine's ex-husband, and Ray's father."

The detectives promise to look into it.

*　　　*　　　*

233

And then begin the media interviews. They go like clockwork, one after the other, with me chauffeuring the mother and daughter from one to another until we take a dinner break about eight at night. By ten o'clock, they start again, and as I have predicted, the journalists are kind and helpful, and the Keplers are extraordinarily effective on the air. Both of them cry, when interviewed. Both of them look straight into cameras and plead for mercy for their Johnnie, and they plead for the man called Ray to surrender himself.

And the more they do, the more discouraged I feel.

This is not going to work, I am thinking but not saying to them.

Ray can't read, so the print interviews are pointless. And there's no reason to assume he is anywhere near a television set, or a radio. And even if he sees and hears these women, will he care? Will he even believe they are who they say they are?

By ten-thirty, it is finished.

The last television crew has left my house, and the Keplers and I are working our way through a bottle of wine out on my patio overlooking the bridge. The canal looks very beautiful tonight, and they are enchanted with my view of it. We are all exhausted, but they seem hyper, encouraged, optimistic, though I doubt that will last. I suspect it's just a reaction to the lights and cameras, the sense of action that breeds hope. I stay up with them for another hour, rehashing every interview, reviewing all the possibilities for what might happen next, and listening again to their memories of Johnnie.

It is spooky to think of him out there somewhere, and his mother and sister, in here with me. With the help of the wine, after a while they seem almost relaxed for the first time since I've met them. I get the impression neither of them drinks very much, so this may sedate them into a good night's sleep. God knows they can use it. The wine is having an opposite effect on me, however: I'm feeling increasingly, irrationally jumpy. I fight an urge to look over my shoulder, turn on all the lights in my house, take a flashlight, and check the shadows under my cypress trees.

*   *   *

Franklin calls, just as I am dropping off to sleep upstairs.

He knows I often work late into the night, and that I welcome his interruptions, especially when he's calling to say that he could come over, if I want him to. Tonight, he knows I have house-guests, so he only wants to talk.

"Nice people," he says.

"Um," I agree, and roll over to turn on the light again.

"So are the McCullens," he adds, pointedly.

"I couldn't agree more."

"But you don't want me to go for the death penalty."

"I don't know anymore, Franklin. All I know is that his mother's sleeping in my house, and for the past three days, all I've heard is tragedy. It kills me, to think of her watching him die."

"I thought you wanted him to die."

"Yeah, I thought I did, too. When I think about Natalie, I just want Ray wiped from the face of the earth. But now I've met his mom, and I've heard his story, and I'm confused."

"I'm not. I don't care if his mother was the Virgin Mary. He deserves to die, and if I get another chance, I'm going to make sure he fries."

"I think you may be wrong about this."

"No I'm not. You are." Suddenly, he laughs. "This is how lawyers have foreplay."

"Don't call me a lawyer," I retort, and then I have to laugh, too.

"So." His voice softens. "Tomorrow night?"

"I'll still have guests."

"Marie?" The softening has turned to suspicion. He has heard some quality in my voice that lets him know I am putting him off again. The man is accustomed to cross-examining expert wit-nesses, and I'm a cream puff by comparison. Getting to the truth is what he does for a living, every bit as much as what I do. "You wouldn't stop seeing me, just because we disagree about the death penalty?"

"Just?" I say, in quotes, avoiding his question. "Wouldn't that

235

be more honorable than breaking up with somebody because he . . . snores, for instance?"

"Are you saying I snore?"

"No, Franklin, I'm saying some differences are important."

"Snoring doesn't seem trivial if you're the one it's keeping awake."

I can't tell if he's trying to tease me out of my mood, or if he, too, is avoiding his own question. "All right! Snoring is important, we'll stipulate to that, all right?"

"It would make a hell of a lot more sense to stop seeing me because I snore, than because we disagree about some philosophy."

"Ray is not a philosophy, he's a person."

"Ray is a monster, not a person."

We sound like a couple of schoolyard kids trading taunts.

There's a silence, before I say, "Look, I understand that if anybody seems to deserve it, it's Ray. I get that. But I feel really uncomfortable about this, about flirting with you one minute, and sympathizing with Katherine the next."

"What are you saying?"

"Let me sort this out."

"You want me to stay away for a while?"

Dammit. "I guess I do, at least until this is over."

"One way or another."

"Yes," I say, feeling sad, "until it's over one way or another."

"All right, but this is entirely your choice."

His anger and hurt crackle through the phone lines.

"I know. I'm sorry. Good night, Franklin."

"'Good night, Marie."

I am left staring at my own phone, and thinking in dismay, How did that happen? And also, What have I done? Maybe the right thing, maybe not. Maybe I'm a woman of principle, and maybe I'm just an impulsive, pigheaded fool. One thing for sure, I have definitely proved it is not wise to date any of the principals in my books before they're published. I already knew that, but Franklin DeWeese could charm the freckles off a tomboy's face. If

Ray is recaptured, will Franklin charm a jury into sentencing him to die? If he does, I don't know if I can go on feeling the same about him as before. Maybe I can, but maybe not. I know he's put other people to death, but that seemed far removed from me. I could almost overlook it, as terrible as that sounds. But this hits close to home—as close as down my stairs, where Ray's mom is sleeping.

I'm too tired to trust my feelings, which are raw.

I lay back on my pillows and stare out my windows at the canal. My bed feels too big for me, alone, and this view is too beautiful to keep to myself. I miss him already, but I know there won't be any give in his position. Why should there be? He's the prosecutor, for heaven's sake, in a capital punishment state, and I knew that going into our relationship. He's not going to change his mind, and I'd be crazy to expect him to. But can I balance passion for him with compassion for Katherine, and for a little boy named Johnnie?

Eventually, I lie awake long enough to remember that I haven't checked my messages since I turned down the ringer on my telephone to accommodate the television crews.

There's one from my editor, and guilt floods me when I hear her voice: "Marie! Were you going to call me today? I can't wait to hear how the book is coming. Call me tomorrow, for sure, okay? If you're not quite finished with the manuscript, maybe you want to send me some chapters?"

I definitely do not want to do that, but I swear I'll call her.

Now my agent has jumped in: "Sweetie! Your editor showed me your new cover today, and I love it, except your name's not big enough, and I told her that's got to be bolder. Give me a call tomorrow, and let me know when I can expect my copy of your manuscript. Bye, love."

I can imagine the conversation between them: *"Have you heard anything from Marie?" "No, have you?" "Not a word. You don't think she's having trouble with the book, do you?" "I think she'd let us know." "Yeah, I'm sure you're right, she'd let us know . . ."*

I have to let them know, it's only right.

And then I discover I've missed the most important call of all, a second one from the anonymous woman:

"I called once before, looking for Marie Folletino," she says, sounding really nervous this time. There's a long silence while the tape plays, and I wait with my fingers crossed. Finally she says, hesitantly, and so softly she might be whispering into the phone: "She's got to hear what I have to say. She's just got to. I think I can call back at eight o'clock tomorrow night, but that's the last time. I won't be able to call anymore after that. Please . . ."

She hangs up.

Feeling so frustrated I could scream, I lie back down on my pillow.

After Ray had his hypnosis session, I got one, too. Turns out I'm not nearly as good a trance subject as he is. Humbling, that. All I "saw" was a dreamlike sequence in which "I" was a baby, lying on a blanket in the backseat of an old-model car. I "saw" the back of a man's head in the driver's seat. Dark hair. It's night in the scene. I'm hot in my baby clothes, but my face is cold. Is the man my father? Maybe that's a memory of him driving me to the motel on the edge of Birmingham where they left me. And maybe it isn't. Maybe it's just a scene from a movie, my own *Raintree County*.

I wish this weren't happening to me now.

Bad timing, is my last thought before I sleep.

11

Raymond

"Nothing's going to happen right away," I predict to the Keplers over breakfast on my patio. I've forced Katherine to sit down for once and let me fix them pancakes. We have coffee, and grapefruit picked from a tree in my yard. "So there's no point in sitting by the phone all day. I could be wrong, but I think it would be safe for us to leave the house. Is there anything you'd like to do?"

Mother and daughter glance at each other, as if to ask: Is there?

All of Bahia Beach stretches out around us, on a gorgeous day with the temperature in the low eighties and no clouds in the sky. Now and then we hear a vehicle honk on the bridge, or a boat on the water. There's a faint citrus smell to the air, and a lovely breeze off the canal.

I'm thinking they might like to be distracted for a little while, although I should know better than that, just as I should have allowed Katherine to cook, if she wanted to, if it made her feel better. Foolishly, I'm thinking they might like to do some sightseeing. Maybe I can be excused for thinking that, because I love my hometown so much I want everybody else to enjoy it, too. Already, I know that they think it's too hot and sticky down here, and they're afraid of our crime.

Lots of people feel that way, a sentiment to which I have a knee-jerk defensive reaction: Well, of course, what rational person wouldn't prefer shoveling snow to the bother of washing sand off your feet? It's so annoying to have to keep that hose in the yard, right? As for our crime, not all of it's horrible, some of it's hilarious in its own warped Florida way. My favorite is the gang of transvestites who stole courturier clothing from retail shops some years ago. When caught, they were wearing the evidence. As Dave Barry, one of our famous south Florida writers says, I am not making this up. And as Carl Hiaasen, one of our famous novelists says, in south Florida fiction is just nonfiction waiting to happen.

But what's not to love about gorgeous weather, relaxed people, and an easygoing lifestyle? Sure, there are traffic jams, and crowds in the malls, and in high tourist season it can take an hour on a Friday night to drive a mile along the beach, but so what? Big deal. There's a trade-off for everything, right? What's the upside of ten feet of snow, I ask you? Skiing? Pretty leaves in the autumn? Thanks, I'll visit that. I'd rather live in the sunshine. There are so many compensations here—the beach itself, which you can stroll every day if you like, and the canals, and Butterfly World, and Cuban food, and restaurants on the water, and boats, and convertibles, and fresh fruit, and Cuban coffee, and—

Katherine says, "I need to see where my son has been."

"Of course," I say, slammed back to the harsh reality of their lives, where sightseeing takes a very low priority. I feel ashamed for even thinking she might be interested in trivial pursuits. "Do you have any place in particular in mind? We can go anywhere you say."

"Can you drive us by the jail where they kept him?"

"Yes. And the courthouse is near there."

"Good. And what about that place where he worked?"

"Checker Crab? I think it's closed, but we can drive out there."

"Thank you, and . . . I want to see where he killed that poor man."

240

She's referring to the aging hippie who owned the trawler from where Ray made his phone call to me. I keep my tone carefully neutral. "Okay. Would you want to see where Natty's family lives?"

"Yes, I want to see that, too."

"Mom!"

"I need to see these places, Kim. You don't have to go."

Her daughter looks fearful, undecided, but finally blurts, "I want to go with you, but I just can't. Do you mind if I stay here?"

"Of course not, honey."

So that's what we do: Katherine and I leave Kim at my place, and then I drive her past the recent landmarks of her son's violent life. It takes a long time, because it turns out that she doesn't feel satisfied merely with staring at them from my car. She wants to get out, and actually go into the jail. We have to park, and walk up to the courtroom, slip into a trial that's in progress, see the judge's bench, the table where Ray sat, and get a glimpse of the elevator on which he rode down on the gurney. Then she wants to go down to the basement garage, to see where he staged his attack and escape, to see where he ran, holding his lawyer as hostage.

We follow a path down to the New River.

Katherine wants to sit there for a long, peaceful time, staring at the water and the boats going by, while I sit silently beside her.

Finally, she says, "I've been thinking about what you told me about the pineal gland, Marie. And I put that together with how my son looks from his pictures . . . as if he never grew up, not normally, not physically. And I was wondering, do you think that could be why he took it? Out of some strange notion that it might help him develop into a man?"

"It's an interesting theory." It had crossed my mind, but I eliminated it for the reason I'm about to give her. "But the pineal gland is markedly larger in a child under the age of six, and Natty had just turned six. If that's what he was after, I think he would have taken a younger child."

241

"Maybe he didn't know her age."

"Maybe he didn't." She hasn't mentioned her older son in all the time she's been here, and I've gotten the feeling that Kim doesn't know that part of the tale. "Katherine, how's Cal?"

"Not good." She shakes her head. "He doesn't want to talk about it, he doesn't want to tell anybody, not his wife, not even his sisters. He would die if he knew I had told you and Jack, and if you put it in your book—"

"I'll figure out a way to leave it out."

"I don't know what we're going to do, he's been so badly hurt. How could I let such a thing happen to him? How could I not know? There aren't enough days left in my lifetime to say I'm sorry." She glances at me, and I glimpse pain deep in her eyes. "Marie, all these years I've been grieving for Johnnie, and there was Cal who was hurt, and needing me, too."

"I suspect Cal and Johnnie aren't the only children he . . ."

"No, probably not." She takes a breath, to steady herself. "Where did Johnnie go from here?"

We visit the trolley stop where he got a ride.

She even wants to go to the beach, to see the rest room there, which was the last place he was officially spotted by anybody. Over a long lunch down at the beach, she has me tell her again everything I can remember that her boy ever said to me.

"He could survive for a long time, couldn't he?" she asks me.

"It sounds as if he could," I agree.

"He did survive for a long time, before any of this."

"Yes, I guess he did, Katherine."

"And Donor Miller taught him how."

She shakes her head, as if there are no words to describe the hideous irony of that. "I want to see that boat now, where he killed that man."

"Are you sure?"

"Yes, and then show me where the McCullens live."

"Okay, Katherine."

*   *   *

242

The trawler that the old hippie called home is still tied up to a mooring on a canal just outside of Bahia. When Ray called me he was only fifteen miles away from my house, a fact I have been slow to grasp until now, as I stand beside Katherine five feet from the deck of the boat. It is strung with multicolored drapes of old fabric, so it looks as if the biblical Joseph has strung his coat over it.

"The old man's body was found in the river," I tell her.

"Why do they think Johnnie killed him?"

I hesitate before answering her. These are very difficult things to tell a mother. "He died the same way Natalie did, with pressure to his carotid artery. Things are knocked around inside," I point to the boat, "As if they struggled. But he was a lot older than Ray, and probably couldn't have put up much of a fight."

She reaches for my hand.

"I'd like to say a prayer, Marie."

Under the broiling Bahia sun, the mother of the killer offers up a prayer for the soul of his most recent victim.

"Amen," I echo.

"Okay," she says, in a tiny voice. "Now let's go see where the little girl lived."

This time we only drive by, because Katherine doesn't want Tony or Susan to see us. There's nobody visible on the whole cul-de-sac. It's as if all the parents have become afraid to let their children play outside. Katherine urges me to drive around it quickly, and then head back out again. I tell her that they wouldn't know who she is, but she's afraid they could have seen her on television, and she's scared to death of offending them. She turns and looks behind her until we have driven far out of sight of their house.

It's another world back along the New River.

It's late afternoon by now, and Katherine and I have driven into a place of shade and coolness, of Spanish moss hanging from tall trees, of twining vines as thick as your arm, and huge, green leaves that fold in on themselves like hands. There are dank aromas here, and a sense of a million things crawling, eating, flying, biting. We have the windows rolled down, and our elbows hanging out, and we hear bird calls and twitters, and a murmur of verdant life, always moving, never still in the backwoods.

"It's beautiful," she says, "but I don't like it very well."

I know what she means. Although I have friends who live in wonderful homes back in secret places like this, I don't think I could do it. I need salt water and sunshine and fresh air; in a place like this, I'd go to sleep worrying about what might be crawling over the sheets to bite me. These are subtropical regions, where even cute little lizards or frogs can be poisonous, and snakes and spiders proliferate.

I've been out here once before, on research for the book.

The road turns and turns again, and suddenly we're there, at a barbed wire fence in ill repair, with a "gate" that's only an open drive with nothing to block the entrance. There are indications that there may have been an actual gate at one time, but Donor Miller didn't keep it, or anything else, in good repair. There's no sign saying CHECKER CRAB, but we drive past other signs saying NO TRESPASSING and PRIVATE PROPERTY, KEEP OUT.

The owner's gone; there's nobody to keep us out.

"Is it okay to be here, Marie?"

"No reason not to."

We see the buildings: the office, the repair shed, and an outbuilding that's falling down and wasn't used for anything. As we move in closer, the docks come into view, but now all of the boats are gone except for the water taxis.

I say, "It's not much to look at, is it?"

"How long was Johnnie here?"

"That's hard to say, Katherine. Donor Miller told the police that Johnnie showed up here about a year to a year and a half before the murder, but we know now that's probably not true. He may have been here the whole time Donor was here, and I believe Donor bought this place about ten years ago."

She knows the police are now tracing Miller's past life.

For now, we still don't know where he went after he left

Kansas with Ray, or where they went after that, although we suspect they came directly to this state.

"I'd like to get out and walk around," she says.

We both get out of the car, and walk toward the marina.

I try to follow close enough to answer any questions she may have, but far enough away to give her a little private space. When we get to the river, she turns to me, and asks, "Which boat was it?"

"Number six, but it's not here, Katherine."

"Oh. I guess the police have it."

"That's right."

"Do you think we could look in the office?"

"Sure, let's see if we can."

It's not even locked, we discover, but when we step inside, Katherine gets overtaken by emotion, and pushes past me to get back outside again. I hurry after her, and rub her back as she takes deep breaths.

"Are you all right?"

"I'm okay."

"Do you want to leave now?"

"No, not yet. If you don't mind, Marie."

"We'll stay as long as you want to."

"Would you wait here for me?"

"Of course. Do you want some time to yourself?"

She gives me a tiny, grateful smile, and just nods.

I watch her go off toward the repair shed, and my heart follows her, even though I do not. There's really no place to sit where I won't have to worry about bug bites, or snakes—

"Katherine!" I call out. "Watch out for snakes!"

She raises a hand in the air to show she's heard me.

I wander down to the docks to throw sticks in the river, while the sun begins a slow descent behind my back. As it gets lower in the sky, the air turns cooler, back here in the woods. At home, my patio will be really heating up right now, driving Kim inside, if she's been sitting out there.

Thirty minutes later, Katherine has not returned, and I wonder when she will. Fifteen minutes after that, I begin to feel a little anxious. Has she wandered off into the thick vegetation around us, and gotten lost? I don't even know if Katherine can swim, and there's water all around us.

That's crazy, I chide myself, about my own nervous thoughts.

Stepping in the last direction I saw her, I call out, "Katherine?"

There's no reply from any direction.

She has just sat down on a tree stump to cry, I tell myself, and any minute now, she'll come walking out of the woods, ready to go home again. I near the repair shed, peek in to find rusting equipment. I walk past it toward the third building that's in falling-down condition. Once there, and seeing there's no place here where Katherine could be, I call out for her again, "Katherine?"

There's still no reply, but there is a path leading into the woods.

I feel better, upon seeing that path.

That's where she went, on a walk into the beauty of the forest.

But it's getting late, and will be dark before very long, and although I hate to disturb her reverie, I think I'd better round her up and get her out of here while we can still see our way to the car. There's a flashlight in it, and I consider going back for it, but that seems ridiculous. It's only twilight, after all, with plenty of light to see by. She can't have gone that far down the path, can she?

I start down it, after her.

A hundred yards later, the path is narrower still, and I'm brushing Spanish moss out of my hair, and fretting about critters that might land on my face or my shoulders.

I start to call out her name, but then pause.

There is a thread of music weaving through the trees, and my heart stops as I realize what it is: a guitar, with a tune being plucked one note at a time. *Yesterday, all my troubles . . .*

I am suddenly terrified, for her, for myself.

It's Ray, I know it is, it has to be.

Should I run back for help, or go on looking for her?

As soon as I pose that dilemma to myself, I know the answer: I can't leave her, not without knowing where she is, what kind of situation she's in, and if Ray's there, too.

I can't step off the path, the vegetation's too thick, and I'd be noisy, and quickly lost, as well. My only choice is to tread as quietly as I can toward the music, following the notes that seem to keep a steady beat now with my pounding heart.

Something moves in the woods to my right, and I nearly scream.

. . . all my troubles seemed so far away . . .

The guitarist plays steadily, apparently unaware of me.

And then I almost miss the second path, a tiny, overgrown branching off that leads to the left, deeper into the woods. When I step onto it I feel as if I am stepping into an envelope that is closing behind me, and being sealed. The music is louder now, though still soft, because it's being played with great delicacy.

There is a patch of sun ahead, and I see Katherine.

She's standing, looking down at something.

I move close enough to see what it is: Ray, seated on a fallen log, looking down at the strings of a guitar while his mother stares at him. He looks much the same, though dirtier, grubbier. They are talking, over the sound of the music, kind of between his slow notes, and I stop in my tracks to listen to their words.

". . . northern Florida, that's where Donor had a cabin."

"How long were you there, Johnnie . . . Ray?"

"Dunno. Long time, I guess. Then here."

"Do you remember anything about your other life?"

He looks up, and I flinch, thinking, what must she feel upon seeing him at last? This is no beauty, her son. He looks as I remember, maybe worse.

"Huh-uh," Ray says, meaning no.

"Nothing at all? Not me, or your father?"

"Huh-uh."

"You have a brother, and two sisters."

"No kidding." He doesn't sound very interested, or even as if he particularly believes it.

"We've never stopped loving you, Johnnie."

He squints at her, as if to say, Huh?

After a minute, Katherine asks so gently, "Why did you kill her?"

"Didn't want her to die."

I am baffled by that answer, and I can tell that Katherine is, too.

"What do you mean?"

Ray plucks a few strings, and then he says, "Donor told me, go pick up a little kid, and bring it back to him. He said I was too old for him now, and he was feeling too old, and he needed a new little kid. He said I should find a kid for him, like I used to be. So I found her."

"But you killed her."

"I wasn't supposed to do that!" He looks around, as if he's still afraid of getting caught. "I had to, though. I had to kill her so she wouldn't die."

"I don't understand." I hear tears in Katherine's voice.

"This is death!" Ray tells her, looking upset. "Don't you get it? What we're in right now. Life is death. Death is life. That's what I figured out. If I gave her to Donor, she'd die. He'd do to her like he always did to me, and she'd die, like I'm dead in here." He took his right hand off the guitar strings, and struck himself first on his chest, and then on his head, to show her where he was "dead": in his head, in his heart. "But if I killed her, she wouldn't have to die like me."

Oh lord, my own heart turns over, hearing him.

If I'm understanding Ray, he killed Natty to "save" her from Donor. He saved her from the terrible fate of becoming Donor's little girl, as Ray was Donor's little boy.

Please, Katherine, ask about the bridge . . .

She's openly weeping now, though he doesn't seem to care.

"But you mutilated her brain, you took that—"

"Did not!" This was the Ray who sounded more like a child than a grown-up. "I did not do that! Donor did that! I brought her back here, and I came off in the woods for a while, and then I took her to the bridge."

248

"Why . . . the bridge?"

"Scared."

"What were you scared of, Johnnie?"

"Donor. He'd of made me go get another kid. A new kid."

"You didn't want to do that, did you?"

He shakes his head, without speaking.

"You were trying to stop Donor."

"Yeah."

"But you didn't understand the police would put you in prison, and convict you, and want to put you to death."

"That would have been okay, the death part. It was just the jail part I couldn't take anymore."

Katherine sinks to her knees on the spongy earth.

"Johnnie? Why did Donor do that?"

"What?"

"Take that part of her—"

"I guess 'cause he wanted a soul, whatever the hell that is. He said if he could get an innocent little soul he would be . . . some word he used . . . oh yeah, redeemed." Johnnie shakes his head, looking unsure of himself. "I never knew he meant it like that. I thought he just wanted a kid, like me."

For a moment, neither speaks.

"Are you really my mother?"

"Yes, Johnnie."

He nods as he plays a tune I've never heard. I wonder if he wrote it. I wonder what kind of creativity is latent in this strange, sad person, that will never emerge. But now I have to figure out what to do. Make myself known to them?

Or slink away, and race for help?

Is Katherine in danger? Am I?

There's a sound behind me. I turn, but before I get all the way around, something shoves into my back, violently propelling me forward toward the clearing.

"Shut up, Ray! Shut up!" a man's voice shouts.

I'm being kicked and shoved, and I'm falling, then crawling to get away from the kicking feet and whatever else it is that is striking and hurting me. Jesus, it's a shotgun! I twist around, look up, and see a man whose face is so twisted in fury that I don't even recognize him. "Move, bitch!"

I stumble to Katherine, who grabs me, looking terrified.

The man levels the shotgun at the two of us, huddled together. Then he swings it toward Ray. "What'd you tell them?"

"Nothin', Donor! I didn't saying nothin'!"

Katherine shudders in my arms as I think: *Donor!* If this is Donor, then who is the man who was found dead in the Everglades, with Donor's wallet and scorpion necklace?

"You two," he shouts at us, "get up!"

We struggle to our feet, doing as he says.

"Come here, we're going someplace."

As we get close to him, he grabs Katherine by her hair, swinging her around back of him, while he's staring at me, as if to say, You make a move, and I'll hurt her more.

I am frozen, but Ray shouts, "No! Let her alone!"

Suddenly Ray is flinging himself toward us.

Donor releases Katherine and swings the gun toward Ray. I launch myself toward the barrel of the gun, but it goes off before my arms strike it. I feel as if the woods have exploded. There is a flash of fire, a roar of sound. Ray looks as if he's flying for a moment, and then he goes down. I fall against the side of the gun, which knocks me to the ground. Donor grabs for me and jerks one of my arms, yelling, "Get up!"

Katherine screams, and tries to go to her son.

But Donor puts the gun to my head to stop her. I know, as he must know, that if he had put the gun to her head, he would have had to shoot her before she would halt. The expression on her face is so desperate, so painful, I turn away, unable to bear it.

"We're going someplace together," he says again.

He marches us back down the trail, Katherine first, followed by me with the shotgun in my back, then him. We are leaving Ray on the ground, and once again he's been shot, and again, I don't know if he's dead or alive. Katherine is stumbling, weeping, crying his name: Johnnie.

I am driving us away from the marina.

Katherine is behind me in the backseat, and Donor is seated beside her with the gun pointed into her right thigh.

"You're the writer," he says to me.

I nod: yes.

"What?"

"Yes. I am."

"Take us to your house."

"Why?"

"Shut the fuck up, and drive."

We drive in utter silence back into Bahia, up cheerful familiar streets under streetlights, stopping at stop lights, passing hundreds of cars. My mind is frantically trying to figure out a way to wreck my car without getting Katherine shot, and I can't imagine a way to do that. I don't know what to do, but drive. If it were just me, with the gun pressed to my side, I swear I would drive up the steps of a post office. I would find a police station, and drive into the side of it. I would ram this car into a fire plug. But it isn't me with the shotgun pressed against my thigh, it is Katherine.

I cannot even imagine what she is feeling at this moment.

There's nothing for me to do but exactly as he says.

We glide on past the guard at the gate of my cul-de-sac, and there is no way to transmit a message to him.

Into my garage, we go, and now all I can think of is Kimmie.

She's waiting inside my house for us, not knowing, coming innocently to greet us when we walk in the kitchen door.

I have to make this horror stop right now.

After I turn off the engine, I say quietly, "May I ask you something?"

"What?" he says. *A killer's ego,* I am thinking, *a killer's ego.* "Ray says you took Natty's pineal gland. Most people don't even know where it is. How'd you know how to do that?"

He bangs the end of the shotgun against my skull.

I cry out in pain, and grab my head.

Blood runs down my fingers.

"It's up there," he says, meaning in my head, where he hit me. "I know all about that shit, from being a medic in Korea. That's where your soul is. I could take it. I could steal your soul. I could take yours, but it wouldn't be innocent enough for me."

You are crazy! You are a sick, perverted lunatic!

He forces us out of the car.

"What do you want?" I ask him, because I have to know.

He pushes Katherine into my kitchen, before he answers.

"You're going to drive me back home to Kansas."

He starts to laugh at the expression on my face.

"Don't you know who I am now?" he asks me.

I shake my head as he reaches into his back pocket while still holding the shotgun level with my stomach. He pulls out a wallet and tosses it to me. When I open it, I see a driver's license with a photo of a man about his age, and the name: Fred Kepler.

"I'm Fred Kepler now," he says, laughing. "And he's me, feeding the alligators in the Everglades. First I got me a new soul. Now I get born again as Fred Kepler. I'm going back to Kansas, as Fred, and then I'm going to disappear. Everybody thinks Donor Miller is dead. But Fred Kepler is alive and he's going home to Kansas!"

He shoves me into the kitchen.

I hear my telephone ringing, and see that it is eight o'clock, and the woman who knew my parents is calling right when she said she would. It rings again.

As he's coming through behind me, I step aside.

And that allows retired deputy Jack Lawrence to shoot him.

"I came to Florida to track Donor Miller," Jacks says, when he learns who he has killed, "and I guess I found him. Kimmie let me in."

My phone rings a third time, and I have a choice of either running to answer it, or embracing Katherine Kepler. I take Katherine in my arms, and Kimmie wraps her arms around us, too, and after one more ring, my phone stops.

Hours later, Johnnie Kepler dies in a hospital bed, his mom at his side. His sister is holding his other hand, and I am standing with Jack in a corner of the room. There was never a chance that Johnnie would live after he was found with a massive wound in his chest. It was a miracle that he survived long enough to hear his mother say she loves him. I'm praying there really are such things as souls, and that he has one. If he does, I know that it is still as innocent and unchanged as the day he was taken from his family, and that now it will be given back to him, sweet and whole again.

The Little Mermaid

By Marie Lightfoot

~

CHAPTER TEN

etectives Flanck and Anschutz started with Donor Miller's claim that Fred Kepler was the dead man in the swamp, and tracked backward from there. With the bounced check in their hands, they went to the address listed on the front of it, and traced it to a condominium on which the mortgage had not been paid for the last two months.

"I haven't seen Fred in ages," a neighbor told them.

"Does he have any next of kin?" they asked her.

"Why, is he dead? What happened to old Fred?"

None of the neighbors knew him well enough to provide any useful information, but the bank that held the mortgage showed them his loan application on which he had listed two job references and an ex-wife as a personal reference.

The ex-wife wasn't Katherine Kepler, but a woman named Ellen.

When they found her, Ellie Kepler turned out to be a pleasant, middle-aged woman with two teenaged children, neither of them Fred's. She invited them into her small home, and cried when they told her that her ex-husband had been murdered. When she asked them who did it, and they said Donor Miller, comprehension flooded her eyes.

"That man," she whispered.

"You've heard of him?"

"He kidnapped Fred's little boy, years ago."

"You know about—"

But she interrupted them, asking as if the whole world depended on their answer, "Did Fred get to see his son?"

"His son?" Robyn parried.

"Ray Raintree, the man who killed that little girl."

"What do you know about that, Mrs. Kepler?"

"Fred came over one day to see me, and he was so upset. It was all over the papers, about how a young man named Ray Raintree had been arrested for murdering a child. Fred was practically hysterical. He said that his son who got kidnapped used to have an imaginary playmate named Raymond Raintree, just like that murderer's name. He said he was scared to death that was his son. He was the right age, and the worst part of all was that he was employed by a man who used to teach music to Fred's older boy."

"How'd he know that?"

"It was the name, a really unusual name."

"Why was he scared about it?"

She frowned, trying to figure it out. "It was guilt, I think, and shame. It killed him to think his own child could have turned out like that, and suffered so much. It was so strange. You'd think that if you found your long-lost child you'd get to be overjoyed. But this was terrible. Fred was just a basket case when he came over."

"Did he do anything about it?"

"Well, I know he was going to. He read in the paper where Ray Raintree had public defenders, and he told me he was going to make sure that at least he had decent defense lawyers. Fred never had much money, but he was going to give the boy every penny he could scrape together. The last time I talked to Fred, he hadn't decided if he actually wanted to see his son. I think he was scared of the boy, of the whole thing. I know that sounds terrible, but Fred wasn't a very brave man, I hate to say. He was always running away from things, from responsibilities."

"Did he say anything about the other man?"

"The music teacher?"

"Yeah."

"He was really upset about that. He was in a rage. I've never seen Fred behave like that, I thought he was going to have a stroke. He claimed he was going to find that man, and accuse him of stealing his child, that he was going to beat him up, kill him . . ." She stared at them. "I didn't believe him. I didn't think Fred was brave enough to do that, I thought he'd end up going to the police, and letting you arrest that man."

Paul said, "But instead, Miller killed him."

"Oh, my god," she said, and put her face in her hands.

"If we put what you're telling us together with what we already know," Robyn said, "it looks as if your ex-husband went out to the Checker Crab marina to find Donor Miller. Some of Miller's employees heard him in a shouting match, and that was probably your ex-husband. Miller was a tough man, Mrs. Kepler. I doubt most normal men would have had a chance in a fight with him. I think Miller killed your ex-husband, dumped his body in the Everglades, and then assumed his identity."

Before they left the neat little house, she asked them again, "Did Fred ever get to see his son?"

They had to tell her no, he never got the chance.

"Mrs. Kepler?" Robyn asked, on her doorstep. "Your ex-husband tried to keep his first wife from finding out about their son's identity. Do you have any idea why he would do that?"

Ellen nodded, as if the answer to that was easy. "He was a weak man, Detective. He was always afraid to face the truth, and he assumed everybody else was, too. It was really very brave of him to go out there to see that man. As far as I'm concerned, Fred died a hero, not a coward, and I'll always be proud of him for that, even if it was a foolish thing to do. Will you tell her that? Tell her how he tried to help their son. Tell her how he died."

Robyn promised to do that.

As they drove away, Paul remarked, "I'll say one thing for Fred Kepler. For a worthless son-of-a-bitch, he had good women."

"Like you," Robyn joked, meaning herself as his partner.

"Who you callin' worthless?"

There were other things they knew now, too.

The three baby teeth they had found in one of Ray's backpacks were his own teeth, which he had saved all those years, like a little boy still waiting for the tooth fairy to put a dime under his pillow. The medicines he stole and saved were his own strange way of taking care of himself. He wasn't allowed to see doctors, and there was nobody to tend him when he got sick.

"You got to be prepared," he told Katherine, in the woods, "because you never know what can happen to you."

He was just cruising the canals, like Donor told him to.

It was good, getting to take one of the taxis out, which Donor didn't let him do very often. Anybody who took one out was supposed to tell Donor, or sign a chart. Ray hadn't felt like doing that tonight. He'd just taken a boat. Donor would be mad, but these days it seemed like Donor was always mad.

Most of the time, Ray was supposed to stay out in the woods, take care of himself, not come in unless he was

257

starving, or something. Donor had softened a little bit in the last few years, and let him spend nights on the empty boats fairly frequently. But Ray wasn't as comfortable in a bunk, in small spaces, as he was outside in a lean-to he'd built himself. Donor had taught him how, Donor had taught him everything he knew, from playing the guitar, to survival in the wilderness, and especially how to hide from the view of any kind of authority at all.

The Intracoastal was choppy, so he turned down a side canal.

For so many years, he'd been living like this, and he was used to it. He didn't know how people could stand to live in houses, go to jobs, although sometimes he watched them coming and going inside their houses and their cars, and he wondered, What would that be like?

"You're an imbecile," Donor told him, had drilled into him. "You're retarded, you're a moron, and morons don't get driver's licenses. They don't go to school, they don't have friends, and nobody wants to know them. You're damned lucky I'll take care of you. Don't you ever forget that I'm the only person who will ever help you. You come to me if you need anything. Don't ask anybody else, or they'll lock you up in a loony ward, or throw you in jail for the rest of your life. I won't be able to help you then. You'll never see me. I'll pretend I never knew your ugly face."

This was a residential canal, with houses lining its banks.

Ray puttered down to the end of it, and pulled up to a dock to get the taxi in position to turn back around again. He was startled to see a little girl come running down the yard of the house toward him. She looked excited, at seeing his black-and-white checked boat. And suddenly, Ray knew this was who Donor had sent him to get.

He had a bag of popcorn in the boat, and he held it out to her.

"Want some popcorn?"

With his other hand, he grabbed a post to steady his boat.

She took a handful of popcorn, not even looking at him, she was so entranced with the checkered boat. And before he even knew it, she had hopped in with him.

Damn, this was going to be easy.

"Get me a little kid," Donor had instructed him. "You're too damn old for me, I want a little kid like you used to be when you were little and cute. You go get me one, Ray."

It sounded crazy to Ray, but Donor was crazy these days.

Donor'd always been crazy mean, but now he was just crazy some of the time, and meaner than ever. Ray was seriously considering staying out in the woods more and more, and not coming in, except that Donor would find him, and beat him up if he did that. Donor always found him. Things always hurt like hell around Donor.

"You like boats?" he said to the little girl.

She didn't seem to hear him.

"Hey! You like boats?"

She still didn't look up. Instead, she kept staring at the houses.

"You deaf, kid?"

Jesus, she was deaf, he decided, and with that thought, something began to go weird in his body and his mind, like it was filled with a sadness that he couldn't stand to feel, and vague memories came flashing to him, as if from somebody else's life. But it was his life. It was his life with Donor that was coming to him, and he looked at the child and realized that was going to be her life now, too.

They swung out into the big Intracoastal channel.

In his mind, Ray screamed, No, no no!

She didn't know, didn't even notice him in the back of the boat.

He kept steering in the direction of the river, as if he

couldn't stop the boat, couldn't stop what was going to happen to her. But he could! He could! He could save her from dying a little more every day until she was a walking dead person like he was, and like he had been for more years than he could remember. Sometimes he felt dead, other times he felt like he was other people in his own head, and they had memories different from his, and feelings different from his. And sometimes he got all fuzzy and things got blank and black—those were the worst—and later he couldn't remember anything he had done, or anywhere he had been.

The water taxi turned into the mouth of the New River. It was darker in here, and the little girl turned around.

Ray saw the fear dawning on her face, and it ate at his heart, and he couldn't stand to look at it a second longer. He had to save her from that fear. He had to save her from dying every day. He turned off the motor, and let the boat drift. And he began to drift as well, into a place that he wouldn't remember later.

When he pulled up to the docks, she was lying in the bottom.

Ray didn't know what was the matter with her.

Donor was coming from the office, walking toward him. There wasn't anybody else around. The marina was dark except for a couple of dim dock lights.

"Ray, you stupid shit, what are you doing taking one of my boats out without me telling you to? I thought somebody stole it, you moron! I called 911 on it! What have you done now, you dumbshit?"

"You told me to get you a kid!"

"Hey! You did it already?"

"You shouldn't do this, Donor!"

"Don't you tell me—"

"You shouldn't hurt kids like you hurt me."

260

"Hurt you? How can you say that? I've been nothing but good to you—"

"Don't hurt any more kids!"

"I'll show you a world of hurt, you moron. Come here!"

Ray took off running for the woods, and didn't look back.

He didn't know how long it was before he got up the nerve to peek out again. There was nobody down at the docks. Donor wasn't there. Ray ran down, and untied the boat, and took it out again. There was a tarp in the bottom of the boat, and he knew she was under it.

Donor would tell him to go get another one.

If Donor couldn't have this one, he'd want another one.

Ray couldn't do it. He didn't know why he couldn't, he just knew that he couldn't. But if he didn't, Donor would hurt him again and again. He needed to make sure that Donor couldn't make him go get another little kid, and he needed to be safe from Donor. But how could he do those things? Where in the world could he be safe from Donor?

Jail. Donor wouldn't touch him there.

Donor had always told him that if he got caught and put in jail, that's the last he'd ever see of Donor.

He had to get caught, he had to go to jail, he had to show the world what Donor was doing, so Donor couldn't do it again.

He started the engine of Boat Six, and slipped away from the marina. Once he reached the Intracoastal, he slipped down a side canal with a bridge at the end of it.

When he returned the boat, Donor said, "What did you do with her?"

"I got rid of her."

261

Donor said, "Good. Wash out the boat. Get rid of any evidence."

But Ray didn't feel like doing that, not if he wanted to get caught and go to jail, and be safe from Donor.

He waited until Donor left for his apartment, and then Ray wandered off into the woods to wait for the sun to come up.

12

Raymond

Katherine is waiting on their doorstep with the flowers.

I drove her to a florist's, where she purchased a lovely arrangement of white roses and baby's breath, and now I have brought her to the McCullens' house.

My heart aches for her, and for the young woman who answers the door. What will Susan do? Will she turn Katherine away? I'm so hoping she won't, though nobody could blame her if she did. Oh, yes! She's stepping aside, and Katherine is walking into the house.

The front door closes.

I relax my head against my car seat, and close my eyes.

I've got a car phone now, and it can dial 911 automatically with only one silent press of a button. With any luck, I'll never need it. But at least for a little while, I want the security of knowing I can summon help whenever I am in my car, and whoever might happen to be there with me.

I haven't given the number to anyone yet.

If I want to talk to someone, I have to be the one who calls.

I pick it up and dial the office of the state's attorney.

"Did you finish your book on time, Marie?"

"Barely, but at least it's a whole book now."

"That's good. I'm glad. What did you say about me?"

"That you work prosecutorial magic."

"Thanks. It's too easy when there's no defense."

We think we know why Ray never confessed the truth: He understood Donor's last words to him as a warning that if he talked, Donor would harm other children. Ray kept quiet, hoping to protect them. Even if he had told the truth, he still would have been convicted, because he killed Natty. His reasons may have been confused, even well-intentioned in their own cruel way, but the fact remained that he murdered her.

"I was wondering," I say, "if you'd like to discuss philosophy over an omelette at my house this evening. If I haven't broken too many eggs, that is."

"It may be," he says, as if we had never stopped talking, "that writers are not as used to arguing about things as lawyers are. It may also be true that writers are better than prosecutors at thinking of defendants as real human beings."

"You're saying we could both learn something?"

"That, and I could pick up some wine."

"I won't argue with that."

It's hot in my car, so I take my new phone with me and I step out into the street, and then I walk up onto the McCullens' lawn and stand under a palm tree that provides about six inches of shade. Suddenly, we're arguing, laughing, flirting. I'm sweating, and the mosquitoes are biting, and a coconut falls inches from my head and lands with a crack that could have brained me. For a few minutes, at ten cents a minute, it's just another perfect day in Florida.